Through the Mind's Eye

—————

A Richie Radcliff Adventure

Written by:

Chris Reynolds
and
Jedd Birkner

www.AuthorChrisReynolds.com

Retail Distribution Available through Ingramspark.com

© Through the Mind's Eye Copyright 2020 by Chris Reynolds

Cover design by Chadwick Pelletier

Library of Congress Cataloging-in-Publication Data
Ghost Gold by Chris Reynolds

ISBN 978-1-734-8939-7-7

Contact Info
11932 N Lake Drive
Boynton Beach, FL 33436
www.AuthorChrisReynolds.com

Acknowledgements

Many characters in this book are based on friends or people I have met along the way. Thank you for allowing me the leeway to veer from your true nature.

I would like to thank Dawn Alexander, Nancy Smay, Lisa LaPaglia, all who have been instrumental in helping shape the final story and keeping me on point.

A special call out to my life long friend and writing partner Jedd Birkner. For without him this book would have never happened.

Lastly and most importantly, I would like to thank my wife and family for their unwavering support and encouragement.

Follow us at:

 AuthorChrisReynolds.com

 AuthorChrisReynolds@AuthorChrisRey1

 AuthorChrisReynolds

 Chris Reynolds The Manna Chronicles
This is A Public Group open to those who want to explore the unusual

The Past, Present and Future
All Intersect
Within the Mind's Eye

Prologue
Egypt, 1958

From a distance, the archeological dig looked more like a patchwork of abandoned craters than an organized expedition. Hundreds of workers toiled under the blaze of the desert sun.

Bartholomew Miles had lost faith and no longer believed there was anything to find. He did not hear the cry of triumph rain down from the ridgeline, unaware of the excitement echoing from one worker to another until it had swept through the entire camp.

"Professor, Professor," shouted a small boy who weaved his way towards the lone tent set apart from the others.

Inside the tent sat Professor Bartholomew Miles. With his great bulk hunched over a small desk, he was dripping sweat onto piles of bills and ledgers, wallowing in his worries. He was oblivious to the winds of fate that were changing.

My funding has come to an end. There is no more money to pay the diggers. There is barely enough money to get me back to Cairo.

"Professor, quick . . ." the young boy exclaimed as he came bursting through the closed flaps.

"What is it, Saba?" The professor was startled. He never liked this ragamuffin. He was a street urchin from the slums of Cairo who seemed to be underfoot every time he turned around.

"On top of the ridge, Sir! The diggers, they found something! Something big!"

The professor's breath hitched on the boy's words. *They found something?*

With his heart thumping he leapt to his feet and poked his meaty head out to see workers streaming in from all directions. The elation was contagious.

"Oh please, let this be it," he mumbled. He hastened to the ridge unaware that his fat jowls were flopping in rhythm with the bounce of his belly.

Cresting the hill, the professor stopped to catch his breath. The entire expedition was here, gazing into the freshly excavated hole.

Could this really be it? Could all the years of failure and ridicule be over?

As a young grad student, he had stumbled upon a fable of a lost city in a fellow student's notebook. Stealing the book, it became his fixation. While colleagues laughed at his obsession, he was desperate to prove them wrong. And now, after years of searching, success was so close he could taste it.

Itching with impatience, he brushed aside a worker. He descended into the pit on a rickety ladder that groaned beneath his enormous weight. When he touched the floor, he stood transfixed. Two doors had been cleared of sand, though the desert hid the structure that lay behind them. His desire concluded this was his lost city.

"These doors have not been opened for five thousand years," he proclaimed in a gesture of triumph. "This is my city, my victory. And it shall become my glory and my fame!"

Alone – his declaration was filled with bravado.

"Professor, can we open the doors tonight?"

When Bartholomew Miles saw Saba stepping from the ladder, his face flushed with anger. He turned his gaze upward. The sky had dissolved into shades of red. In the desert, night fell quickly.

Professor Miles pulled himself back to the surface. Bathed in sweat under a labored breath, he barked his orders. "Rajiv, place guards here around the clock. No one goes down there without my permission. Is that clear?"

"Yes, Professor," Rajiv said, unruffled.

"Tomorrow I am going to make history."

What he did not know was that tonight, while he dreamt of fame and fortune, the cards of fate were being reshuffled and all the players were going to be dealt a new hand.

⚬ℳ•◆•⻊•●⻊⤧ℳ

Saba embraced the desert nights. Pulling the threadbare blanket tight, he stared into the star-spangled heavens. A lone jackal howled in the distance.

The constancy of the twinkling lights gave him comfort. Orphaned after his parents had died in the great cholera epidemic, the young boy had come to appreciate simple comforts.

A full belly, a safe place to sleep and the friendly companionship of others, what more does a person really need?

Taking out a worn pad and a pencil, he considered the day's happenings. Though only nine, inside him burned a keen intelligence. Struggling to survive the streets of Cairo, he had never been to school and had never learned to read or write. But with a desire to record observations of the world around him, Saba had taken to blending slants and symbols into a unique language that only he could understand.

Safely tucked below the cosmic ocean, Saba wondered about those who built the structure that had lay so long below the desert sands.

Did they sit here gazing into the heavens? Did these same points of light watch down on them? With thoughts hovering at the edge of consciousness, he drifted off to sleep.

Once freed from the shackles of reality, his dreams grasped a current that pushed him out past the crescent moon, beyond the solar system, into the endless sea of celestial light.

$$\textit{e}\,\text{ɱ}\,\bullet\,\blacklozenge\,\bullet\,\mathcal{H}\,\bullet\,\bullet\,\mathcal{H}\,\nearrow\,\text{ɱ}$$

The next morning the workers had all gathered under the searing sun as it baked the desert with temperatures that were becoming unbearable. Saba watched as the professor stood before his doors of destiny, brushing greasy bits of mutton from his shirt.

Workers had toiled all morning clearing away sand, baring more of the façade. Rajiv spoke in reverence. "Allah has blessed us by entombing this place in the ancient sands. Look at how deep are the blues, and how striking are the yellows and reds. It is a luster time should have taken long ago."

The professor ignored him. "How can I get these blasted things open?" he growled. The doors appeared to be solid, insurmountable barriers, each weighing several tons.

3

As the professor paced back and forth, Saba saw his frustration turn to anger. He looked past him, and his gaze roamed over the colossal ornamentation when something jumped out at him.

That's not right . . .

"Look, professor . . ." he pointed with an extended arm.

"Leave me alone!" the man bellowed.

But Saba insisted and reached towards the intractable doors. "Sir, there is something wrong with the Maiden's Pitcher. I think you call it the Big Dipper." Before the man could intervene, Saba ran his hands over the door.

"Look there is an extra star in the pitcher's handle."

Professor Miles hesitated. He clenched and re-clenched his jaw. He was mumbling under a hushed breath. "The boy needs to be put back on the streets."

Saba ignored his comments and reached for the extra star. His fingertips felt the hardened stone. He gave it a tug and there was a little movement, so he pulled a little harder. With a soft *pffft,* it came free.

"Hah," he said with a sigh of satisfaction. The group behind him let out a collective gasp. But before anyone could say a thing, the doors groaned inward. With a sibilant hiss, air from the twentieth century rushed into the stale vacuum of antiquity.

"You see, professor," Saba said. "There are only four stars in the pitcher's handle. Just as you explained it to me." His quick wit allowed the professor to save face and tension turned to anticipation.

Saba's imagination soon turned to visions of treasure, walls made of gold, diamonds the size of potatoes and rubies the size of one's heart. He heard the rustling of those all around him, noting he was not alone in his anticipation.

"Quiet!" the professor shouted, stilling the clamor around him. He ordered the workers to wait outside. The professor entered, followed by Rajiv carrying kerosene lanterns, and Saba, who assumed it was all right for him to tag along. They stepped into a very old darkness.

Dust motes swirled in the pale-yellow glow of the lamplight. The stale air felt dusty on Saba's tongue. Rajiv went ahead, setting out lanterns. Following the main corridor, they continued deeper into the shadows.

A seemingly unending stream of pillars faded into the darkness. Each was covered with intricate paintings, carvings, and bas relief.

Turning away from the wide corridor with a lantern in hand, Saba watched the light grow smaller as the professor counted off over a hundred steps, yet still he had not reached another wall.

"The size of this place . . ." His booming voice was swallowed by the cavernous room.

The boy marveled at the stars and constellations so realistically painted upon the ceiling. It occurred to him that since the North Star opened the way in . . .

If there are matching stars in here, it might be important . . .

Following the heavenly trail, Saba ventured farther into the darkness. Entering a second chamber, the dim light from his lantern mingled with the temple paint and the room began glowing with a soft radiance. Dominating the hall was a flat-topped pyramid. On one side were steps that led up to a platform. He stepped back for a better view. To his surprise he saw a huge statue peering down at him.

A dog? It's not Egyptian?

Upon closer inspection, images of the same canine were painted on the surrounding columns. Saba knew many of the Egyptian gods, but not this one. Searching the room for more clues, the dog-god seemed to cover every surface. Each pillar was unwinding a story of this unknown dog-god.

He must have been really important.

Venturing deeper, Saba saw the Maiden's Pitcher. He walked over to the wall and his lamp caught a glint of something lying on the floor. It was an odd-looking thing. A cylinder with a hole in one end. It was so different from anything else in the room. He picked it up and examined it.

It's so light. What is it made of?

While considering what it could be, he saw something else, something far more amazing. His heart thumped as a knot formed in his belly.

How?!? Who? Impossible!

Etched onto the wall was a familiar set of slants and symbols. As he read and reread the script that only he could possibly understand, his mind raced.

Who could have written this? It's my language. I invented it. Then on an analytical note. I have never shared this with anyone.

"What have you got there?" the professor demanded.

Startled at his unexpected voice, Saba handed him the cylinder. It was a tactical diversion. He used his body to shield his greater discovery.

"You dirty little monkey!" he roared in anger. "What in the devil are you thinking, littering my temple with rubbish? What's wrong with you, boy?"

"Sir, I did not bring this in with me," Saba replied defiantly. "I found it here, on the floor."

The professor's jowls continued to shake long after his head stopped bobbing. He paced back and forth talking to himself. "If he didn't bring it in here then who did? And it's written in English . . ."

He squeezed the container. It flexed under his grip. It was painted with splashy letters.

Saba saw his lips move as he read: *Fizz Cola—Always Refreshing—All the Time.*

And then drawing it close to the lantern, the professor read the inscription on a strip of black and white numbers. "July 2021. Impossible!" he scowled. "It must be a hoax."

Bart leveled his eyes at the boy. Weathering his stare, Saba pressed his body against the wall, blocking the hidden message.

$$e_\mathsf{T}\mathsf{M} \bullet \blacklozenge \bullet \mathcal{H} \bullet \bullet \mathcal{H} \mathcal{K} \mathsf{M}$$

Saba was surprised that the professor now seemed more focused on the object than he did on his discovery. It was like he had suddenly forgotten the incredible temple they were in.

"I could make a fortune producing such a lightweight container," he muttered. "And get rich . . ." At that moment, an unquenchable desire for money began its conquest of his soul.

The professor turned the object over and over mumbling quietly to himself. "2021 is over sixty years into the future. How did it end up here in a building that has not been opened in over 5000 years?"

As the can disappeared into his rucksack, the professor moved toward the entrance. "Come along, boy." His tone had become surprisingly upbeat.

Saba hesitated, waiting until the professor had retreated to the other room. Still perplexed, he set out to memorize every single word written in his private language.

ℯ𝑇𝔐 ✦ ◆ ✦)(✦ ●)(⤢ 𝔐

Man makes plans and the gods laugh. One never knows what the stars have in store. That day in the chamber, forces were unchained that would sweep both Saba and the professor down into the river of destiny where each churning bend would impact the fortunes of mankind.

The discovery of the lost city of Osiris made Professor Miles one of the leading archeologists of his time, but he no longer cared about the world of academia. He was consumed with an unquenchable desire for wealth and power.

With a single-minded ruthlessness, the discovery of that can became the basis for Miles Industries, a global network of mines, factories, and industrial applications to dominate the production of aluminum, the lightest industrial metal ever produced.

As the twentieth century was nearing an end, his business practices were so unscrupulous that even the most crooked businessmen were taken aback by his greed. Even as technology and the advent of the internet dramatically changed the business landscape, Miles Industries grew to become one of the largest conglomerates on Earth.

Still, despite all his wealth and power, Bart was not satisfied. Two things remained that irritated him. One was the date of that can. And the other was the thing that was driving him mad.

How did that filthy beggar dominate Wall Street and become so enviously rich?

He had sorely underestimated the street urchin. Six decades before, Bart had ushered the filthy monkey back to a life of begging on the streets. That should have been the last of him. Instead, little Saba had grown to become S.B. Halim, one of the richest men in the world. Far, far richer than Bartholomew Miles.

He was haunted by jealousy. Was the source of Saba's success a result of that can found so long ago? Surely the man's wealth should be his. After all, it must be a result of that day of discovery.

Years before, Bart had learned that the black and white numbers on the side of his can were called a bar code. It was an information strip detailing where it was filled, as well as where and when it was shipped. Now, sitting at his desk in the fall of 2021, at the ripe old age of eighty-eight, he was finally closer to an answer. His eyes fell to the report laid open upon his desk. Rereading the item highlighted in yellow, a smile played at the corners of his mouth.

"So, my can had been shipped to Santa Martina, California."

For the umpteenth time, Bart's thoughts returned to the same question.

How in the world did it end up in ancient Egypt?

Chapter 1
Santa Martina, California, 1998

The evening air was stifled by the Santa Ana winds that brought an unbearable warmth to the California night. Sleep was impossible and Richie lay in bed filled with anxiety. As the sun hid below the horizon, his thirteen-year-old brain worried. He worried about the next day at school, he worried about the kid who wouldn't leave him alone, and mostly, he worried about his Dad.

He rose from the rumpled sheets and moved to the lone window that looked out over his yard below. There was a panoply of stars high above. A shooting streak blazed across the heavens.

"Out here in the country the stars spread across heaven like a spilt chest of silver coins," Richie recalled his mother telling him as a child. "When I was a little girl, you could reach right up and touch them. Where do you think you came from, my little star? I just reached up and plucked you from the heavens and brought you down from that velvety sky."

My little star, she always called him that. At the time he hated it. But now that she was gone, he longed to hear her say it just one more time.

From the corner of his eye, he caught another shooting star flaming across the sky. His heart made a wish. The same wish he always made.

I wish that the mining truck had never been there, and Mom's car never crashed. I wish we could all sit down as a family together. I wish Mom was alive today.

He said it out loud in case someone was granting wishes. But he knew the sad reality. She was gone—forever.

In the yard below, Richie could see his dog Kippy. With his nose pointed heavenward, his white coat gleamed in the bluish moonlight.

Kippy turned his head slowly, like he was tracking a bird or something. Then the barking started, shattering the late-night quiet. In seconds, all the dogs in the neighborhood joined the chorus.

"Great!" Richie could already imagine the phone ringing, his crabby old neighbor complaining. Then, as suddenly as the dogs started barking, they stopped.

Weird . . . He craned to see beyond the shadows as Kippy passed through a disheveled hedge into the field beyond and trotted toward a stand of oaks a hundred yards distant. *Something was out there that got his attention. Richie thought.*

Keeping his dog in his line of sight, Richie was only able to catch glimpses as shadows danced across the lawn to the rhythm of the freshening breeze. The shift in the wind stirred the trees and chased the stifling heat from the bedroom, which gave Richie the relief he needed to finally go to sleep. Searching for one more glance of his wayward dog, the interplay of dark and light created an illusion.

Kippy appeared to be levitating. Then the passing clouds threw a shadow over the moonlight and he was gone.

𝑒𝕋𝕞 • ◆ •)(• ●)(⤢𝕞

Kippy saw that something huge and unfamiliar had landed in the field. Sniffing the air for danger, his snout detected only the scent of dry grass and dew as he circled the vehicle.

No smell?

He inched closer with his ears perked. A slit in the night opened and a soft glow revealed a ramp coming out. The fur along the nape of his neck gave rise, but nosiness was pushing him forward.

Kippy hesitated halfway up . . . He was torn between curiosity and concern. Curiosity won out and he entered the open door.

Inside he saw two boys and a girl who appeared to be similar in age to his master. Wagging his tail, he offered his universal greeting.

One of the boys was slightly different than most of Richie's friends. He was much shorter with a slightly larger head. He was the one who spoke. Kippy did not understand, but the tone seemed friendly enough.

"Ruff, ruff," Kippy responded. He sensed this one was their leader.

He looked to one of the others and said something to him. The larger boy reached past the lone girl and flipped a couple of switches on a console arrayed with an assortment of blinking lights.

"How's that?"

Fricken cool. Kippy could understood everything they were saying. Even better, he found he could talk back.

"This is awesome," Kippy said with genuine elation.

"You know we're not supposed to be sharing stuff with these guys," the girl said uncomfortably.

"Come on Reshea. It's just a dog. We're only supposed to avoid contact with the 'higher' forms of intelligent life." She said this as a form of justification.

Reshea slunk down in her chair and leveled a look at her two companions.

"We're not even supposed to be here. 'In and out,' you guys said. This wasn't in the plans. I'm sure he . . . You are a he, right?" she asked, glaring at Kippy.

"Far as I know, I still lift my knee when I have to pee," Kippy said, thinking himself quite the comedian.

"Gross!" Reshea shook her head in disgust. "Like I was saying, I'm quite sure this four-legged fur ball here has never even seen a star runner before, let alone come inside of one. Oztin, imagine explaining this to your father if we get caught . . ."

"A star runner?" Kippy turned and looked towards the sky. "You're from out there?"

Considering the possibilities, Kippy studied the interior of the craft. It was about twice the size of Richie's bathroom. In the back center was a fluted column that looked like two funnels. Their flared ends rose from the floor and dropped down from the ceiling to join in the middle. The ship's interior was made of a spongy white material that gave off a soft glow, evenly lighting the inside of the craft. Meanwhile the larger boy in this group was pleading a case.

"Come on Reshea, how else are we going to find what we've come for? Tell her, Oztin."

"Squib's right," the one called Oztin conceded. "Dogs aren't exactly the higher intelligence on this planet."

Kippy believed he had just been insulted and would not let it pass unchallenged. "What? Are you kidding me? You're saying that you think dogs are less intelligent than humans? Let me ask you something. How often does a dog go to work? Never. You know how often humans go to work? Always. We sleep all day and play all night. Now, tell me, who's smarter?"

"Oh, really?" the girl pounced with a sarcastic wit. "If dogs are so intelligent, how come you've never invented anything? Please tell me, oh, wise furry one."

He may have been a novice at talking, but they would soon learn not to underestimate his intellectual prowess. Without so much as a nanosecond of hesitation, he answered her question. "Thumbs."

"Thumbs?" she questioned.

"Look at your hand."

She spread her palms and looked down.

"See that thing sticking out of the side of your hand? That's right, it's your thumb. It's the big physiological difference between humans and dogs."

She waved her hand with an uncomprehending expression.

"Have you ever tried to open a can without thumbs? Or grab anything? Good luck! Since we couldn't develop our mechanical skills, we were free to develop other abilities instead, like our minds."

The little guy, the apparent leader, offered a conciliation. "Sorry. You seem a little sensitive about this intelligence thing. Let me introduce myself. I am Oztin. This is my cousin, Reshea. Over there is Squib. You are right, we are from up there, way up there." His stubby fingers pointed towards the sky.

"My name's Kippy," he said as he considered how young these guys were and how far from home they must have traveled. "Aren't you guys a little young to be tooling around in outer space alone?"

"I'm twelve and Squib is thirteen," Reshea replied indignantly, as if this should be more than a sufficient answer.

"Almost thirteen—and a half," Squib added, throwing his shoulders back with pride.

Kippy was not sure that he could see any difference between these visitors and the local neighborhood kids. *Are humans the same on all planets? Are all planets like this one, with humans, animals . . . do they have dogs?*

"We have come here for a specific reason," Oztin set out to explain. "We were told we could get some liquid Fizzle Sweet here. And, well . . . we're kind of hoping you could help us."

"Fizzle Sweet?" Confused, Kippy tilted his head.

"It's what we call it back home," Oztin said worriedly. "It's a brown liquid and if you open it up too quickly, it will create a gaseous foam that rapidly expands and usually ends up spraying all over the place. We were told that this planet is the only place in the entire galaxy where this drink is brewed."

"And this is our third time here and so far, we've found nothing . . ." Squib blurted out.

"A brown, foaming, gaseous liquid? Jeez, you make it sound so appealing!" Reshea placed a finger in her mouth and pretended to gag.

Only available on our planet? Hmm . . . Kippy knew what they wanted, and his mind churned. *If I tell them what they want to know, they'll be gone in a flash. But if I can convince them that I can help them, perhaps . . .*

It was every dog's dream to be able to converse with his master. Kippy was worried about Richie. This boy was a mess. As a dog, he saw all his master's best qualities, the ones that others did not always see. Somewhere along this stream of thought, fantasy morphed into a scheme.

If I had a voice box, I could talk to him.

He assessed the disparate crew of kids and began calculating. *The girl is worried because they are not supposed to be here on Earth. The little guy—who is obviously the brains of the bunch—is not going to be fooled easily. And the big blond guy, well he's the least of my worries.*

That's it, Kippy realized. *Go after the weakest in the pack.* And since this is a matter of brains, not brawn . . . Kippy eyed his adversaries.

"It's called cola," Kippy told them. With those three simple words, the atmosphere of the room changed. Dogs are experts at reading body language. Tens of thousands of years of breeding and selection have honed this skill. These were eager customers.

"Can you get us some?" Squib said on a rushed hope which caused Oztin to shake his head. He stepped in and took charge of the conversation.

"If this is a hassle . . . well, we're sorry to have bothered you," he began dismissively. "In fact, we are running a bit late and our parents will start to worry if we have the star runner out much longer. Perhaps some other time?"

"But the Buzzard . . ." Squib complained, but Oztin shot him a silencing look.

Kippy had been right about this young pup. The last thing in the world he wanted to do was walk back out that door. It was time to make his move. Engaging Squib, he leaned in toward his victim.

"There is no such thing as Fizzle Sweet. And it is not something that just happens to be lying around. For those who are even fortunate enough to have access, it is considered a very sacred brew." He paused long enough to see if they were falling for it. *So far so good.*

"Fizz Cola is the most sought after of all the colas. Of course, Fizz Cola is also the hardest to get. This is not something for everybody."

He locked eyes with Squib, "Are you man enough to handle it?" Before Squib could reply, he continued. "Only select initiates can have Fizz Cola. As you know, it can't be found anywhere else in the galaxy or the universe for that matter." The honey of his lies rolled effortlessly from his tongue.

Watching Squib turn a deep red, Kippy planted the final hook. "It just so happens that you have come to the right place . . ."

"Why, why do you say that?" Squib said, giving up all pretense of having any negotiating skills.

"Because my master is able to get all the Fizz Cola you would ever want." Then lowering his voice, he added, almost as if it were an apology. "There's just one little problem."

No one said anything, the only sound in the craft was a faint humming from somewhere in the rear. Kippy wondered if he had pushed too far. *Have I lost them?*

Finally, it was Reshea who broke the spell. "What problem?"

"It's a communication problem," Kippy said with relief. But his nerves were tensing and when he got nervous, he tended to get gas. He could feel the pressure building. He was so close and knew he had to be very careful.

"If there was a way I could communicate with my master, I am sure I could get him to part with some of his Fizz Cola."

"Why can't he understand?" Squib asked in frustration. "Just go and talk to him." Kippy turned to Oztin and gave him a look.

"He needs to borrow the translator," Oztin explained with a growing worry on his face.

Kippy could see the shifting body language and knew he needed to close the deal before the smart one changed their minds.

"That's right," replied Kippy. "Just let me use this voice thingy and in three days you'll get twelve precious cans of Fizz Cola."

Squib threw back his shoulders and gave a quick look to Reshea. "This is like the last chance for us. You know if we fail then the Buzzard is going to mock me every day for the rest of my life." Squib was pleading his case to her.

"You should have never taken the bet," Reshea admonished.

"What was I supposed to do? He said I didn't have the balls to come here. Basically called me a coward in front of everybody." He avoided making eye contact with Oztin; setting his jaw in determination, he made the choice for them.

"It's twenty-four cans. And you only have two days, not three."

Can it really be this easy?

"Deal!" Kippy enthusiastically agreed before anyone could object.

Oztin sighed.

No sooner had Kippy begun to savor his victory when Squib made a quick lunge and grabbed him by the neck. Kippy let out a long silent stream of gas.

"Here you go Oztin," Squib said handing him the band. "No one will see it under the collar, but he'll be able to talk." Oztin fixed the miniature translator into the back of the leather seam and refastened it on Kippy's collar.

But before he could relish the moment, Reshea crinkled her nose and eyed him suspiciously.

"What's that disgusting smell?" It was Kippy's cue to leave.

𝑒ᴛ𝔪 ◆ Ж ● Ж ↗𝔪

Chapter 2
A Change in Fortune

Roaring out from behind the fleeing comet's tail with an adoring Kayla strapped into the seat at his right, Richie navigated the space cruiser through the perilous trail of ice and debris.

As he fired the reverse thrusters of his advanced battle cruiser, he was surprised to bring his weapons to bear upon the rear guard of the invading lizard race known as the Dragos. He knew he was the last chance that Earth had to stop these aliens before their final assault. The fate of humanity hung in the balance.

He gave Kayla a smile of reassurance, then dropped below the formation of the advancing armada, skillfully lining his blasters upon the command cruiser of the alien fleet.

The shrill cry of alarm bells began to sound. He realized that a very clever trap had been set—one for which he had fallen hook, line, and sinker. Hiding in the rubble of comet debris were two alien cruisers waiting, prepared to eliminate Earth's last hope.

The alien ships fired multiple photon torpedoes at him. He leaned hard on the controls trying to avoid the danger.

Drowned out by the din of the ringing klaxons, Kayla was shouting, trying to warn him, but he couldn't make out her words.

"T-me-o-g-t-up!" she hollered.

"What? What is it?" He asked her, again and again.

With the Dragos' deadly torpedoes closing in, Kayla's voice rose above the bleating cry of warning bells, heralding unwelcome news . . .

"Time to get up!"

The voice of Richie's father thundered from Kayla's mouth, catapulting him from the bold adventures of dreamland back to the dullness of reality.

"A dream. Of course, it was just a dream," he muttered.

How could I think I would be cruising among the stars with Kayla Carlyle? Why would the most beautiful girl in school have anything to do with me?

His father yelled his usual rhetorical question from the bottom of the stairs, "You don't want to sleep your life away, do ya?"

Morning? How could it be morning already? It felt like he just closed his eyes, but sunrise said otherwise.

"Just because Dad needs to get to the store at the crack of dawn doesn't mean I have to," Richie groused under his breath. At that moment, sleeping his life away didn't sound like such a bad idea.

Stepping into the tiny bathroom, Richie washed his face, brushed his teeth, and then rummaged through the closet for something clean to wear. The floorboards squeaked upon entering the kitchen. His dad was seated at the table, nose buried in the paper.

"Morning, Dad. Anything interesting today?" His dad was old school, still had the newspaper delivered seven days a week.

His father peered across the top of the *Daily Herald*. His brows were furrowed with anger. "Damn Miles is at it again!" Mr. Radcliff snarled, dropping the paper to the table.

'Damn' was the strongest language Richie ever heard come from his father's mouth. However, the subject of Bartholomew Miles presented a special case.

"More talk about the factory that that pompous crook wants to build here," his father continued. "He's working every official in town. By now they've all been bought and paid for! Don't they see what he's doing? Bart doesn't give a damn about the community, only the money he stands to gain."

Richie had heard the tirade before. He could almost mimic his father's next statement word for word.

'If that factory is built where Professor Miles wants to build it, in five years Santa Martina will wallow in its own filth! Smokestacks will pollute the skies and the streams will become filled with cadmium, lead, and arsenic! They could forget Lacey Creek for trout fishing.'

He loved his dad, and the truth was, that if Miles had never been here in the first place, his mother would never have been killed by the mining truck that swerved onto her side of the road. He knew that was part of his dad's resentment toward the man.

Richie just nodded and tried to change the subject. His father said nothing, and Richie could sense the gulf between them grow another inch. After a long pause, Mr. Radcliff let out a sigh.

"I'm sorry, Richie." His tone was sad. "I've gotta get to the store early this morning. Make sure you feed that dog of yours and lock the house before you go to school. There's pizza in the freezer. I'll probably be home late."

His father got up from the table, and his gaze fell upon his son. Sorrow was etched at the corner of his eyes. Then choking on his words, he told him. "I had to let Kenny go yesterday."

Kenny is gone? Richie's eyes lingered on the closing door. *I know business is slow, but . . .* Kenny and his new wife were about to have a baby. Richie now understood the pain behind this morning's anger. His father prided himself on his loyalty to his friends, family, and employees. He had often commented that Kenny was a good man. Honest and hardworking. Richie liked him and he could sense how his father must feel about having to lay him off.

Who's gonna run the store when dad's not there? Kenny was his last employee.

Solemnly Richie poured cereal into the bowl and grabbed the newspaper. Absentmindedly, he shuffled through the various sections until, in the local news he saw a picture that caught his eye.

Mrs. Capon from the local museum was shaking hands with a distinguished gentleman. Looking at the article, Richie's thoughts drifted back to his dad. It felt like everything in his world was falling apart. "This sucks!"

He heard Kippy barking outside and put the paper down. Richie looked out the kitchen window to see his mutt barking up a tree.

As if he could ever catch that squirrel, he thought. It helped dispel the gloom of Kenny's dismissal. He called through the screen. "Kippy, come on boy. It's time for breakfast."

Kippy heard his master's voice. "Okay Robin, I promise, if you do this for me, I'll make sure that cat never bothers you again. Deal?"

Still marveling at the wide spectrum of his new communication skills, the hungry canine ran across the lawn and in through the doggie door.

He viewed his master with a fresh eye. Lanky, with a lick of hair that poked from the back of his head, he seemed to be weighed down. Like he was draped in perpetual defeat.

Things are going to change, Kippy vowed.

"What's up boy?" Richie rubbed the tufted fur behind Kippy's ears. "Can I fix you something to eat? What's it going to be, Kal-Kan or Purina?" It was a rhetorical question, but Kippy got careless.

"Purina," he replied with a happy-go-lucky voice.

Richie dropped the stainless bowl and Kippy froze, realizing he had slipped. He was not yet ready to divulge his secret. He had a plan forming in his head and he wanted to see if Mother Robin fulfilled her role first.

"Ruff, ruff-ruff," Kippy recovered.

"Man, I'm losing it." Richie mumbled and then lunched into the unilateral conversation he usually had with his best friend and confidante. "I saw you out prowling. It must be great not having a worry in the world."

Kippy replied with a high-pitched butt-belch. This was followed by a wall of stink that spread through the room.

"Jeez, Kippy," Richie reeled, crinkling his nose in disgust. "You gonna peel the paper off the walls if you keep letting 'em out like that."

Kippy ignored him and kept eating.

eтℳ · ◆ · ℋ · ● ℋ ↗ ℳ

With a little time left to kill before he had to leave for school, Richie browsed through the rest of the paper. He found the article with Mrs. Capon in it. He liked her, she was always nice to him, and she seemed to be one of the few adults in town who really understood how much he missed his mother.

Fizz Cola CEO Donates to Local Museum
Mr. S.B. Halim, Chairman and CEO of the global consumer powerhouse, Fizz Cola Corporation, made a personal donation of $1,000,000 to the Santa Martina County Historical Museum. Said Mrs. Dorothea Capon, director of the small county museum, "This is the largest donation we have ever received. The funds will be used for exploring the origins of local Native American tribes, their lore, myths, and legends.

"Have a good one, Kip," he said when it was time to go. Richie lived inside of the bus zone, so he had to either walk or ride his bike to school. Until last September, he had ridden his bike every day, hooking up with Ned at the old oak tree.

In his mind's eye Richie could see Ned now. With his head of unruly red hair and big, black-framed glasses always sliding down his nose, Ned navigated these paths as if he were in control of the world around him.

But he had moved away nine months ago. His father was out of work and had received a call about a job in Bakersfield. And just like that, two days later, a U-Haul lumbered down the road and Ned was gone.

Richie no longer rode his bike to school. Mainly because whenever he did, he had to push it home. The butthead bully, Chucky, always let the air out of his tires.

If I stood up to him just once, he would quit picking on me.

He knew it was because Ned had embarrassed him, and since he was gone, Chucky took it out on him instead.

As he walked down the hill, he could see Santa Martina Middle School in the distance. Dad's tirade at breakfast was a bad start to his day. By the time Richie approached the school, he realized that it was about to get worse. A swarm of kids cluttered the walkway, partially blocking the front entrance. Holding court was the overweight bully, prancing around as if trying to enchant Kayla.

Seeing the girl of his dreams with her soft brown hair floating in the morning sun and the glowing wattage of her smile, Richie was reminded why he felt she was the prettiest girl in the entire world. The thought of Chucky getting any attention from Kayla—good or bad—made Richie want to retch.

I wonder if she even knows I'm alive?

With eyes cast down, Richie hoped to get by without any problems. *Please, not today, he prayed. Not in front of Kayla.* Almost to the safety of the steps, he heard the dreaded words.

"Hey, Radcliff, come over here!"

There was nowhere to hide, so Richie turned and faced the group, steeling himself for the worst. Pulling back his shoulders, he lifted his chin in defiance. Electricity flowed through the crowd. He could tell they sensed something was going to happen.

21

The morning light cast his shadow far out in front of him. Richie fought to maintain control. He wished he were as large as his silhouette mocking him from the concrete.

He shuffled his feet forward, knowing that Kayla was watching. Be brave, he told himself, repeating the mantra over and over and over again. Then something out of the ordinary occurred. His shadow vanished.

Following the gaze of the gawking crowd, Richie looked skyward. *What in the world?*

Bearing down on them came the wump, wump, wump sound of beating wings. Thousands upon thousands of birds circled overhead—coming closer and closer. Curiosity soon turned to panic. Kids began to break and run. It was like something out of a horror movie. So many birds had gathered that their mass was blocking the light.

He saw that Kayla was trapped in a trance. *I need to help her.*

Richie ignored the chaos surrounding him and nudged Kayla away from the gathering storm. He tried to ignore the birds as they swooped down. They were now whirling about faster and faster until it all became a blur. Air rushed past as the flock tightened into a tornado that enveloped the lone bully.

"Kayla," he said gently shaking her. She did not respond. "Kayla!" he said more forcefully. She responded and gave him a weak smile. But it did not cover her fear.

He turned his attention to the growing flock of angry birds and saw that Chucky was paralyzed. Richie's instincts pushed him to act. Raising an arm, he used his hand to protect his face and began pushing his way into the whirling cloud. Running on autopilot, he felt nothing. His only thought was to help his classmate, even if he was a jerk. His intercession disrupted the flow of the birds, and soon the avian tornado began to part.

Rising up they first cleared at foot level, then waist, head, and eventually every last one of them departed towards the sky. Chucky was a quivering mass of guano. In unison, everyone on the playground erupted into an uncomfortable laughter.

"Phew . . . you stink," was all Richie could think to say.

Not daring to open his mouth, Chucky was speechless.

Kayla stepped alongside Richie. After one glance to see that Chuck was alright, she smiled at Richie. "We're going to be late for class. Will you walk me?"

Richie's heart thudded against his chest, and he worried it was another dream. *What do I say?*

Kayla coughed softly, waiting for a reply.

"Uh, sure," he finally managed.

ℯⲦⲘ ⬩ ◆ ⬩)(⬩ ●)(⤬ Ⲙ

Smelling worse than a septic tank, Chucky was livid. He took the shortcut that ran past the old cemetery as he walked home, and all the while his mind roiled with thoughts of revenge. "I'll get that Radcliff," he spit.

Reaching the top of Graveyard hill, Chucky stopped, trying to catch his breath without ingesting the poo that covered him. He knew the burial grounds behind St. Paul's Episcopal Church were creepy, but in the bright light of day, they seemed harmless enough. Once he had been here at night when clouds scudded across the moon and tree branches swept shadows across the yard. He shuddered at the memory.

Just beyond the gnarled tangle of rusted fence was the graveyard. Standing alone, he paused to scrape more of the bird crap from his clothes.

"What was that?" Something was moving in the bushes. He peered into the thicket but saw nothing. The hairs on his neck prickled as the sound of a deep throaty moan got his unwavering attention. Like lamentations of the dying, the sound sent fear coursing through Chucky's veins. Quietly, he strained to understand the words floating up from the bramble.

"Chuuuuuuuuuuuuuuuckeeee . . . Chuuuuuuuuuuuuuuuckeeee. . ."

Stunned at his own name, he stammered out a reply, "Who. . . who is it?"

"You are a baaaaaaad boy," the throaty voice moaned. Then a mocking laugh pierced the thicket, and finally, silence.

His mind went blank with fright. Chucky jerked to his right, jumping around the bush. *Someone is playing a joke on me! Yeah, that's got to be it!* But no one was there. His heart rate accelerated his anxiety.

Up above he saw two old crows sitting in a tree. *Caw, caw, caw,* they called as they stared down at him. Their eyes were dark pools. Chucky's imagination was getting the better of him. His heart was beating in a rapid pulse. Fear filled his throat. He knew if he screamed, bird dung would probably choke him.

Cutting through the silence he heard the beating of wings and turned to see an incoming black blur. He dropped to the ground as the massive crows swept by so close that the wind of their wake was like the devil's breath upon his cheeks.

He began trembling, crying as he pressed his hands into his face. When he finally dared to open his eyes, the birds were gone, but he was not alone. A dog stood hovering over him, sniffing. And then it crinkled its nose and backed away. Whether due to fear, or the inexplicable events of the morning, Chucky dared not move. He lay paralyzed, wishing it would all go away.

Kippy was laughing so hard his ribs hurt.

Mrs. Robin certainly lived up to her end of the bargain.

He was thrilled this new voice thingy was working out so well. His devious mind came up with additional torments. Racing ahead, he prepared for his next act.

Chapter 3
The Oriana Star System

Oztin stood by the open doors of his father's study. Enoch was on the halo-phone engaged with members of the counsel. Seeing his son, he waved him in, but put a finger to his lips for silence.

His father was a brilliant and well-organized man, though a cursory glance at the disheveled office would leave one with a different impression.

His study was a wall of books. Volumes on navigation, philosophy, astral physics, agronomy, and history surrounded the community leader. There were tomes on almost every subject.

Beyond the windows, Oztin could see the rising moons of Gondor. Like the eyes of night, the twin moons were protective sentinels reflecting the pale green light of the helium-fired sun that anchored their solar system. His father was wrapping up his call.

"This is very, very serious," Enoch said. "The sooner we meet the better. Thank you, Lachman, please call me back as soon as you know." Disconnecting, he looked up from his desk.

"How's my favorite son today?"

"I'm your only son, dad," Oztin said, falling comfortably into the script they replayed so often.

"Ah, that is true, but you are still my favorite." It was his father's cue. "You look like you have something on your mind. Care to discuss it with an old codger like myself?"

His father could put him at ease with a simple smile and a few choice words. "Dad, I'm confused about something," Oztin told him. "How come there are so many populated planets that do not know the Federation exists? I mean, couldn't we help them?"

"That's a good question," Enoch said. Standing to stretch, he came around the desk. "As you know, the universe is vast. What we call the Galactic Federation is nothing more than a collective of nine regional councils. A coalition of governments that share common values." His hands moved restlessly, as if he had more thoughts than words and they were trying to escape through his fingertips.

Beyond the big bay windows, a soft breeze stirred the treetops. Enoch paused long enough to open the window, allowing the cool dry air to float in on scents of frangipani and lilac.

He then paused to crack his back. Oztin knew the tell-tale signs. His father was worried about something.

His father scratched his head and continued. "The Federation does not govern every planet or culture in the universe. We have our enemies, and though they do not subscribe to our philosophy of freedom and individual rights, we have been able to maintain an uneasy truce with them."

"You mean the Dragos, right?" Oztin asked.

"Yes," he affirmed with a dour expression. "For some inexplicable reason, the universe is dominated by two distinctively different forms of life. Every living planet is either populated by warm-blooded humans or the cold-blooded reptiles."

Oztin had read about the Dragos at school. Just the thought of them sent a chill down his spine. Still, he hoped for a more definitive answer to his question. But he knew to proceed cautiously, lest his father become suspicious.

"Dad, what I want to understand is why it is forbidden for us to make contact with humans who do not know of the Federation?"

Enoch took a long look at his son before replying. "Like music, the cosmos are tuned to many harmonics and frequencies, the rate and speed in which matter vibrates," he clarified. "Every planet is governed by these immutable laws. . ." he continued.

To Oztin, the explanation seemed contradictory, but perhaps, this was simply because he was determined to assuage his own guilt. They were interrupted by the soft chiming of the phone. Enoch stepped behind his desk and picked up the receiver.

After listening he replied. "Good Richard. I will expect to see them soon."

"Son," he said with a paternal smile. "Think of all your actions—no matter how small—as if each were a stone cast into quiet waters. The ripples from each stone continue to push out into ever greater circles, eventually touching distant shores, even as the stone appears to sink harmlessly to the bottom of the pond. We have no idea what effect our smallest dealings can have on the development of an entire civilization, or upon which shore of destiny our ripples may touch."

Oztin had never really considered this. *Am I affecting the other world simply to get some sugar water?* It was simply a different aspect of the same worry. He was defying the rules of the Galactic Federation and more to his heart, he was disobeying his father. This bothered him the most.

As these thoughts ran through his mind, his mom popped her head into the doorway. "Enoch dear, Loon Sambrk and his Bocan emissaries are here."

"Okay darling, we're just finishing up."

Turning back to his son, he hastened to wrap up their conversation. "Remember, everything you do will not only affect your life, but the lives of others as well. One day it will become clear to you. Now I need to meet with these fellows. It's important."

Oztin was curious about their visitors, and he was smart enough to understand that their visit was somehow tied into that faraway place that had a lock on his father's attention.

"Dad, who is Loon Sambrk, and why are there people from Bocah coming by the house at this hour?"

Enoch studied his son, as if sizing him up. He answered the question by asking a question. "Do you remember the Diageo Treaty from your studies?" He waited only a heartbeat before giving Oztin a summary.

"Three thousand years ago the Galactic Federation and the Dragos signed a treaty. The essence of which was that they would not interfere with any developing civilizations, and we would remain neutral as well."

Oztin vaguely remembered some of this from his classes at school. Suddenly his innocent little trip did not seem so innocent anymore.

"If we fail to adhere to the strictest measure of this treaty, can you imagine the can of worms we would open with the Dragos? This is why parents put the restrictor plates on their children's space cruisers. We're not just being over-protective. If the Dragos found that citizens of the Federation knowingly went to territory that has been mutually deemed off-limits, it could set off a galactic struggle that would last for centuries."

Oztin felt sick to his stomach. Even the cool air flowing in through the window could not arrest the sweat breaking on his brow.

"The only reason they have stuck with the treaty so far is fear of our superior technology. Right now, they are so easily recognized that if they were to approach a humanoid planet, we would quickly find out."

Oztin saw the deep seriousness etched at the corners of his father's eyes. He had seen pictures of Dragos in his history class. They always seemed to be a faraway idea, but not really relevant to their lives. Now he wondered. This led back to his guilty conscience. *What if Kippy had entered our craft and seen Dragos instead of us?* A roil of discomfort coursed through his veins.

"I'm going to share something with you in the strictest of confidence. Can I trust you?"

"Yes, father," Oztin answered solemnly.

"The planet Bocah is near the edge of our treaty boundary, very close to the Dragos' border. Loon is here because he has disturbing news. The Dragos have learned to morph into human form. We know they are up to something—we just don't know what it is."

ℰℳ•◆•ℋ•●ℋℤℳ

Oztin's father worked with the Bocans behind closed doors until his mom called them to dinner. She had set the table for six. As they filed into the dining room, the interplanetary guests did not bother to wait for the hostess to assign them seats but grabbed chairs and began serving themselves.

Oztin watched in shock. He had never experienced a ruder group of people. It seemed their culture was one of every man for himself. Once they were done, Enoch led their guests back into the study and Oztin helped his mother clear the table. In the kitchen, Oztin pulled a stool up to the sink to dry dishes as she washed. He asked her a question about the Bocans, why she thought they acted so rude.

"Honey, it is not our place to judge," she mildly admonished him. "But don't ever let me catch you acting as if you are the center of the universe."

"I promise!" he grinned. "Is it okay if I go down to Ricca-Madness?"

"Not too long." She smiled.

Stepping out the front door, Oztin tasted the cool evening air. Starting his walk towards the gaming pavilion, he could see the peaks of the Plebian Hills in the distance. Outside of the city there were winding roads and wild rivers, but here, the center of town was on a systematic grid of north-south and east-west streets and boulevards. Coming to the end of Pike Street, Otzin paused before stepping onto Stiles Boulevard.

Walking under the neon moons of Candahar, crimson from the rooftop sign of Ricca Madness, he entered the brightly lit arena and became engulfed in the sounds of laughter.

Oztin saw Reshea seated with friends. He noticed two girls next to her that he had never met before. They looked like twins. One of them turned her head and Oztin followed her gaze towards Squib.

His smile was full of triumph and satisfaction. Knocking down a perfect bole, and acting as if was no big deal, like he did it every time. Oztin secretly admired how Squib mastered the trick of becoming the center of attention without actually appearing to show off. Squib was his friend, it was just that being a dwarf was difficult, and most of the time it was the only reason he ever got any attention.

Scoring a perfect bole was not as easy as it looked. The trick was to finesse the ten-inch ball off the recoil bumper with just enough impact to miss the first line of traps. This was the part that was most difficult for him. With his little arms there was no way he would ever be able to control the toss like that.

Oztin shuffled through the crowded aisle and joined his friends. "Hey guys, what's going on?"

"Hey," answered Reshea, "Oztin, do you know my friends Lithe and Lil?"

"Hi Oztin," they said in unison. Their voices had a playful hint in them. He wasn't sure who was who. "Is it really true you guys are getting some Fizz Cola?"

"We would love to try some," said the other. "If you have enough."

"Oztin, come sit next to us," they chimed together. He immediately forgot the petty jealousies he had felt.

He looked over at his cousin and she smiled at him, saying nothing. One thing he liked about Reshea was she always made sure that he was part of the group. Fresh on the memory of the rude Bocans, he vowed tonight he would thank her.

Sitting between the pretty girls, Oztin could smell their hair as errant wisps touched him like an electric current. He was sure they could hear the amplified beat of his heart as his pulse raced across sweat dampened hands.

He was used to the stares, the whispers, and people treating him as an oddity, but tonight, there was none of that. Tonight, amongst friends and these two gorgeous creatures, he was just one of the crowd. Even if it was for just a fleeting moment, it felt great.

When it was time to go home, sliding from the seat, he accidentally slid a hand across Lithe's jean-clad leg as he went to steady himself. He froze, nervous, unsure if he might have offended her. But the slight twist of her lip said without words, "it's okay."

"I have to head home," he stuttered slightly, in unfamiliar territory.

They giggled at his blush. "Goodbye, Oztin. Good luck with the Fizz Cola."

Conscious of his waddling gait, Oztin threw back his shoulders and headed towards the door. He had a lot to think about as he walked home that night.

The Bocans, the treaty, the ramifications of getting caught visiting the blue planet, and the girls. It all weighed heavy on his mind. The desire to be able to share Fizz Cola with Lithe and Lil suddenly burned inside him. It was an unfamiliar fire. But his annoying conscience kept posing the same question.

If I go back to the blue planet, am I like a Bocan, only thinking of myself?

ᘓᛖᛗ ⬧ ◆ ⬧ ⵁ ⬧ ⬤ ⵁ ⤜ᛗ

Chapter 4
A Dog's Life Indeed

Kippy walked down Second Avenue with a question still seeking an answer.

How am I going to get those guys their Fizz Cola?

His strategy for Richie was working, but if he failed to deliver the Fizz Cola . . . He knew they would take back their voice thingy. Pondering this, he saw a sign.

Fizz Cola Always Refreshing. On sale now at Davey's Locker. Lowest Prices in Town!

Awesome. I also understand what they write. "This is just so cool," he grinned with a dog smile.

Davey's Locker was the new store on Main Street. Walking through town, Kippy realized there were signs for everything. 'Buy this. Tastes great. Less filling. Eat here. Save now. Borrow. Low prices. Best value. Instant credit.'

The town seemed awash in messages telling people what to do and where to go. 'Look younger. Lose weight. Remove wrinkles. Fuller hair!'

Kippy admired people and all they could accomplish. Yet all around them were messages that from his perspective were made to make people feel bad about themselves. He could not remember a time when he wished his tail were longer, his ears were perkier, or his breath sweeter.

Why on Earth do people worry about that stuff?

Trotting along the sidewalk, Kippy spied two boys vaping in the alley.

"Hey you!" Kippy shouted from behind a garbage dumpster. "I'm going to tell your mothers!" The boys took off running.

"I love this . . . " he said, laughing. This just raised the stakes on keeping the translator. He had to figure out how to live up to his side of the agreement before the space kids returned.

Rounding the corner, he saw the store's grand opening sign in the window.

'DAVEY'S LOCKER. Lowest Prices in Town - We Guarantee It!'

Kippy walked through the parking lot and sat beside the front door plotting his next move.

"Do you realize my bill is over forty dollars less than when I shop over at Radcliff's?" asked a middle-aged woman who wore pants that were awkwardly tight.

"I know, me too," said her friend as they stepped onto the sidewalk. "Maybe he's been ripping us off for years."

"It serves him right then that he is going out of business," replied the first.

Going out of business? Richie's dad was going out of business? This comment hit Kippy with a thud. It also explained the stress that filled the Radcliff house. And as one who was loyal to his family, it left him concerned.

He saw a large delivery truck turn down the drive behind the store. Emblazoned on its side were two simple words: Fizz Cola.

He decided to investigate, maybe get an idea of a plan. Darting around back, Kippy found a husky uniformed man unloading cases and cases of Fizz Cola. *How would I move some of this? I don't have hands.*

"Hey pooch," the driver said, spotting him. "What's up boy?"

Kippy bit back a desire to punk him. *Wouldn't he be surprised . . .*

Out of the back door came a man in a white shirt and loud tie who handed the driver a clipboard.

"That's a lot of Fizz Cola you're moving," the driver noted, signing the drop off form for the store employee. "How the heck can you stay in business when you're charging less than what you pay?"

"Beats me, I just work here. But everybody in town is coming because of these prices. Miles Industries owns the store, I guess their strategy is to run everyone else out of business. Then they raise prices sky high. Seems like a slimy way to do business."

"I guess," said the driver. "Competition is rough. Too bad. I always liked Radcliff." Pulling down the rear door, the driver climbed back into his truck and with diesel fumes filling the alleyway, he drove off.

If it hadn't been for this translator thing, I would never have understood how quickly things are turning bad for my master's family. And who's behind it. I can't let this happen. I don't know how, but I need to stop this before it is too late.

℈ℳ•◆•Ж•●Ж⤢ℳ

From across the field, Kippy saw Richie turning into their driveway. He forged his snout through the tall dry grass racing to stay one step ahead of his master.

He had mentally bounced back and forth about sharing his new ability with Richie. He had promised not to, but he needed his help. *If they learn I broke my promise, they may take this thing back. But his dad is in trouble . . .*

Leaping the steps of the back porch, the doggie door was still swinging when Richie came strolling in through the front.

"Kippy! I'm home! Here boy! There you are." He had a grin on his face as he reached down to rub his buddy's furry mane. "I'm starving, how 'bout I fix us something to eat?"

This perked Kippy's ears. Sitting up on his haunches, he put a hopeful look on as his master opened the refrigerator door.

Turning with hands full of milk and sandwich fixings, Richie laughed. "Don't worry boy, you know I always take care of you."

Kippy licked his lips, his tail thumping hard on the linoleum.

"Guess what? I walked Kayla Carlyle home today. Not only that. You should have seen what happened to Chucky. He got dive-bombed with bird poop! You should have seen all those birds. It was crazy!"

Kippy had given a lot of thought to this and made his decision.

"If you thought your day was crazy so far," Kippy said in a husky voice . . .

Richie's jaw dropped along with the cup of milk. It bounced once before spilling all over the floor. He stood there—his mouth wide in disbelief.

"Look at the bright side," Kippy said with mischief. "Your day has definitely gone better than Chucky's."

"I knew today was too good to be true," Richie muttered.

"What's so bad about a talking dog?" Kippy asked, his tail thumping the floor.

Richie eased into a chair and let out a long breath.

"No one else knows about this and we should keep it that way," Kippy said in earnest. "Let me tell you about Chucky and maybe you'll feel a little better."

Kippy proceeded to tell him about his deal with the robin and unfolded the various machinations of his plot.

"So how long have you been able to talk and how did it happen?" Richie said with a little color coming back into his cheeks.

"I have always been able to speak. We just didn't understand each other's languages," Kippy replied. "Run your hand along the inside of my collar."

Richie reached over and stroked two fingers under the red leather band.

"Feel that? I got it last night. It's some sort of voice translator. So today was actually the first time we could understand each other."

"Wow. Where did you get it?"

"You said it was a crazy day. Alien kids let me borrow it."

"Aliens?"

"Yea. Three kids, just like you. Even about your age."

"Aliens? Kids—my age? They just dropped by and let you borrow it? Why you? Or for that matter why me?"

"It was a trade."

"A trade? For what?" The questions reeled of doubt.

"Tomorrow we have to deliver them a case of Fizz Cola. You're going to meet them."

e⊤𝕞 • ◆ • ⋊ • ● ⋊ ⤳ 𝕞

Chapter 5
Boy meets . . . Aliens?

"How much longer before these guys get here?" Richie asked, shivering in the backyard as he watched a shooting star streak across the sky. "Make a wish!"

"What did you wish for?" Kippy asked.

"Something special, probably impossible, but special."

"Well don't count on it coming true. That's not a falling star, it's our interstellar neighbors."

"Really?" Richie suddenly had a flood of questions come to mind. *What do they look like? Do they speak English? What do we talk about? What if we can't communicate?*

Kippy interrupted his deliberations with a tidbit he conveniently forgot to mention. "Humans can't actually see their spaceships, only the sparks from their craft when they enter our atmosphere."

"I can't see them?" Richie asked with fresh concern.

"I'm working on it," Kippy said with weak assurance.

The canvas of stars stretched across the broad horizon spanning the gentle breeze that carried the chorus of distant dogs who had begun barking down in the valley.

"They're here," Kippy announced.

"Here?" Richie didn't see anything. "Where?"

"Just wait. I'll be back in a few minutes."

Richie watched as Kippy's feet left the ground and each step carried him farther into the air. When he was eye level with his master, Kippy stopped and winked.

"Remember, Fizz Cola is rare and sacred. You're bestowing a great honor on them with this gift."

Richie managed to nod his understanding, then Kippy disappeared.

An invisible ship, an invisible ramp. This is what I saw the other night!

He crossed his arms and stood guard over his case of Fizz Cola. He felt foolish, but he didn't know what else to do.

As the seconds turned into long minutes, Richie had time to think, and this meant he had time to worry.

My first encounter with beings from another world and I'm supposed to start out by lying to them.

Stepping into the galley, Kippy tried to act with an air of nonchalance. It was a false bravado. "Hey guys, welcome back," he said glancing to each of them. No one returned his greeting. Kippy knew they saw Richie standing outside. They had been very clear about having no contact with humans.

Squib had a scowl on his face and got up from his seat. His body smelled tense and angry as he brushed past the dog. Ducking his head through the door he went down the ramp. The other two shifted uncomfortably in their seats, but still, no one said a word.

A momentary fear turned into concern for Richie who was unaware that Squib was coming his way. Turning heel, Kippy growled as he followed Squib out the door. "You better not even think of touching him," the canine warned with bared teeth.

"Just wait!" Squib ordered with a commanding voice. Kippy stopped at the top of the ramp, but his gaze never wavered.

◆•⋈•●

"What was that?" Richie gulped. He heard the growling. Fear welled up and his mind raced through all the things that could go wrong. He was ready to do something, anything, to help his friend.

Then, as if by magic, the prize over which he was standing guard rose up and floated away.

"What the . . ." he stumbled backward. He had read stories about UFOs with tractor-beam rays that could snare unsuspecting humans. He tried to put distance between himself and the fleeing cola. Tripping on a tuft of wet grass, the next thing he knew he was sitting on his backside, his pants soaking up the evening dew. Meanwhile, the soda slipped into the night and vanished.

"What are you thinking, bringing him here?" Squib glared while wiping droplets off his hands.

"I brought the Fizz!" Kippy retorted defensively. "That was our deal!"

"No, you broke your promise!" Squib said. But his words were not quite as harsh as he eyed the soda.

Kippy shot a pleading look towards Oztin, but there was no sympathy in that corner.

"I think we should call it a day," Oztin said with firm decisiveness. "We need the collar back."

Kippy had to do something, and fast. *Words, I need to spin some more words.* Cast in the soft glow of the ambient walls, Kippy tried to read their expressions. What makes each of them tick?

"I know how important it was to make sure I delivered as promised," he said in his most humble voice. He had his tail tucked up under him, it was a dog's way of showing shame.

"But it was the only option left. Really, I had no idea how difficult it is to get this stuff." That was partially true, but not for the reasons he had implied. But he could see their expressions soften. This emboldened him to continue.

Looking at Oztin, Kippy realized how hard it must be for him as a dwarf. All kids want to fit in. If I can get him on my side . . . He angled his body so that they were naturally facing one another.

"Do you realize what you have in your hands? You are now about to be the coolest kid on your planet. The talk of the universe." It was an all-or-nothing gambit. He was not about to let something as mundane as the truth get in his way.

"It's not that we're not appreciative," Oztin replied. "But we're not supposed to let humans see us, and I think we made that pretty clear to you."

"And we definitely can't interact with them," Reshea exclaimed, each word elongated and edged with criticism. "It's totally against the rules of non-interference . . ."

Kippy could see that their fear of getting caught was going to win out if he did not act quickly. He began back-filling his story with small kernels of truth.

"Do you guys really think you are the only ones that come here? Honestly, you're not that naïve, are you?"

Looks were exchanged between the three visitors. Confusion and even disbelief replaced the clarity that had reigned supreme just moments before. Kippy was emboldened and pushed on.

"Shoot, my four-legged friends and I have been watching you mess with humans for years. Not exactly what I would call non-interference. No sir, it seems more like a freeway here most nights."

Reshea looked at Kippy with skepticism, but her curiosity was clearly piqued. "You say you see ships coming here all the time? I find that hard to believe."

Kippy was about to reply but Reshea cut him off. "Don't lie to me. If you ever want to see us again, I want the truth. You understand? No crap, no stories, just the truth."

Kippy took a deep gulp. The air smelled damp, it was the dew-soaked cardboard. He decided it was no time to lie. Truth was his ally.

"Not every day for sure. But ever since I was a pup, I've seen ships coming and going. You're certainly not the first, nor I expect will you be the last. The other ships, at least the ones I have seen, they're much different from yours. They're bigger. And . . . well, something about them always gives me the creeps. Not like you guys."

Kippy's tail remained tucked in humility, a subservient position all dogs understood. He recalled the crawling sensation he'd had the time he had seen that other craft pass overhead.

"I wonder who they are?" Reshea asked with eyebrows furrowed in skepticism. Turning to her two companions, she leveled them with an unflinching look and then laid out the obvious flaws in Kippy's statements.

"No one's supposed to be here unless they have monitoring status from the Federation. And though their ships may be a lot larger, they still look pretty much like ours. Besides, they wouldn't come here that often, if at all."

"Look," Kippy said. "I'm telling you the truth. Really, cross my heart. You are not the only ones who show up here."

"Could this be what Dad's worried about?" Oztin asked, thinking aloud.

Kippy did not know what that meant but he sensed an opening. "Why not take a sip of your prize?"

Squib took one of the cans and popped the top. *Phhhhht* . . . Little gas bubbles dribbled around the opening.

He took a long swallow and then belched. It was deep, loud, long, and vibrant. Reshea laughed. In an instant, the tension had disappeared. He passed her the can.

"Try it. It puts the concoctions of Candahar to shame."

Reshea wiped its edge with her sleeve and took a sip. She closed her eyes and smiled.

"Look you guys, I am sorry that I made you angry, but my master is the one who was able to get the Fizz Cola for you. I tried, but I couldn't do it without his help. You may not appreciate that fact, but it's the truth." Kippy knew he had a very small window to make his pitch.

"He's a good kid and he can keep you guys in a regular supply of this stuff. But he also has his own problems. Please understand what I am about to ask of you is not for me, but for him."

He glanced towards Oztin, instinctively knowing that he would be most sympathetic to his request. Whatever he decided, the rest would agree too.

"Richie doesn't have a lot of friends. He's an only child, lost his mother a few years ago. He lacks self-confidence. All in all, he feels that he just doesn't fit in and he is drifting towards becoming a loner. I want to change that before it is too late. If I could keep talking to him, I'm sure I could help."

Squib popped another can and passed it around while Kippy continued.

"Please consider a trade, this voice translator in exchange for an ongoing supply of Fizz Cola."

He pleaded to Oztin specifically, thinking of the three of them, he more than most would likely empathize with wanting to fit in.

"Okay," Oztin agreed. "If everyone is okay with this, here's the deal. We let you continue to borrow the translator, but only as long as your master continues to supply us with Fizz Cola. If at any time we need it back, you hand it over, no questions asked."

"Deal!" Kippy answered before anyone could interject or change their mind. His spirits were starting to soar. He had done it. He was drooling a little saliva, and his tail would not stop wagging.

"Hellooo, hello, anybody out there." It was Richie, he had apparently mustered up his bravery. Oztin pushed some buttons on the control panel and the video monitor came to life.

"He's sort of cute," Reshea said. Quickly adding, "In a geekish way."

"He looks harmless," Squib retorted at her observation.

"There is one other thing," Kippy ventured. He had promised Richie that he would meet these kids and well, he had to take a shot. "Don't you think it's only fair that he sees you like you see him? After all, we are going to be partners, and you guys are roughly the same age."

Oztin looked long and hard at Kippy. He then opened another panel and took out something that looked like a wristband. Kippy could see apprehension on their faces.

Holding out his hand, Oztin warned him. "We will get in trouble beyond your wildest imagination if this blows up in our face. I mean *all of us*. Take this out to your master and tell him to put it on his right wrist. Not his left, his right. Then bring him in."

𝑒𝓂 ⋅ ◆ ⋅ ⚹ ⋅ ● ⚹ ⤢ 𝓂

Richie exhaled relief seeing Kippy and his wagging tail step through a crease in the night. "Are you alright?"

Kippy had something dangling from his mouth and dropped it at his feet. "Put this on your right wrist."

Richie hesitantly took it. It was cool to the touch and flexible. He trusted Kippy and laid it across his wrist. In an instant, a craft the size of small semi-truck appeared mere feet from his face.

"Whoa," Richie said jumping back. In a moment of panic the band slipped from his hand and *poof*! the craft was gone as suddenly as it had appeared.

"What the heck . . .?" His heart raced as he gulped in shallow breaths.

"It's the bracelet," Kippy told him, grabbing it in his mouth and offering it back to his master. This time Richie kept his head down as he attached the clasp.

And there it was again. A blue spacecraft close enough to touch.

"Jeez, this is unbelievable!" The expanding feeling of awe was causing him to feel lightheaded.

"They're waiting," Kippy told him. "Remember the story line."

"Yea, yea, sacred brew, special . . . I got it."

When they entered, Richie felt awkward. Not really knowing what to say, he started by introducing himself. "I'm Richie."

That was the catalyst that broke the spell, and within minutes they had all done the same.

"Reshea, Squib and . . . Oztin right?" he asked, making sure he got it right.

"Thanks for the Fizz Cola," Squib said, asserting himself. "Kippy told us how hard it is to get."

"Ah sure. No problem," Richie managed to say. He could not believe these kids were aliens. They looked just like any kids here on earth. Except maybe for Oztin, but Richie had seen dwarves before, so he didn't really consider that outside the ordinary.

He could not imagine his dad letting him drive the car across town, let alone go trolling across the galaxy. Did their parents let them do this? As a million questions passed through his head, he realized they expected him to say something, so he mustered a little bravado.

"A deal's a deal?" he said without conviction. "Though my four-legged friend here really shouldn't be making promises he can't keep by himself. Right Kippy?"

Kippy settled onto the floor but stayed silent.

"Why can I see you guys now, but I couldn't before?" Richie asked as his curiosity overcame his apprehension. "And why is it you speak English?"

"It's the bracelet," Oztin explained. "It's sort of a slimmed-down version of the voice translator that Kippy is wearing. It raises your frequency . . ."

"Frequency?" Richie asked with a scrunched face.

"So you can see us," Oztin explained, detailing how all matter vibrates and these vibrations on the eyes and ears allow sight and sound.

"Got it," Richie said, not really understanding. He just didn't want to seem like an idiot. "So where exactly are you guys from?"

"We are from Orion," Reshea said with a hint of pride. "It is in the same Galaxy, but nearer to the center."

"Oh?" Richie had never given any thought about where Earth was located within the Milky Way. "Are all kids allowed to travel around the galaxy? I mean, do your parents allow you to go this far from home?"

The question hung unanswered and Richie sensed a discomfort. He noticed a small surfboard and deflected to change the subject. "What's that?"

"That my friend, is the heart of my cruiser," Squib said with puffed up pride.

"I use my body's motion to navigate through the stars. It controls speed, direction, everything!"

"Like a surfboard," Richie said. "We use ours to ride on ocean waves, letting their momentum push us forward. But we control the speed and direction by weight transference, and stuff like that." In actuality, Richie had never ridden on a surfboard, but he had seen plenty of movies.

"Right, right, exactly," Squib said with excitement. "We do the same thing. Except our waves are more like anti-matter . . ."

Their conversations continued into the night and ricocheted from subject to subject like a pinball—two worlds meshing. This lasted until it was time to go.

"It's getting late, guys," Richie finally announced. "I need to get home."

"Before you leave, there is something we must agree on," Oztin said seriously. "You cannot tell anyone about us. Nobody!" he stressed. "Not a single solitary soul. Promise?"

Richie hesitated as he rubbed the bracelet and considered how his best friend could now communicate with him.

"You have to promise. It is very, very important. We'll let Kippy keep the universal translator. In return, you get us a reasonable amount of Fizz Cola but tell no one. I need your promise, and you cannot break it, for any reason."

"And I keep the bracelet so I know when you guys are here?"
They all nodded.

"Absolutely!" Richie agreed. "It's a deal."

erM ✦◆✦)(✦●)(xↀM

42

Sunlight spilled through the bedroom window as Richie heard his father's call to breakfast. Exhausted, he stumbled out of bed and headed down to the stairs into the kitchen. "Morning, Dad . . ."

His dad turned, a vacant look on his face.

"Ruff, ruff-ruff," Kippy started barking. It startled his father into deflecting his train of thought.

"What's the matter, boy?" he asked, reaching down to pet the dog.

Richie understood. *The wristband! If my frequencies are still raised, it must mean Dad can't see me.* He stepped around the corner, removed the bracelet, and tried his entrance again.

"There you are. I swear it sounded as if you were standing right here . . ." His father turned his attention back to the stove. It was Saturday morning, and the smell of bacon and eggs permeated the room.

So, this thing not only makes space kids visible, but if I wear it, humans can't see me. I could be the invisible man!

Chapter 6
Miles Industries World Headquarters

Sal O'Mander stood in the offices of his boss Professor Bartholomew Miles. High atop the glass cathedral of Miles Industries, he noted that age had not been kind to this man. His jowls were fleshy and his girth expansive. He had a cartoonish quality about him. But Sal took pleasure in knowing he was the cause of the red face flushed with anger.

"Why are we holding up that factory?" Miles shouted with total exasperation. "Why is that Radcliff land so damn important anyway? We have our permits! We own the adjacent land—that should be sufficient to get started!"

Sal O'Mander did not say a word. With eyes like dark bottomless pools, he glared at his boss. He often fantasized about taking this measly piece of dung and slow boiling the fat from his meaty bones, but that would have to come later.

"Am I getting through to you?" Bart railed. "We need this factory built and we need it done now!" Catching his breath, his cheeks flushed a deeper crimson and sweat dripped from his brow.

"I'm sorry, boss," O'Mander finally said in a hiss. The words carried no meaning. "I will increase the pressure on this Radcliff fellow and see what other alternatives are available." Smiling, Sal's thin cold lips turned at the corners and he walked out of the room.

Something about the way O'Mander had stared at him sent a tremor of fear down Bart's spine. He remembered the day that Sal joined the organization. At the time, he had been impressed with Sal's ruthless manner and efficiency.

Somewhere along the way, the lines of boss and underling had blurred, and now Bart was not so sure who was in charge. More concerning was his nagging conviction that if he ever tried to fire O'Mander, it'd be the last thing he ever did.

"Where does Sal disappear to?" Bart seethed, as he stewed on the fact that Sal had left before he was done yelling at him. Days would go by and nobody ever had any idea where he'd been. And when asked, his answer was always vague and fuzzy.

The Professor grabbed the phone and shouted into the receiver. "Rocky, get in here. Now!"

Moments later, his assistant came running into the office. "Yes sir?" squeaked the harried voice.

"What's the real deal with Radcliff?" the Professor demanded. "Why haven't we put him out of business yet? Doesn't he know what's good for him? If he doesn't surrender soon, I cannot be responsible." His blood pressure was near boiling and his words came out raspy and rushed.

"Well sir, uh . . . these things take time . . . I mean, we already sell everything in our store at way below our cost. He must be hemorrhaging. In time he will go out of business. What else can we do?"

"I don't care!" he seethed. "I want that factory built before those environmental clowns have a chance to change the minds of the commissioners. We need this done while we still have them on our side. Look here," Bart whispered. "Here's what I want you to do . . ."

$$eT\text{Ⓜ} \cdot \blacklozenge \cdot \cancel{)}(\cdot \bullet)(\nearrow \text{Ⓜ}$$

The Invisible Boy - Santa Martina

Richie wondered if the incident with his father was merely a fluke, or if he really was invisible. With his pooch at his heel they set out for town. Just before St. Augustine Street, Richie slipped on the bracelet.

"Kippy, am I invisible?"

"Beats me," his dog replied. "I mean, I can see you either way. You're still making a shadow," Kippy noted at the silhouette. Looking at his feet, a frown ticked the corner of Richie's mouth.

"Your dad couldn't see you today," Kippy reminded him.

Richie struggled to find an answer. "Does it mean that I can be seen in sunlight? Or that my shadow can't hide? Let's go see if anyone else can see me."

They continued walking towards town. Two kids on skateboards raced out from a walk hidden by hedges and ran smack into Richie. All three of them went sprawling.

"Jeez, Johnny, watch it man," said one of the boys as he examined the scrape on his elbow.

"Me?" The other replied indignantly.

Richie winced as one boy accused the other. *They're looking right through me as if I don't even exist.* This helped to ease the pain. *So I am invisible—but shadows are not . . .*

Once the two boys had stopped bickering and departed, Richie's excitement grew with anticipation at all the possibilities.

"Let's go try something else," Richie said. "Let's go down to Davey's Locker, maybe have a little fun."

They walked across Elm Street and down past the little shops that lined both sides of the town's main thoroughfare. The sidewalks were getting busier as the morning bargain hunters crowded the streets.

Someone bumped into the back of Richie and almost knocked him off his feet. Catching himself, he turned to see the startled look of a middle-aged man pulling himself up off the sidewalk. He realized invisibility came with a price. People drifting left, drifting right, stepping into his path without warning. You had to anticipate everyone else's movement or risk collision.

"Kippy, look," he whispered, pointing across the street to Marimba's Dress Shop. "It's Kayla—she's with her mother." His heart leapt into his throat. Without hesitation, he dodged the throngs and crossed the street. Kippy followed his lovelorn master.

"I'm going in," he told him. Richie sensed disapproval. "Just wait here, I'll only be a minute . . . Don't worry, I will keep out of sight."

At that moment, the door opened, tinkling with a little brass bell. Richie slipped in behind a wide-ended woman. Once inside, the store's tiny footprint meant Richie had to keep moving out of people's way. There were racks of clothing on three of the walls and along the fourth was a bay window with mannequins dressed in what he assumed were the latest fashions. He melted into the clothing rack where Kayla and her mother were browsing.

For some inexplicable reason, whether it was a smell, a thought, a texture or whatever, sadness followed on the heels of a long-forgotten memory.

Mom brought me here once. It was on a Saturday just like this one, right before her accident. All I wanted to do was go out and play with my friends. If only I could have that last day all over again.

He was pulled back to the present when Kayla reached into the rack for one of the skirts near his arm. He openly stared with the boldness of anonymity. From her mother's incessant chatter, Richie gathered a party was involved and a nice dress for Kayla was what they had come to find. More shoppers arrived. In ones and twos, the small shop began to fill. Richie pushed himself deeper into the clothing as hands reached in and moved the dresses back and forth.

"Look Mom! It's Richie's dog." Kippy was standing with his front paws on the sill, trying to keep an eye on his master.

Her mother turned and scowled.

"I wonder if Richie is around," Kayla gushed. "Mom, he is so cute . . ."

Startled at her comment, Richie's feet got tangled and he fell forward, sending dresses sprawling across the floor. The store owner scurried over to see what the commotion was all about.

"Don't give us that look, Helen," Kayla's mother said sharply to the woman. "We didn't do that!"

She turned back to her daughter, wagging a finger mere inches from Kayla's face. "I forbid you to talk to that boy! Do you understand me? Do you?"

"What? Why?" Kayla asked.

"His father is causing trouble for this whole town, that's why! You know that aluminum factory they're trying to build? He refuses to sell them the land they need. His damn unreasonableness is going to cost this town a lot of jobs. Jobs your Uncle Jack and Aunt Marge are desperate to have! As someone who's lived here all his life, you'd think Radcliff would appreciate that our town is crumbling before our eyes."

"But Richie is a really nice guy," she said. Her voice hinted at defiance and her mother glared.

"Radcliff is a selfish man. He's holding out for more money, trying to cheat the factory people, and the people of this town! I do not want you being influenced by selfish people like the Radcliffs.

"Bad karma will come to him, and I don't want you around when he gets what he's due. From what Mr. Baylor told me just last night, there's a committee forming to take that land of his.

"Now that Davey's Locker has opened, no one is shopping at Radcliff's anymore. He'll be broke in no time. So you stay away from that boy. Do you understand me?"

"Yes mother," Kayla mumbled.

Richie couldn't believe the malice in her voice. She was attacking him, his dad, and their business. What had they done that was so bad? He needed to get out of the store—he needed room to breathe. The store owner was crowding him, and the walls were closing in. Overcome by memories of his mom and sucker-punched by Kayla's mother's accusations, he fled the store.

"What's wrong, Richie? What's happened?" Kippy asked trying to keep up.

Richie fought to control his emotions. But right then, more than anything, he just wanted to be left alone. "Girls," he replied, his answer punctuated with finality. It was the first thing he could think of.

"Is there anything I can do to help?"

"No!" Richie snapped, immediately regretting the tone of his voice. He bent down on one knee and petted his friend's head. "I just need a little time alone. I'll catch up with you later. Please?"

"Okay." Kippy's gummy frown made his disappointment clear.

"I appreciate it," Richie replied with evident relief.

"Don't forget. We agreed to get a case of Fizz Cola for tonight," Kippy reminded him. With a nod they set out in opposite directions. Richie heading towards the far side of town, and Kippy going back the way he came.

eᴛ𝔪 ✦ ✦ ✦ ℋ ✦ ● ℋ ⤢ 𝔪

Chapter 7
Intruders

Every person that Richie passed was talking about the same thing—his father. It was as if overnight a conspiracy had mushroomed against them.

Oblivious to the wispy clouds drifting in the mid-morning light, Richie continued down Main. He passed the outlying commercial section of auto repair and body shops and continued beyond the industrial buildings and junkyard until he came to the Department of Transportation, which marked the town's outer limits.

Over and over he replayed his thoughts, his mind gnawing at unfulfilled answers.

Is Dad being selfish and unfair? Doesn't Dad know how many people in town need these new jobs?

Richie passed overgrown fields shimmering in the sun. His sneakers slapped the asphalt with a hypnotic beat. A breeze brought the tang of wild clover and the wispy smell of dry grass. And with it came the memory of long-ago games of catch in these very fields with his old friend Ned.

It was a recollection tinged with sadness. If there had been a factory in Santa Martina, Ned's family would not have had to move away. Richie's reflection was bitter and for a moment his mood turned foul. Then he caught himself. He couldn't blame his father for Ned moving away. His friend moved because of family.

This sparked the answer. Not from the head but from the heart. *Family sticks together. I love my dad and he needs me now more than ever . . .*

"Dad doesn't want the factory built here. And it's our land!" The sound of his own words emboldened him, gave him strength, and understanding. Mom would never want us to sell it. "That's why he won't sell!"

The call of cackling birds gave Richie pause. Bathed in the warmth of the midday sun with waist-high grass brushing against his pants, he found himself alone in an open field. To his surprise he had walked miles beyond the town line to the land that had been long held by his ancestors.

He could feel the stress evaporate. There came a sense of peace under the azure sky. Indecisiveness gave way. This was their land. Passed down for generations, going back almost four hundred years.

"No one is taking this without a fight!" he vowed, stepping under the boughs of ancient pines. Richie felt a renewed and deep love for his father. Sitting down on a large rock, for the first time he truly understood.

Dad is lonely. He misses Mom as much as I do.

With clarity of conviction, he knew that only if they stood together would they survive. He had no idea how long he sat on those rocks. The afternoon shadows grew long. The surrounding trees swayed soothingly. Richie felt a calmness of his soul, reminding him of his mother. Like a soft breeze, her tender spirit came to sit quietly beside him.

He realized that this was exactly where he had to be, away from the clamor of town, to the peace and stillness of their land. "I remember Mom," Richie said softly. "'Never sell the land.' We will keep that promise."

The sun was sinking low. Feeling better, it was time to leave.

Dad's going to be worried. I need to get a move on. Shoot, I need to stop by the store and get a case of soda.

Making his way down from the rocks, his warm sense of tranquility dissipated like smoke in the wind. He saw something dart by without seeing him. Something that was not human, but not animal either.

A chill ran down his spine. Blood pounded through his veins and the rush of adrenaline caused his breathing to come in uneven raspy breaths.

He checked his wristband. He was still cloaked in invisibility.

ꑉ ◆ ᚼ ● ᚼ ꑉ

The long shadows gave way to darkness. Hidden behind a cluster of rocks, he watched the intruders. He had been coming to these woods his entire life. They were like a second home to him. Richie had never seen anything like this.

Large lizard-like creatures with darting tongues and glistening skin were pouring in and out from a gash in the side of the hill. As he watched the trespassers, he felt tingles creasing his brow, like nerves guiding his thoughts through forgotten memories. Searching and then stopping, a favorite memory opened before him like a cherished book. It was a childhood story his mother had told him.

'There's a legend that's been passed down through our family. It is said, the ancients were waiting for the chosen one. When he comes, he will be the key, he will be the one who will rewind the clock of the ancients and prevent unimaginable evil from destroying the world.'

Though Richie never really understood most parts of the story, he loved the way she could bring the courageous heroes and awful villains to life.

From behind the protection of the rocks, Richie watched as a strange alien craft lowered into the glade. More creatures came streaming out of it. They stalked about their business with such a malevolent air that the hairs on his neck stood on end as if an electric current was running up his spine.

The steady procession of creatures carried crate after crate into the side of the hill, a cave he had never seen before.

The hours passed slowly. Watching the continuous procession from the vantage of his hiding place, Richie had plenty of time to considerer his mother's ancient tale. *Is this the evil she had spoken of?*

With a waning moon, diffused light drifted down to the forest floor. It was getting very, very late. Cramped by fear and immobility, Richie dared not move, dared not take his eyes from their comings and goings. If they saw him . . . He was no match for their size and numbers, and he had no doubt that they wouldn't think twice about disappearing any witnesses.

Unexpectedly, the lizard men looked up and a nervous chatter arose amongst them. Richie followed their gaze and saw a streak of light flash against the night sky.

Could it be Oztin returning? This idea filled him with a sense of relief.

The creatures wasted no time clearing the area and then boarded their spacecraft. Silently the craft lifted and took off, low and slow until it cleared the tree line. Then in a sudden flash the ship shot up and was gone.

$$e\!\!\!\!\:\tau\mathfrak{m} \cdot \blacklozenge \cdot \mathcal{H} \cdot \bullet \mathcal{H} \nearrow \mathfrak{m}$$

Chapter 8
The Great Discovery

"Yes officer . . . I understand officer . . . No sir . . . Of course sir . . . No sir – you don't need to send anyone out tonight. I'll call back first thing in the morning . . . Thank you for anything you can do."

Standing in the fluorescent glow of the kitchen light, Mr. Radcliff replaced the phone in its cradle.

"It's after midnight for Pete's sake and no one has seen Richie all day. Boys will be boys—my butt," he mumbled. "Something's wrong. I can feel it."

Kippy wanted to help but knew that he shouldn't. The only way he could think to effectively lend a hand was to tell Mr. Radcliff about when he had last seen Richie, but that would open a can of worms he could never close again. And it would break the promises they had made to Oztin and his friends.

And thinking of them, his acute hearing heard the ultra-high-pitched sound of the star craft landing out beyond the hedges.

With reluctance, he slipped unnoticed out the back door. Light spilled from the kitchen window casting shadows on to the back lawn. Beyond the hedge, at the far end of the field, Kippy spied the distinct outline of Squib's star glider.

Maybe they will know a way to locate Richie?

When he entered the craft, Squib greeted him much differently than before.

"Hey Kip!" he said with a sense of jocular camaraderie.

"Richie's missing," Kippy said in a quivering voice. It was the only thing that mattered to him. "The last time I saw him was this afternoon and he was really upset. No one's seen him since."

Reshea placed her hand on the dog's worried shoulder and spoke with genuine concern. "What can we do? Do you know where Richie was going?" She gently rubbed him behind his ears

"I don't know," Kippy said hesitantly. "Is there a way you could track him through the bracelet?"

"He had the bracelet on?" Oztin jerked up in alarm. "Don't you realize that if something happens to him while he's wearing the wrist band, no one will be able to see him or help him? Ever!"

Kippy's heart sank at the harsh words.

"I'm sorry, Kippy," Oztin said, softening his voice. "We don't have any seeker devices. I wish we did."

Kippy sank even deeper into despair.

"But we can help you look for him," he offered. "After all, the three of us do have the advantage that we are able to see him."

Kippy perked up—it was a ray of hope.

"We only have two hours before I have to get home," Squib reminded them with annoyance. "My mom said if I'm not home on time tonight . . . " The words hung unfinished.

"We'll probably all get busted . . . " Oztin accepted, looking first to Reshea and then to Squib. "But Richie is in trouble and we're partly responsible. I'm sorry, but we can't just think of ourselves—not today! We're going to help find him.

"Let's split up. I'll go with Kippy. You guys fly low, around the town and surrounding areas. If he has the bracelet on, he will be able to see you. Maybe he will try to call out."

Reshea said nothing but felt a sense of pride. Once again, when a situation called for someone to take charge, her cousin stepped up.

She knew that for Oztin it was difficult being a dwarf. Everything was a little harder to deal with. Everyone either stared at or shied away from him because he was different. It was very easy for kids of difference to lack self-esteem.

But she knew that what truly made Oztin different from the other kids was not how he looked. It was the style and grace he had in dealing with his adversity. She realized that of all the people she knew, by any measure, he was truly one of the coolest.

"Okay," she agreed. "Let's do it!"

Watching the pinpoint light dissolve into the depth of night, Richie heard a rustling sound. Cautiously, he peeked from his hiding place. In the dim moonlight he glimpsed a bald head receding into the forest.

Did he see me? Where was he hiding? Then a sense of familiarity formed just below the surface. *I've seen him before. Where?*

He wracked his brain, but both the man and the memory were fleeting. Whoever it was, he was gone. Richie waited a few more minutes until he was sure he was alone. He had an itch of curiosity that needed scratching.

How did this cave get here? I've never seen it before! What's inside?

Probing, he tried a little experiment. Removing the bracelet, he confirmed his suspicions. Suddenly there was no cave and no path, and instead, he saw a huge pile of stones. Odd, he thought.

When he put the bracelet back on, the stones were gone, and he approached the opening. It was damp. The night's cool air condensed the vapor trapped on the forest floor. Curiosity now dominated his actions. Forgetful of the time, his father, and most importantly, his obligations to his space friends, he inched forward.

Coming to the edge of the opening, Richie noticed etchings carved into the stone. They seemed ancient, like Druid runes from one of the video games he liked to play.

He ran his hand along the surface. The marks seemed familiar, but he knew that was not true. They led into a murky darkness. Crossing the imaginary boundary, he found himself in a narrowing tunnel. His eyes strained against the darkness.

Any lizard dudes still here?

Suddenly the only sound was the blood rushing in his ears—anxiety pumping adrenaline through his veins. But curiosity trumped caution. Step by step, Richie ventured deeper into the mystery. His hands grazed the corridor walls, and he was surprised that they were so dry. Not wet or clammy as he would expect to find inside an earthen hole.

Continuing down the sloping corridor he could see a pale flickering glow. This ratcheted up his anxiety even further. *If something is in that room, they must be able to hear the pounding of my heart.* But he was drawn. Every synapse in his body willed him forward. He was no longer in control—or at least it felt that way.

He kept going, closer and closer, his body needing to find out what lay just beyond. As the tunnel leveled out, Richie poked his head around the edge.

"What the . . . " All hesitation vanished. It was like something out of a James Bond movie. Before him opened a room as big as his school's gymnasium. All four walls were covered with giant floor-to-ceiling television screens.

He slid a finger down his cheek, almost as if wanting to make sure he was awake. Disbelief surged towards awe and inexplicably all his worries fell away.

He stepped into the incredibly large space. It was hard to tell where the room ended, and the walls began. The room began to fill with an iridescent glow. It seemed alive. Expectant, as if it was waiting for something or someone. He wanted to reach out and touch it.

It drew him in. But he stopped as something else captured his attention. There was a large pyramid that centered the room. It had stairs leading to the top. He circled the perimeter. The shuffle of his sneakers was drowned out by the volume of the room.

The overall structure was square. Made from blocks of meticulously crafted stone. His vision was adjusting to the dim light or perhaps the light was adjusting to his vision, he did not know for sure. The shapes and shadows continued to solidify like the room was awakening to the morning's dawn.

They were studying Meso American history in school and it seemed to him to mimic something the Mayans would build. Licking the dryness from his lips, Richie strained to see what was at the very top. It was flat and had a dome held up by pillars.

Who built this place? How long has it been here? Again, the same questions, and again, without answers.

Gazing about, he noticed that what little exposed rock there showed was covered with strange hieroglyphics. They were etched into the floors, embedded into the stairs, and even filled the seams at the corners of the monitors.

He climbed the stairs get a better view. As he ascended, the walls shimmered as they grew brighter. The massive monitors were coming to life, their expectancy becoming more urgent. On the walls, it was no longer just opaque light. Images appeared, darting in and out of view.

The light intensified, and the fluttering imagery was joined by a soft sound. Waffling in and out, like it was being carried in on a distant breeze. A calming melody filled the cavern. His body relaxed into the soothing sound.

When he finally reached the top step, he saw a large box beneath the dome, like an Egyptian sarcophagus. The lights pulsed brighter and the melody grew louder. The room felt as if it contained a lifeforce. Something ancient.

Good or wicked?

The melody was reaching a crescendo. In unison the screens burst into living color. Materializing depth and clarity that surpassed real life, a broad plain swallowed the room with unbroken horizons.

Watching landscapes fill the walls, he steadied himself on the edge of the stone box. He felt as if he had reached the pinnacle of the world's highest mountains, and far below, the ends of the earth were unfolding in all direction.

Are those camels? He stared at a distant caravan moving deep within one of the screens. *And people!*

"Dang," he mouthed. A feeling of euphoria washed over him. Fear, worry, anxiety—that was all gone. Time had lost its meaning.

The details were becoming so crisp and clear that it soon became impossible to tell if the walls were even there anymore. The room melded into some magical land of which he was now a part.

As the room assaulted him with one sensation after another, he could feel a gentle stirring of air carried on soft breezes. In the distance he saw a thunderstorm. Far off, lightning crackled, and a whiff of ozone touched his nose. Instinctively he looked up, checking to see if a storm was gathering above. His mind was losing track of the line between imagery and reality.

How is this happening? he continued to ask himself. He remained amazed, curious, and focused on the moment.

Standing so close to the sarcophagus, he could see into the stars above. But he knew it wasn't a window. It was like everything else in here, something that simply superseded the imagination. The very depths of space came alive with motion and color. Planets of the solar systems fanned out as they rotated around the glowing gases of burning suns.

Looking up was kind of awkward, but he had always had a fascination with outer space, so he sat on the lip of the stone box to pause and take in the cosmic landscape.

As he sat transfixed by the celestial surrounding, he felt a calm, which led to a yawn. He slid his feet over the side and slipped half consciously to the floor of the sarcophagus where in an instant he fell into a deep, deep sleep and began to dream.

Time moved across the heavens.

$$e\tau\mathrm{M} \cdot \blacklozenge \cdot \mathcal{H} \cdot \bullet \mathcal{H} \nearrow \mathrm{M}$$

Back at the Radcliff house his father was beside himself with worry. Anxieties were mounting all around. Foremost was worry about his son, but there was the store, the tenor of the town's attitude toward him because he refused to sell their land. Worry, worry and more worry.

"Where is my son? God please, let him be all right. Don't let anything happen to him." His father begged the heavens.

He lay his head on the table, listening to the duet of the ticking clock and dripping faucet as he unfolded and repacked each of the mounting worries. He silently prayed for his son to be safe. But just below the surface, there was a growing undercurrent that simply thinking what he was thinking, was a betrayal against his dead wife. He lifted his head at the sound of crunching gravel and he saw Richie approaching the screen door.

"Richie!" Richie's dad leapt from his chair and wrapped his son in a deep embrace. Holding tight, he kept saying "thank you" over and over. Finally releasing him, he seemed to be at a loss for what to say to his son.

He was torn between anger and relief. And now more than ever he needed his son on his side. He sensed the entire town was turning on them and now was not the time to vent his frustration out by berating his son.

He was drained and resigned himself that he was no longer willing to fight the town—they could have their damn factory. With a heavy heart, it was time to tell his son they were going to sell their land. As if his thought had leapt out into the emotionally charged room, Richie gave a plea.

"Dad," he began. "I know the whole town is against us. Just, well, no matter what happens, promise me, we won't give up our land. For Mom's sake."

The tremor in his voice touched at his father's heart but more importantly, it struck at the undercurrent of his resignation. He knew his wife would never want their land sold, but the mounting pressure was just too much. His son's words galvanized his resolve and stripped away what should have been deep anger at his son's actions.

"It's a promise, son," he said. "You and me together—for your mother."

"Richie, I need to get cleaned up and head on down to the store. When I get back this evening, we need to have a little talk about why you were out all night."

"Yes, sir," he replied, sounding relieved.

"Make yourself some breakfast. You gave me a heck of a scare. I'm not sure I could handle losing you."

"I'm not going anywhere Dad," Richie said, shifting to a more serious tone. "But there is something I need to tell you." His voice gained confidence. "There's trouble brewing in town. People are spreading bad rumors about you, about us. They're planning on doing some kind of legal thing to make us sell our land. If we don't sell, they're going to stop shopping in our store and run us out of town." His words rushed out in a tumble. "What are we going to do?"

"Don't worry about it, son," his dad said with feeble assurance, wondering how he had found all this out. He had only come upon this information yesterday.

"Stories are stories, and lies are lies," he answered, putting an arm on his son's shoulder. "Let's just see them try to take our land."

After a brief moment, he dropped his arm. "I gotta go get ready."

$$\mathcal{e}\text{T}\mathrm{M} \cdot \blacklozenge \cdot \mathcal{H} \cdot \bullet \mathcal{H} \nearrow \mathrm{M}$$

Alone, Kippy looked up from his spot on the floor and studied his master. Richie had changed somehow, but he couldn't quite put his paw on what it was.

"So you want to tell me about it?" Kippy's voice had an edge to it. Though relieved that he had arrived home safely, their space friends had traveled far and had left empty-handed. He was surprised they had not demanded back the translator, but then again, they had helped search for Richie until they had no choice but to get home.

"You know our friends came back last night. As promised. They were expecting their next installment. Remember?"

"I'm sorry."

"Well they got pretty worried when I told them you were missing. And not about the Fizz Cola either. About you. Especially Reshea. I think she likes you.

Richie said nothing.

"So what really happened?" Kippy asked, sensing his preoccupation. "You were pretty upset when you left me yesterday. You stay out all night, come strolling in at the crack of dawn . . ." His anger was fading along with the hollow pit he had felt through the night.

Richie unloaded the thoughts that had culminated at the cave. Kippy listened patiently. When the torrent turned to a trickle, Kippy relayed something that previously seemed unimportant.

"The first time I met our friends, they said they weren't supposed to come to our planet. It was off-limits to all space travelers. They said that if they got caught here, they'd get in really big trouble.

"When they mentioned this, I kind of embellished my story a little. You know, sort of used that knowledge to my advantage. Anyway, I told them that dogs see spaceships coming here all the time."

"You embellish?" Richie asked with exaggeration. He reached down and scratched his friend behind the ears. "I'm shocked."

"Whatever," Kippy said, enjoying the contact but ignoring Richie's sarcasm. "The truth is, I have seen a few spaceships in the last couple of months. But they never stopped near our house. Maybe they were heading towards that cave."

At the sound of footsteps bounding down the stairs, they reverted to silence. Richie's dad poked his head into the kitchen. "I gotta go." And he was out the door and the car pulled away.

"I don't think you are far from the mark," Richie told him. "There is a legend my mom used to tell me about that land. About a long-ago uncle named Silas. I used to think it was just a wild tale, but I'm not so sure anymore."

"What's a legend?" Kippy asked.

"It's sort of like a story—maybe true, maybe not. It goes like this," Richie began.

"'When Silas was a young man he trekked out of Old Mexico and up along the coast of California. He was looking to find El Dorado, the fabled Lost City of Gold.

"Hearing a call for help, he came upon a young Indian girl. Her leg was pinned beneath fallen rocks. Silas knew that if he did not act quickly, the inevitable rockslide would bring an agonizing end to this girl's life.

"He started dragging logs and boulders to a spot above the trapped maiden. Silas reckoned he was only going to have one chance, and it was now or never. Grabbing the large rock that had her pinned, he wrenched it aside. The entire ledge above sheared away. It came crashing down, splitting boulders and uprooting trees.

"The rocks surged forward slamming hard into the temporary dam Silas had rigged, giving him just enough time to pull the maiden to safety before tons of rock engulfed the spot where they had stood moments before.

"When the dust cleared, fierce-looking warriors appeared from nowhere. They were surrounded. Silas helped the maiden to her feet, and she spoke to him.

"You have come as my dreams showed you would. You are the one who was prophesized. For through the mind's eye, the past, the present and the future will intersect. Guard this land from the lords of darkness, for I have seen them, they will come. It is your seed that will unlock the ancient clock. He will restore our great mother to her rightful place, back amongst her brothers and sisters in the sky.'

"Silas abandoned his quest for El Dorado, settling down on that very land. More settlers came, and he eventually took a bride and had children of his own.

"One night many, many years later, there was an eclipse of the moon. At the edge of the clearing in front of his house, he found a wizened old Native American man sitting by a campfire. Silas cautiously approached the fire. The old man sat, rocking back and forth, singing in a low voice. He stopped as Silas approached, opened his eyes wide and grinned a toothless grin that put Silas at ease.

"'So you are the chosen one," he said appraising him. 'Funny. I expected more." And then he laughed.

"Silas came to understand that the young maiden that he had saved was not so young after all. She was almost two hundred years old and was the spiritual leader of the Haida, an ancient tribe from across the sea.

"'When she touched you, her job was done. She infused you with the tribe's authority, fulfilling the prophecy,' the old man told him. Abruptly he stood up and looked Silas in the eye. 'Be wise. Be brave Viracocha. Protect this land. Your seed will be the key to the clock of the ancients. Into the Mind's Eye.'

"My mom said that Silas went to his grave never finding the answers to his questions. But before he died, he charged his children and his children's children. *Never sell this land, keep it sacred and always protect it.*'"

When he was done, neither said anything. The only sound was the clock ticking in the background.

"I am Silas's direct descendent. Maybe it isn't a coincidence that our space friends just happen to show up now. Maybe we are all part of the prophesy."

"And these lizards, or whatever you saw, could they be the evil that is mentioned in the legend?"

Richie ate a bite of his cereal before answering. "I don't know . . ."

Kippy studied his master. A transformation had taken place. From boy to man.

"Come on Kippy, let's go back to that cave . . ."

e⊤ℳ • ◆ • ⋊ • ● ⋊ ⤳ ℳ

Chapter 9
Back to the Cave

Richie filled his backpack with some snacks and soda and headed out to the woods. Sunlight spilled down to the pine needle floor, but warmth had yet to penetrate the thick treetops.

"There is something else about yesterday that I forgot to tell you," Richie remembered. "Last night I saw a human darting into the woods after the lizard men left."

"Did you recognize him? Could he have seen the aliens too?" Kippy asked.

"All I saw was the back of his head. He was too far away."

"Hmmm, let me do a check of the area." Pushing his snout to the ground, Kippy didn't take long to locate the lingering stink. "Richie, can you smell that? This smell, it's—I don't know how to explain it. It's not natural. If it's the lizards, they emit a very distinctive and very foul odor. It's burning my snout."

Richie tensed. *Could they be back? Are they hiding nearby?*

"It's not fresh. I think it's safe to say we are alone, at least for the moment."

Richie let out a long breath. He did not realize how keyed up he was and realized he had let his excitement about this place dismiss the obvious dangers that could be present. He was glad he had his buddy with him.

"Do you think the lizards built this thing?" Kippy asked, looking towards the cave. "It was never here before—was it?"

Richie had been thinking about this all the way over. He knew it was the truth behind his family's legend. So, it had to pre-date the aliens.

"Maybe it's always been here but it was buried under the rockslide," he speculated. "Remember my mom's story? If the story is true, then that slide wasn't an accident at all. She wanted this cave covered until the legendary seed of the Viracocha showed up."

"Of course. But why now? And how did the lizards find it?"

Richie speculated aloud. "You said that you have seen space craft heading into these woods for the past year. Maybe they found the place, cleared out all the real rocks and put some sort of cloak or something on it to keep it hidden?"

"Make sense. By the way, I don't think we need to worry about them right now. They only come here at night," Kippy said. "Think about it, they know they can't escape their shadows!"

"That's pretty smart thinking," Richie said. "You really are a wonder dog."

Relieved his dog's scent picked up nothing, Richie's anxiety was dispelled, which accelerated his impatience to go back inside the cave. "Let's go exploring."

Following the passage into the bowels of the hill, they entered the large room. Upon entry, the walls appeared solid. But once inside, something was triggered. The fluorescent glow morphed into like 3-D. There was no distinct horizon where the sky met the curvature of the Earth. Like before, it was as if the globe had been flattened. And like before, Richie was captivated with awe.

Within the depths, what at first he mistook for butterflies became some form of ancient writing. It was very faint, present one moment and gone the next.

Dwarfed by the giant screens, Richie became captivated by a pinpoint of kaleidoscopic light. "What could possibly cause such intense rays?"

Peering deep into the panorama, the fractured rays soon shaped into a jeweled top structure far off in the distance. Subconsciously he willed them into focus.

"What the?" Kippy said cowering up and behind his master's legs.

The imagery on the front screen was racing toward them like a rocket, splitting the landscape into left and right as it whipped down and raced past them on the two walls of the room, like they were on a fast-moving train and the imagery was flying by. Until finally merging together again on the far rear wall where it flowed away into the distance like a great river seeking the sea.

Richie stood mesmerized as the images of a great and mighty desert continued flying by. "Whatever it is, it's getting closer," he said. "Oh my God! Look!"

The huge sentinels drew closer and closer as the windswept sands passed on every side. Richie stared in wonder while Kippy squeezed his eyes tight.

Suddenly, everything came to an abrupt halt. Kippy let out a low whimper followed by a defensive growl.

"Easy boy," Richie said soothingly. He felt no fear. A giant structure rose before them. Silent, imposing, and magnificent.

"It's the Great Pyramid of Giza," Richie whispered in amazement. Pristine white, capped with stones glistening like diamonds, it was beautiful.

Richie's thoughts were already racing through an ocean of endless questions. Is it reading my mind? What is this place? How does it work? Can I see anything anywhere?

Move back, he thought in his mind's eye, willing the massive structures to retreat. In an instant they receded, widening the view to a living, breathing Egypt.

"That's it!" he exclaimed. "I did it. It's my thoughts. Look Kippy, all I have to do is look in the right direction and think of a place. And there it is!"

Richie worked it back and forth. Everything rushed to his whim—his thoughts were in command. With each passing minute he honed his skill.

Kippy was uneasy and kept watch as his master continued indulging in the novelty of the room.

If the aliens figured this place out they are going to return sooner or later. Hopefully later.

He thought of something Richie had mentioned in passing. The lizard dudes were carrying in crates but left without them.

So where are they? And what could be inside? He went to check out the rest of the hall.

Nosing around the base of the pyramidal structure, he smelled the same pungent odors that he had noticed near the entrance. The same scent permeated everywhere he explored. It was strongest at the base of the stairs. It set his hairs on end. He finally figured out what it was that bothered him, and it sent a shiver through his spine. It was the smell of evil!

Still, he kept searching. Turning the corner, he saw Richie climbing the stairs. With each step, Kippy noticed that the walls were becoming more energized, brighter—more focused. The life force was filling the room and he heard the faint strains of a melody, but it was not music.

From every corner of the room, glyphs were peeling free. Swarms of free-floating symbols came flowing in from all corners. Advancing to their own rhythm, they continued, undulating to and fro, like a ballet of fireflies on a summer night. They danced up the stairs, drawing closer and closer to his master.

Something's not right Kippy's hairs were standing on end and he soon had a stream of nervous gas pass out of him. He ignored it.

Richie reached the top of the platform and swung his legs into the sarcophagus. "Keep an eye on the screens."

"Everything okay up there?" Kippy asked in alarm.

"It's soooo peaceful."

Though faint even for a dog's ear, the sound of his master's voice did not ease his panic. Meanwhile, the images were increasing in speed and tempo. All the rapid movement was making Kippy dizzy, but in the whirl, a reassuring voice managed to penetrate.

"No worries bud," Richie reassured him. "No worries . . ."

If my thoughts can trigger the walls, can it move the stars above me?

Focusing his attention on the ceiling, Richie considered a date in time. They had studied Pharaoh Tutankhamen in school, so he focused on him.

And just like that, the stars in the dome's underside started moving in rhythm with the changing monitors on the walls. He knew from their science class that most of the constellations were assigned to signs of the zodiac. As the constellations traversed the sky, he tried to remember the names of each group. Gemini . . . Cancer . . . Leo . . . He could see a pattern emerging. Each time the constellations did a full twelve-sign cycle, they rose a little higher in the sky.

Faster and faster and faster they moved, until it was no longer possible to differentiate. They were now moving so swiftly that he was getting motion sickness.

That's it, he rejoiced with triumph. The stars are the key. It all made sense to him now. The ancients marked long passages of time by the rising and the setting of the stars. Just like this chamber used the stars to locate a specific era we then see up on the walls.

I can watch everything everywhere, at any point in history.

With arms extended as an amplification of his triumph, he began to turn around and around and around, slowly, in awe of his surroundings and grasping the idea of the four corners of the world.

From every corner of the room, butterfly-like glyphs advanced like an army and rushed up the stairs. They flowed onto the platform pressing forward until the base of the sarcophagus was surrounded.

Richie stood in an ark, oblivious to what was unfolding at his feet. With a final surge they flooded into the chamber engulfing the twirling boy.

Kippy raced to the top of the stairs when, BAM! There was a bright flash and a loud pop.

Richie was gone!

Chapter 10
Through the Veil

The bright flash and loud bang had Richie's ears ringing and his eyes trying to focus. Spitting, he tried to expel the acrid taste from his mouth.

"Don't worry Kippy, I'm fine," he called down as he ran an adrenaline-juiced hand over his body. "That was something, wasn't it boy?"

The only response was the faint echo of his solitary voice. He looked down but there was no Kippy. *Did something happen to him? Where did he go?*

Shaking his head, his gaze darting all around the room, he grabbed his backpack and raced down the stairs.

"Come on, boy! Don't be scared. Everything is all right. Come on, Kip," his tone was now full of worry, begging that Kippy would show himself.

Everything was slightly askew. Even the texture of the air had changed. Before it had been dry, but cool. Now it was hot, almost oily.

Something about this place is off—his need to find his dog grew more urgent. "Kippy! Here, boy! Come on, boy!" He called louder, just short of shouting. "Where ya hiding, boy? Come on!" The room absorbed his words unheeded.

He turned the corner at the bottom of the pyramid and froze in his tracks. Dozens of crates were stacked along one side of the towering edifice.

How'd they get here? When? They look like the ones the lizard men were carrying last night.

Anxiety was pushing towards panic. "Here boy! Come on, it's okay." Richie called out, his voice quivering in fear.

Did he run out of the cave?

Richie turned and raced up the corridor expecting to see tall pine trees, moss-covered rocks, and a warm spring sun. Instead of a forest, the cave exited into a huge cathedral. Instead of towering pines, there were hundreds, if not thousands of stone columns reaching towards a high ceiling. And most disturbing, instead of a solitary glade populated exclusively by Mother Nature, hundreds of people were busy milling about, construction workers building something.

"Whoa—what is this place," he said swallowing fear in great gulps of breath. "Damn it." He fought to squash panic that had his mind running in a million directions. *Where am I? Where's Kippy?* His heart was beating hard against his chest. His breathing came in short, shallow gulps.

He checked his bracelet. It was still clasped to his wrist. Relief temporarily dulled the panic. Stepping back into the shadows, he tried to sort through the confusion.

There are people everywhere. This is some sort of construction project and everyone is busy working, swarming about, and preoccupied in their endeavors. I need a plan to find Kippy.

He was starting to concede that maybe he had actually been transported to another place—maybe even another time. This led to certain doubts. Like the awareness that Kippy wouldn't be here if that was the case. But he had to be sure.

Stepping forward, he hid behind the nearest column. For a long time, he watched, taking in his surroundings. He did not know where he was, whether these people would be friend or foe, or how they would react if he was discovered. It was a chance he was unprepared to risk.

The room was as big as any he had ever been in. It appeared to be a giant rectangular hall, with rows of colossal pillars running down both sides and a large highway-sized open space in the center.

The lighting was hard to figure out. There were no overhead lamps, and though the air was filled with dust from the construction, there was a soft persistent glow. Looking down, he checked his shadow. It was nonexistent.

Turning his attention back to the hall, his attention was drawn to the artisans chiseling into the stonework. And there were workers high atop scaffolding, laying on their backs painting a celestial panorama on the ceiling.

He watched in hiding for a few more minutes studying the people. Feeling bold, he moved to the next column. *So far, so good,* he thought, trying to slow his breath and dial back the adrenaline.

The constant clanging of hammers intermingled with yells and the sounds of construction combined to create an atmosphere of chaos.

Hiding is not the way to find Kippy!

He had to be sure. So he sucked up his courage, took a leap of faith that he was still cloaked in invisibility and walked towards the nearest group of men. They appeared to be studying blueprints. Perhaps they were architects? He kept moving forward.

Good, good, so far nobody is paying any attention to me. Here goes.

"Hey guys, what's going on?"

♏ ◆ ⋊ ● ⋉ ♏

"Who said that?" asked a large man who looked up with a blank stare. The other two looked left and right, after a few more puzzled gestures, they returned to their plans.

Confident he was invisible, Richie backed away. Remembering the problems he had walking the streets of Santa Martina, Richie moved along the wall to avoid most of the workers.

He saw a door at the far end of the hall and headed that way. He passed under scaffolding and sidestepped pails of vibrant paints. Hugging the perimeter, he made quick progress. Sunlight spilled through the opening, which drove his curiosity.

What's out there if there are people in here?

Part of him wanted to believe his familiar forest still lay just beyond. The entrance was a mere three steps away but there was a steady procession of people coming and going, so he willed himself to be patient. When there was a gap in the flow he darted out the door.

"Wow!" he exclaimed. Not in a million years had he been prepared for this. Before him lay the most beautiful city he had ever seen. Polished marble buildings, towering obelisks, giant sphinxlike statues and long cool reflecting pools with rainbows cast up by a fine spray of water that glistened under a vibrant sun.

"This is definitely not Santa Martina."

♏ ◆ ⋊ ● ⋉ ♏

Kippy called out to his master. Over and over his cries went unanswered. The loyal canine jumped onto the lip of the stone chamber, but nobody was there.

Where is he? Where could he have gone?

He looked all around and saw nothing. Looking down, Kippy scanned every inch of the giant room. The monitors had paused, and it was deathly quiet. He strained his ears, seeking any sounds. Again nothing—even the eerie music had silenced.

Did he go down the back stairs?

Kippy trotted down the stairs and methodically traced every inch of the room. Sniffing for unfamiliar smells, tastes, looking for any clue that would reveal where his master disappeared to, he learned nothing.

"Richie, what's happened? What has this stupid room done with you?" he whined with accusation.

He continued his inspection, noticing that the glyphs had retreated to their stations, probably waiting for their next victim. He re-climbed the stairs and jumped back into the box, hoping to find a trap door or hidden opening in the floor. Anything that would explain how Richie had vanished.

He descended the staircase on the other side a second time, examining every crack in every stone, one step at a time. He found a loose piece of rawhide sticking out from a cleft in the stair. Grabbing it with his teeth, he gently tugged at it. It was attached to something that was wedged into the small fissure. Pulling a little harder, he worked it free. Attached to the end was a round amulet of some type. It looked to be made of bone or tusk.

With nowhere left to look inside, he dashed up the corridor and out into the woods. Everything seemed normal. Sunlight wafted down onto the pine-needled floor and the damp smell of forest still hung in the morning air.

His anxiety was now amped at full throttle. With his heart thumping inside his chest he sat his haunches on a rock contemplating where to turn to next. Every fiber in his body wanted to believe Richie was alright. He just needed to figure out where he had gone. Watching the dance of shadow and light play across the forest floor, Kippy kept replaying what happened over and over.

It's all related to Richie standing inside that tub. The answers are in the cave. He decided the best course of action was to try and replicate every action Richie took. Once inside, he raced back up the stairs, but nothing happened. Then he tried a different tact. Going to the bottom, this time he began to climb, but slowly—let the feel of each step matter.

With each stair he ascended, the walls grew brighter, the same as before. He remembered the dancing glyphs. The closer he got to the top, the more he peeled free of their hold and began their dance his way.

This is how it acted when Richie climbed . . . good!

When he got to the top, nothing happened. *Now what?* Kippy wracked his memory. *Of course, the tub.*

He jumped into the granite box and lay down on its floor. Not sure what to expect. His fur began to rise like electricity was pouring in from the walls. It wasn't painful, it was more like a tether of energy was linking him to somewhere else. It was difficult to articulate, but he was encouraged. This is what Richie must have felt.

He waited, expectant but again, nothing happened. Impatient, he peeked over the side. The glyphs made no farther advancement.

Come on man, come on . . . his frustration was beyond anything he had ever experienced before. "A dog's life, indeed," he growled. Then it came to him.

"Twirling! Richie was twirling!"

Planting his paws on the chamber floor, Kippy began to chase his tail. Round and round and round he went, going faster with each turn. Getting dizzier with each successive spin, he began to think that perhaps this wasn't going to work after all.

And then it happened. An exoskeleton of energy surrounded him and . . .

Bam! A wave of sound and light washed over him.

$$\textit{e}\text{ⴅ}\text{ⲙ} \cdot \blacklozenge \cdot \text{Ж} \cdot \bullet \text{Ж} \text{⤢} \text{ⲙ}$$

Chapter 11
The Dog God

Kippy tried to refocus as the light abated. Instantly he jumped from the box and scanned the room looking for Richie. Nothing!

Down the stairs he raced and around the pyramid he searched. Nothing—his hope began slipping back into anxiety.

Raising his snout, his anxiety turned to fear. The smell of the lizard dudes was strong, and fresh. And to add fuel to concern, he saw wooden crates stacked everywhere. Richie had mentioned these the night he returned. His hair stood on end and he emitted a low growl.

He heard voices. *Richie? They sounded human.* Cautiously, he went to the door, peered around the corner, and saw the inside of a giant cathedral.

What is this place? It's not our woods.

He had the shock of paralysis but shook it off. *I have to find my master.*

He did what dogs have done for a million years, he lifted his leg and peed onto the pillar framing the doorway. "Consider it marked," he said with a satisfied grin. "Once I find Richie, I'll follow my nose back to this room."

Looking ahead he saw at least half dozen guys standing there, glaring at him. "Uh oh," he gulped, shrinking backwards.

"How dare you defile this temple," scowled one of the men, probably the leader. "Of all the places in the world, you chose to piss on one of your own?"

This seemed to amuse the others and they chuckled. "Maybe he is the mighty Sirius, the dog god himself."

"Oh, so he can piss on his own temple," laughed a third.

Kippy was torn—be afraid and bolt or act a simple dog and wag his tail?

"Enough!" bellowed the leader. "Grab him."

They blocked his escape. As they came closer, the human noose was getting tighter and tighter still. One of the thugs reached down from behind and grabbed his neck. Kippy had only one chance.

"Back off," he yelled with authority. The attackers' hands recoiled as if hit by a bolt of electricity.

"Back away or I'm going to have to Kung Fu your sorry butts!" Kippy growled and bared his teeth.

I need a plan to find Richie. I know he's here. I can feel it. But this place is huge. Could they have taken him?

This created a fresh wave of worry. The unpredictability of man.

Meanwhile, his spoken word brought the men to their knees.

Worship?

"Yeah! That's what I'm talking about," Kippy said, staring into the face of a man who did not look convinced. As they lay prone on the floor, the worried canine looked beyond the small cadre, checking to see if others were coming.

He lowered his voice to avoid attracting further attention. He began to realize just how large this place was. And in so realizing, he understood the daunting challenge of finding Richie. Assuming this was where he had ended up.

Sizing up the men's fear, knowing that the tide of momentum could turn at any moment, he figured he had nothing to lose in shooting wildly from the hip.

"You," he said to the one with the questioning look. "That's right, I'm talking and I'm talking to you. Sit up." Kippy saw that he was panicked at being singled out.

"Have you seen a boy around here? About thirteen years old, brown hair?" Kippy glared at him. Meanwhile, his insides were a wreck of clenching nerves. And when he got nervous . . .

Now was one of those times. As much as he tried to suppress the building pressure, it leaked out. Silent but deadly. A wall of stink so foul it could become legend.

Crinkling his nose, the leader whispered something to one of his men, who sprang to his feet and took off running.

"Stop!" Kippy commanded, but it was too late. He was already far down the corridor. So he returned to his audience. Time felt compressed. His window might be closing.

"I asked you a question. Have you seen him or what?"

Kippy was conflicted in what response he wanted to hear. On the one hand he wanted some assurance that this was where Richie had ended up. But on the other he was hoping that his invisibility bracelet worked and that he still had it on.

They said nothing. Their faces were etched in fear, doubt, and confusion.

"Maybe you haven't seen him. Have you heard anything strange?" Kippy asked.

Rising from his prone position, one of the men near the back of the group sat up and spoke with a whisper. The timbre of his voice slowly gaining strength.

"Oh great Lord Sirius, Praise your name in heaven and on Earth. Please forgive our egregious behavior. It has been foretold that you would come, but we did not expect you so soon. We are not ready."

Lord? He didn't know what that was, but he liked being worshipped.

One by one the others sat up. Their fear was transforming into something else, something Kippy did not recognize.

"We have continued to follow your specifications just as your Lords requested, but we are far from completion. Please do not judge us too harshly."

Reverence, that's what it is. They are revering me. Why? And who are my Lords?

Kippy was certain it could not be Richie. He couldn't have been here more than a few hours. Then a dark thought dispelled his moment of self-grandiosity.

If they have been taking orders from somebody, what if it is the Lizard men? The ones Richie saw going into the cave the other night.

"I have sent word of your return to Pharaoh," the self-appointed leader said. "He will be greatly pleased."

Pharaoh? He sounds like the boss. A tremor of fear washed away the momentary elation of God worship. Until the man who previously spoke stood tall and bellowed for all the room to hear.

"Oh great and mighty God Sirius, Lord of the Sky, the Earth and the underworld. Lord and Creator, we honor your presence on this glorious day."

The proclamation was like a wave. As the word spread outward, clamor stilled, and a hush of whispers rose. Men began streaming in from all quarters, prostrating themselves before Kippy.

The man who heralded Lord Sirius's return continued speaking. "It has been written by the ancients that you would return to us. We have been preparing since the arrival of your priests."

I could get to like this, he thought. Then a rumble in his stomach suggested a more pertinent idea. *Maybe I should ask for a steak, medium rare.* But priorities came first.

Find Richie, then place an order, that's the plan.

With stealth no longer an option, Kippy decided it was time to find Richie and then figure out how to get the heck out of this mess. With everyone crowding closer and closer, all he could see was a forest of legs. He needed to do something, and he needed to do it fast.

"Richie, are you here?"

He tried to muster up what a god would sound like, though he really had no idea. "Where are you, Richie? Can you hear me?"

Walking though the hall, the sea of humanity parted before him. "Richieee, where are you? Are you here, Richieee," they repeated. Wave after wave, like a sacred mantra, the crowd continued.

This is helpful. If Richie is here, he will surely take notice. Deep within the vastness of the great hall, the chorus rolled through the temple.

"Richie, are you in here? Richie, are you here?"

Over and over the crowd thundered, as if it were a hymn. The refrain of sound bouncing off the chamber walls was muddling out any individuality.

"I would recognize that sarcastic mutt's voice anywhere," Richie breathed out with a great sigh of relief. Somehow his loyal friend had managed to find him, even here.

"It's me . . . Kippy," his dog called. "Are you here?"

Richie navigated around the back wall until he was within calling distance of his little buddy. Then he saw him. "Over here, Kippy. I'm over here."

A hush cascaded into silence. Men cast their eyes down, afraid. "He's opened the well of souls," one man cringed.

"Shhhhhh," said the prostrate worker next to him.

"Do not be alarmed!" Kippy called to the fearful crowd. "I will allow no harm to befall you. Go back to your duties. I must communicate with the others . . ." He let that last word hang ominously.

Kippy turned his back on the receding throng. "Man, am I glad to see you!"

"Jeez, Kippy, one minute I'm in the cave and the next minute—poof! —I'm in a place full of strange people. I think we were taken back in time."

"Well it gets even weirder," Kippy said. "These guys have me confused with their Lord and master. They think I've come from some place called Sirius."

"Strange. Very, very strange," Richie said. Kippy noticed he continually fingered the invisibility bracelet.

"You need to stay invisible," Kippy concurred. Richie nodded in agreement.

"We need to figure out how to get out of here."

Kippy nodded. He was still worried that the lizard dudes could be lurking nearby. He could not shake the fact all those crates were stacked back in the room they had arrived in. The portal room.

"I'm worried the lizards know of this place. Have you seen any of them?"

"Here? No. Why?"

"One of these guys mentioned that my overlords have already arrived, and that they have been preparing for my arrival for some time now. They said that these overseers gave them specific instructions. What do you think they could be building? And who are these overlords?"

"I'm not getting a warm and fuzzy feeling," Richie said, his face drooping into a frown.

Kippy noticed one of the men lingering within ear shot, staring at them as his master continued.

"Before we do anything else, we need to have an exit plan. We need to figure out how to get the heck out of here. I should go back to the chamber and figure out how to make it take us back home. You stay and keep the crowd preoccupied with your Godness, or whatever it is. But don't overdo it."

"Sure, but I have a question. What's a Pharaoh? I think he might be on his way here now." Kippy was not sure if he should be worried.

"A Pharaoh! We really have traveled back in time," Richie exclaimed as a cloud of anxiety passed over his face "He's like a king, but more so. His people think he's a direct descendent from the gods."

"What should I do?" Kippy asked hesitantly, his stomach churning that familiar feeling.

"Be careful. He may not like having competition in the god department."

When Richie departed, Kippy noticed the man who was lurking nearby staring and decided to confront him. As he approached, others nearby cast their eyes to the ground. But from the body language of the individual who stood watching, Kippy could see that he was not in awe.

Okay, show time.

"Where is Pharaoh?" he demanded, targeting the individual. "I thought you told him I was here. Why am I being made to wait?"

The man became nervous. Rocking on one foot, then the other, he was biting his lip. A bead of sweat broke out on the man's brow.

That's better—show me some respect. Kippy pushed. He wanted to find out how much authority he could assert over these people before the arrival of their Pharaoh.

"Not only do I need to see Pharaoh—I'm hungry."

"Yes Lord. Food, I understand. Right away."

The man jumped to leave, heading directly into the groundswell of commotion that had erupted near the front of the building. The man hesitated, and Kippy growled at him sharply. "Go—don't make me wait."

He made a choice. He needed to lead the onlookers away from where Richie had gone. And it was inevitable he would have to meet this Pharaoh guy. So he gathered a procession of followers and proceeded down the long hallway. He estimated by the smell of tightly packed humanity, that maybe as many as two thousand people were congregating.

Entering the front doors were purple-clad soldiers carrying poles streaming with multi-colored banners. Then a man wearing white linen and a golden headdress entered as the security entourage formed two protective lines.

So that's Pharaoh, Kippy gulped. Bile churned in his belly and he did everything he could to control himself.

Well, no holding back now. Kippy hoped he wasn't about to commit suicide.

He watched as Pharaoh halted and held up his hand. And all those who stood watching bowed on bended knee.

Kippy was more than just nervous, he was out-and-out scared. He was not sure what he should—or shouldn't say. His heart was beating like a heavy metal drummer. I gotta get a grip, he counseled himself.

The look in Pharaoh's eye was not one of reverence, but it also was not one of anger. It was more like a curiosity.

"Greetings. I am Khufu, ruler of Upper and Lower Egypt, son of Chefen, descendant of Osiris, God of the heavens. Welcome."

What in the world is he talking about? The man's body language suggested he was not about to kill him . . . yet! His racing heart took a pause. He tried to appear regal.

"We were told that your journey would bring you down from the heavens, but that it would not be for some time. If I may be so bold as to ask, why now?"

Kippy recognized the hidden language of humans, the set of his jaw exposed his skepticism.

"We have only begun to implement the work outlined by your overlords, and it is long before the second age will draw towards a close . . ."

Kippy wondered, *Maybe Gods don't answer direct questions or maybe my tone has offended him.* Not sure how to respond, in a rare moment of wisdom Kippy thought it best to say nothing. And is so doing, saw the Pharaoh adopt a sudden change of attitude.

"We have duly obeyed your appointed overlords," the Pharaoh said with noticeable contrition. "They told us that the One Supreme God would come and that he would not be dressed in the body of a man. Please forgive my humble lack of understanding. We should have known. Sirius is the Dog Star. Lord, we meant no disrespect."

Kippy was willing to bet these overlords were the Lizard men that Richie saw. The crates. The inexplicable arrivals. But one nagging thought left a lingering doubt. Their hideous appearance. Still . . .

What if Richie crosses paths with those creatures back at the time portal? Invisibility will not protect him. He needed to get some answers.

"Pharaoh, master of this world," Kippy began. "You are a great and just Lord. Your people revere you and you have done great work. I am sure that my unannounced arrival has caused you some concern and confusion, but my early arrival was deemed necessary. Please let us talk in private."

He needed to be sure. If these lizard dudes were here, they would have conferred with this leader. Without waiting for Pharaoh to answer, he stepped away from the circle of purple-clad guards.

At the precise moment Pharaoh began to follow his canine God, Richie came running down the corridor from the opposite direction. Though only visible to Kippy, he could tell that his master was both excited and relieved.

He did it. Still oblivious to protocol, Kippy asked Pharaoh if he would wait just one moment and turned away. Kippy saw the look of shock on everyone's faces, that the Pharaoh had acquiesced to the Dog God. With his back to Pharaoh, the canine god began speaking to the spirits.

"I figured it out," Richie gushed on a hushed breath. "I know how we can move back and forth! We just have to get inside the chamber."

"Great," Kippy whispered in relief. "The sooner we get out of here the better. I think those lizard guys are up to something."

"You're sure they are here?"

"Not sure, but just in case, I want to put a little dent in whatever plans they have concocted."

"Okay but hurry up. I want to get back before Dad gets worried again."

Kippy turned back to Pharaoh, scheming. "I have news for you and only you," Kippy said, winging it. "Those overlords of mine, the ones that have come here. They are impostors. One of them thinks he can make himself a God. His plan is to replace you as ruler here on Earth. What I need you to do is keep this little visit of mine as much of a secret as can be maintained. And watch your back!"

Seeing Pharaoh nod in worry, Kippy hammered home his point. "When I return, you will tell me everything that these overlords have instructed you to do."

"Yes, my Lord. Thy will shall be done."

"Good. Now I must go."

"Can you not spare but a few moments to come and see all that we have created in your name?" Pharaoh asked.

Kippy looked to Richie who emphatically shook his head 'no.'

"I've done what I came to do," Kippy began with a fatherly tone. "I am here to warn you and to try and protect you. But you must realize, ruling the universe is my duty. Farewell."

Kippy followed Richie back to the portal and ascended the pyramid into the granite box.

"Close your eyes." Richie reminded him.

There was a loud clap, a bright flash, and five thousand years passed by.

$$e_T \mathfrak{m} \cdot \blacklozenge \cdot \mathcal{H} \cdot \bullet \mathcal{H} \nearrow \mathfrak{m}$$

Chapter 12
Girl Trouble

The Monday morning sun streaked through Richie's bedroom window. Snuggled under the comforter, he absentmindedly fingered the amulet that Kippy had found wedged into the back stairs of the pyramid.

It was made of carved ivory and it depicted three pyramids on one side, with the stars of Orion's Belt on the other.

Did a distant time traveler bring it back here and accidentally drop it? How old is this thing? He wondered as he let it dangle on the rawhide.

As it swayed from the end of his finger, his mind drifted back to Kayla. Her smile, her hair, everything. He thought of how many times she had stood up in class when it was her turn to share a report she had written or a story she had created.

She never ever saw me watching her—like I was simply invisible.

This thought triggered a memory about the time they had been tasked to write an essay about what they hoped to achieve in life. Kayla had read hers to the class. She hoped to grow up and become an archeologist.

Oh my God—she will love this. With his head buzzing, Richie jumped out of bed to get ready for school. His thoughts changed quickly back to the night before.

His father had come in late. He did not know why, but he was starting to feel that the intrusion by Miles Industries, the discovery of the cave, and the introduction to kids from another planet were not one big cosmic accident. It was not just a coincidence. It may be destiny. But it would not go away.

"Kippy, how about while I'm at school, you sniff around and find out what that guy who owns Miles Industries is up to?"

"Okay," he agreed. "And you?"

"I'm gonna see if I can learn anything that might explain the origins of our cave. Maybe some clues to how old it is or how it got there."

And I hope to impress Kayla with the amulet, he thought, but he did not share this part.

◆•)(•●

Three days earlier, Richie had walked to school a shy awkward boy, so unsure of himself. It now seemed like an eternity ago. Riding his bike for the first time in ages, he let the cool air clear out his head. He was still unfolding what he was going to do next.

As he approached the school, the ring . . . ring . . . ringing of the school bell pulled him back to the moment.

Crossing the teacher's parking lot, Richie scanned the crowd for Kayla. Most of the kids were headed for the main hallway. Then he saw her talking to her friend Mary. And, of course, there was Chucky hovering nearby. This annoyed him. Locking his bike, he headed her way.

"Where do you think you're going, runt?" demanded Chucky, giving Richie a painful jab in the chest. Normally Richie would have backed down. But with so much on his mind, Chucky was nothing more than an irritation to be dealt with. He pushed the arm aside, grabbed the bully by the ears and jerked his head forward.

"Chucky," Richie whispered, his face nose to nose with the dumbfounded bully. "I've tolerated you long enough. If you don't move out of my way, and I mean this very minute, I will summon all of my animal friends and you're going to wish that you were already on your way to hell."

His reaction was so swift, it was as if the very embers of Hades had torched his feet as he scrambled to get away. Strangely, this gave Richie no satisfaction.

"Hi, Kayla. Hey, Mary. How was your weekend?"

"Hi, Richie," they answered. The final warning bell began to ring, and Mary departed. Richie was glad they had a couple of minutes alone.

"Kayla, can I meet with you after school? I want to show you something."

She hesitated, and Richie assumed her mother's comments were fresh in her mind. Before she could respond, he removed the ancient amulet from around his neck and handed it to her. It surprised her, which he noted from her smile.

"It's so beautiful," she remarked. "Where did you get it?"

"If you meet me after school, I'll tell you."

"Sure," she replied. She ran her fingers along the face of the carving

Throughout the day Richie had a hard time keeping his mind on his studies. During lunch period he had used his phone to Google anything he could find on the net about myths and legends of the valley they lived in. The only thing that came up was the exhibit at the library that he recalled from the newspaper article with Mrs. Capon.

He shared a science class with Kayla, and as they were entering, she told him she had to do something right after classes ended.

"Can you meet me at the library afterwards?" he had asked. She agreed.

Class by class, the day progressed. The minutes seemed to drag out until at last the final bell rang, setting him free from the confines of Santa Martina Middle School.

Richie raced across town to the longstanding Mission Library. Stepping inside, a blast of frosty air conditioning buffeted him. Walking to the workstations, he could hear the soft rhythm of his feet padding upon the polished floors.

He went to one of the internal archive computers that catalogued everything they had in the library. He typed in the key word "Viracocha," and the search engine came back with the preliminary results.

Maybe this will show me something that is in the exhibit that would point towards the cave or a legend, he thought. The net had given him nothing.

Leaning back on the rear legs of his chair, Richie let his mind wander as he processed the information. What specifically stuck was that Viracocha was an Incan legend about their mysterious god from across the sea. Richie churned through the possibilities.

If those Indians really did call Silas 'Viracocha,' did that mean that the mysterious Haida tribe was of Incan origin?

"Hey Richie, what are you looking at?"

"Whoa . . ." The chair slipped out from under him and he found himself flat on the floor looking up at Kayla's bemused smile.

He felt ridiculous. This was not really how he wanted to impress her, so he shifted the topic and handed her the amulet.

She turned it with her fingertips and saw over his shoulder he was already looking for something. "What are you researching?"

"I'm looking into a local myth, actually more like a legend, that I think may be tied to this amulet."

"Myths and legends. I love that stuff."

He really wanted to impress her. But he wasn't sure how much he could tell her. *If I mention the cave then I've got to mention the bracelet and that will lead back to my space friends. And I promised . . .*

He decided to stay on the subject of the Viracocha. Pulling a chair out for her to sit, he began telling her the story of his ancient uncle Silas. When he was done, he saw the doubt on her face. Before he could stop the words from escaping his lips, he found himself going down a path trying to impress her.

"Kayla, can I trust you with something? Something huge, and no matter what, you can't tell another soul?"

He lowered his voice as she leaned in closer. Her skin and hair smelled good. He took in a deep breath and then revealed his discovery.

"I stumbled upon a cave that is hidden on our property," he said with a whisper. "That's where the amulet came from."

"Can you show me?" she asked.

This was not the response he expected. But basking in her attention was something he had dreamed of. Without hesitation, he thought, *why not?*

"Sure, how about tomorrow, after school."

"You know . . ." she began. "My mom and dad are out tonight and said they will not be home 'til later. Tomorrow she may not let me."

Then she gave him a look in the eye and told him something she did not realize he already knew. "You're not exactly her favorite person right now. If we are going to do this, today would be better."

He thought about it. Kippy was off doing his recon and Dad was working late. "Okay—let's go!"

eᴛm ⋅◆⋅)(⋅●)(ⵊm

As they pedaled their bikes out of town, Richie was suddenly feeling stupid for not thinking this through. *What was I thinking?*

Without a bracelet, Kayla would not be able to see the cave. If he mentioned the bracelet it would lead to too many questions.

They arrived at the edge of the woods. The open glade was buzzing with dragonflies dancing and slashing through the air. It was his moment of truth.

"Let's hide our bikes here in these bushes. Follow me . . ." one fresh worry came after another.

Glancing at the sunlight tipping the tops of the pines, Richie knew they only had a couple of hours until dark. Entering the cool recess of the ancient woods, calm settled over his spirit. He could feel the touch of the breezes, the sigh of the branches, and the sharp incense of pine. Up ahead he recognized the rocks where the cave entrance would be.

His heart raced a little faster. He was excited—each time he showed up here there was a tingling rush throughout his body.

"We're almost there. But . . . some things I need to tell you first."

She stopped walking and crooked her head.

"You will see some things that your eyes may not believe."

"Really . . ." she said with a trace of doubt. "Come on, let's go before it gets too late." But Richie stood firm, his back straightened in a more serious tone.

"Remember you agreed to keep this a secret?" He knew that what he was about to ask would seem stupid. But it was the only solution he could think of to avoid having to discuss his invisibility bracelet and thus break his promise.

"Of course."

"Okay, I need to blindfold you."

"What? Is this a joke?"

Before her anger could ignite, Richie doused the flame. "Here," he said offering her the amulet from his neck. "I want you to have it."

"Alright," Kayla agreed, her tone both doubtful and slightly put off. "This better be good."

"Oh, it is. Trust me."

He took a red bandanna his mom had given him years ago, something he'd carried around secretly since she had died, and used it to blindfold Kayla. She stood stiffly as he fumbled nervously.

"Ready?"

"Duhhhhhhhhhh," she replied impatiently.

He took her hand and Kayla's smooth skin contrasted with his perspiring palms. It made him feel even more self-conscious.

"Okay," he explained. "I'm going to let go of your hand. When I tell you, take off the blindfold."

Without waiting, she let go of his hand and yanked off the blindfold. "Incredible."

He watched her stare in amazement at the giant screen as the walls began to glow. She turned to Richie and her amazement turned to concern.

"Richie, where are you?"

He knew he had been caught, unable to get the band off his wrist fast enough. He pointed to the screen to deflect her questions.

"Think of the great Pyramids in Egypt," he told her, avoiding eye contact.

"How are you doing that?" Kayla asked excitedly as the scenery started moving towards her.

"There's more. Come with me." She followed him up the steps of a stone structure. At the top, Richie helped her into the granite box.

"Okay, now think of the pyramids again, except this time add a specific year to your thoughts. Perhaps 3200 B.C.," he suggested.

Overhead the stars began moving and the imagery on the walls made a metamorphic change to another era. The desert dissolved into a savanna and the third pyramid disappeared. Beyond the flowing river appeared a beautiful city.

"Look at all those people . . ." Her voice quivered in amazement. "How, how is this possible?"

"I'm not really sure."

Lowering his voice he asked, "Are you ready for the biggest surprise of all?"

"There's more?"

"Would you like to go back in time? I'm talking about real life. Real people, seeing how they live, eat and everything?" The minute the words left his mouth, he realized that he had made a grave error.

She has no invisibility protection, and I promised to keep that a secret.

"You mean back, like rewinding the movie on the screen, that kind of back?"

"Yeah, yes—something like that," Richie said, seizing the chance to recover.

She stood motionless, her mouth agape. "Do you realize that if we can zoom into any time and any place, we could discover every mystery across the ages? How old do you think this place is? Who could have created something so incredible? I mean it's almost beyond belief. Where would they have gotten all the data from?"

"I really don't know." He had not really stopped to consider the who, what or how. It was all still too new.

"Is it okay if I look around?" she asked, stepping free of the box.

"Ah, sure." Watching her walk down the stairs he had a sense of déjà vu, a feeling of familiarity. He could not put his finger on it. Closing his eyes, he let his thoughts drift, hoping to make the connection. He knew it was important.

These mysterious people that Ancestor Silas encountered. This place was already here then, centuries ago. And what? He squeezed his eyes tighter. Every nerve screamed to understand. What?

He took a deep breath, sat on the edge of the box, and blew out slowly, calming his mind. A steady stream of consciousness flowed from somewhere deep within until somehow . . .

My dream . . . the lizard men . . .

"Oh my God," he said with a shiver running down his spine. *What if I am Earth's last chance at salvation? What if I blow it and we all die? What if my dreams were prophetic?*

Suddenly he felt a need to flee. To get out of there.

"Kayla, Kayla, where are you?" he shouted as he ran down the stairs. She did not answer. Panic pushed him towards fear.

"I'm over here. What's wrong?"

He had a feeling of impending dread. Or more to the point, that danger was closing in on them. He could not let anything happen to Kayla. He felt responsible for her.

"We have to go," he replied evasively. "It's getting late." Every nerve in his body screamed for him to get out and quickly.

They stepped outside to find darkness had settled onto the pine-filled glade. He was relieved at the silence, hopeful that they could get on their bikes and depart without incident. But that was not meant to be.

"Darn it," he said in alarm and grabbing her by the hand he pulled Kayla behind some moss-covered rocks.

"What's going on?"

"Shhhhhh," he retorted. "Lie still and don't make a peep. I'll explain everything later. Right now we have visitors." His breath was ragged but adamant. Richie could not afford to let the aliens see them.

His dream about traveling through space with Kayla rang over and over and he intuitively understood . . . Fate, the Dragos, and Earth's survival might be unfolding the prophesy within the legend of his ancestral uncle Silas.

"Kayla, trust me. Please. I will explain everything, but not right now."

Time passed slowly, as the thin sliver of the moon rose above the swaying branches. Richie did not want to leave her, but he needed to get closer. He had to find out what the Dragos were up to but could not risk her questions or her life.

"Kayla," he whispered. "I have to leave you for a few minutes. You won't see me. But I need you to stay here."

He looked into her eyes and saw her trust. In spite of the Dragos and all the other crises, Richie knew he would never forget this one perfect moment for the rest of his life. Reluctantly, he let go of her hand to get a better look.

Slipping quietly around the boulder, and using trees as cover, he was able to view the front entrance of the cavern. The Dragos were busy unloading crates from their ship and lugging them deep into the hillside. Ten, twenty, thirty, they came non-stop.

And then Richie spotted him. It was the baldheaded guy he had seen before. *He's human? If humans are working with the lizards* . . . he knew this just raised the stakes. Evil was afoot.

There was no mistaking that he was in charge of this alien horde. The others always bowed when they passed, and his orders went unquestioned. Richie had a growing sensation that he knew this guy. Or he had seen him somewhere before. He couldn't place him just yet, but he knew him from somewhere.

Catching snippets of conversation, Richie was thankful the vibration band worked as well on voice translation as it did on visibility.

They're taking the crates back to Egypt. What's inside those boxes?

With Kayla just a few steps away, it was a question he was not going to risk getting answered tonight. He slipped back beside her, realizing the moon began falling into the west. A damp chill enveloped the forest. He placed his hand on hers, and together, they waited, neither speaking.

Some time passed before the Dragos finally packed up to leave. All except the bald guy. Richie never saw him come out of the cave.

"Kippy was right," Richie mumbled. *It's the only thing that makes sense. Could he be one of the overlords the Pharaoh mentioned?*

The woods were coming to life. Morning was on the horizon.

"We still have a long ride home," Richie said, once he was sure they were safe. He could see Kayla had a million questions. But they would have to wait.

Chapter 13
Sal O'Mander

"Young man, your behavior is absolutely unacceptable," his Dad scowled. His anger seethed below the threshold of conversation. "I let it slide the first time. I thought we had come to an understanding . . . I have enough to worry about without you going missing all night."

Richie could see his father was exhausted with worry. Richie was torn between a growing sense of duty and destiny and his father's heartache. But he could not ignore what he had seen and the fears that would not go away.

"I'm sorry." His hands were nervously rubbing the thigh of his pants. He wanted to tell his father about his night but . . .

"I simply can't take it anymore," his dad said in defeat. "I've got too many people coming after me right now. The lies and deceit, and the erosion of trust from friends. But from my own son?"

Richie took a deep breath, desperately wanting to narrow the expanding gulf between them. The truth would break the bounds of the oath he committed to his friends, but a lie would be worse. So he let his heart do the speaking.

"Dad, I love you—and respect you so much," he began. "I know you won't understand this, but you have to listen to me. I am trying to do what mom would want me to do. I have been going out to our property. There are things happening there that I cannot explain . . ."

Richie could see that the mention of his mom had in part, frozen his anger.

"In the end you'll understand everything. I'm asking you to trust me."

"Irregularities on our property?" his father questioned. "This is where you have been going?"

"I won't lie to you, but I swear to you that I'm not out causing trouble. This is about saving our land!"

Richie could see his father's resolve soften slightly. This was clearly not the response he had expected. And what he said next contradicted the storm Richie had prepared to weather.

"All right, son," he said. "I'll trust you because I respect that you didn't lie to me. But I expect you to tell me all of it."

"Thank you . . . for trusting me," Richie said, feeling a warmth within—that honesty had been the right choice. The only choice.

"Can I expect that this may happen again?"

"Probably," Richie admitted. "I am trying to do the right thing. Thank you for having faith in me." Uncharacteristically, he went around the table and gave his dad a big hug. Richie was reluctant to let go. The universe seemed in harmony for that one fleeting moment.

"You're going to turn my hair gray before whatever this is ends."

Richie went upstairs to shower and change. Kippy followed on his heels.

"Listen," he told the questioning canine. "We went out to the cave and the lizards showed up again. I was afraid if we so much as blinked, they would know we were there. So we hid in the woods all night until they left." His comments came out a little defensively.

"Oh Romeo, oh Romeo, where for art thou," Kippy crooned to lighten his mood.

"You know . . ." Richie hesitated. "Well, it wasn't like that."

"You didn't mention our friends, did you?" Kippy asked.

"No. I took her in the cave. When we came out, those scaly dudes were just showing up. I hid her in a safe place, then I put on my bracelet and went back to see what they were up to."

"And?" Kippy's tail thumped with anticipation.

"I was able to hear bits of what they were saying. They're using the cave to go back in time and I definitely got the impression that they were not there to make Earth a better place." As Richie considered what they could be up to, he let thoughts ramble from his lips. "I wonder if time travel can change history."

"Alter history?" Kippy asked, looking like a bolt of lightning had just struck him.

"Hey Kippy, any chance that our friends showed up last night?"

"Ah . . . that would be a big N-O, they never showed. "Something must have happened."

"Great . . ." Richie added another worry to his list. He had no way to reach them, and now more than ever, he needed their help.

"I have some news though. It's about Miles Industries and your land. You're not going to like it."

Richie groaned—yet another complication.

"I was hanging out at Davey's Locker and overheard the manager talking to some guy in the alley out back. He was telling the guy how M.I. was having him mark the prices so low that your dad couldn't compete and would have to go out of business.

"Then the guy said to him that the town council had a meeting with your dad on Sunday. They told your dad he had a week to sell the land or they were going to take it. For the good of the town. He said there was some law they'd use."

"What?" A part of his world crashed down at his feet. The pieces all lay there. His dad's worn expression, the constant frown, the worry. The tension in their home had been building like static before a storm and now he could see the nearing clouds coming fast.

"It's strange," Kippy continued. "From what this guy was saying, he doesn't even think they really needed our land. A Mr. Sal O'Mander is the one pushing to get the property under their control.

"There's one other thing. The councilman told Professor Miles that at the next town meeting, if your dad gives them any more trouble, they are going to revoke his business license and close down the store."

"A week!" Everything was speeding up as time was compressed by so much coming at him so fast. His heart raced with worry and he clenched and re-clenched his hands as he tried to unravel all that was happening.

"I'm not sure what to do, but I think it involves going back to Egypt. The Dragos are up to no good, which means Pharaoh, and perhaps history itself, is in danger. We need to stop them!"

"What about Professor Miles?" Kippy asked. "If the town gives him your land, we might not be able to get back into the cave."

"You might be right, but I can't just sit around waiting for something to happen."

Richie got up and headed for the shower. He was fixated on the name Sal O'Mander. It rang a bell, but he wasn't going to solve all their problems here and now. The last thing he needed was trouble at school.

Poking his head into the steam-filled bathroom, Kippy offered a more practical suggestion. "If we are going to cover all this stuff, you go to school and see Kayla, and research anything and everything you can about Professor Miles and his company. I'll go back and see Pharaoh. After all, I said I would return. And I am a Dog God . . ."

Richie hesitated, he was not comfortable letting Kippy go to the cave alone, but it did make sense. Weighing the options, Richie reluctantly agreed.

"Okay but be careful. If you're not back by tomorrow, I'm going to come looking for you. Understand?"

"Understood," Kippy said, his wagging tail showing relief.

"And remember," Richie added good naturedly. "Gods don't fart."

"Ha ha ha, it's a divine fragrance."

"All joking aside, be careful."

ℯⲦ𝕸 • ◆ • ℋ • ● ℋ ⤤ 𝕸

Kippy knew it was going to take both of them to find solutions to the growing mound of problems. Being the loyal dog that he was, he knew where the real danger lay, and it wasn't in Santa Martina, California.

He hastened to the cave, did the dance that was becoming familiar, and then let his eyes adjust from the familiar explosion of light. Kippy took a brief inventory of the area. Nothing seemed to have changed, but he could smell something in the air. It wasn't the Dragos, but it was unpleasant, nonetheless.

At the doorway, he peeked into the main chamber, where at first glance everything seemed normal. Workers scurried to and fro, masons and artists were deep in their craft, and most importantly, no one noticed his arrival.

He heard hushed whispers where before there had been unabashed chatter. But mostly, he could not ignore that smell—it was fear.

Beyond the anxieties of the workers was a scent that was much more nauseating. The hair on his neck stiffened. He had smelled it back at the cave.

Dragos! They are the enemy. Richie said in his dream they tried to kill him and that they wanted to enslave all of mankind. Do they eat dogs? Would they eat him?

Sweeping his gaze across the far reaches of the room he saw strategically placed guards watching over the workers.

How ridiculous. He scowled at their odd getups. Trying to hide their lizard-like features, the Dragos had adopted dog-like headdresses. *It's blasphemy!*

This seemed an especially heinous insult to Kippy, but also, it worried him. Seeking a better vantage point, he stayed in the shadows along the wall until he came to an opening. It was another room off the main chamber.

Peering around the door frame, he saw Dragos slapping some kind of dice onto a crate turned into a makeshift game table. Fortunately, they were not immune to the power of the translator. They were in the middle of a conversation, and Kippy could understand everything they said . . .

One of the lizards laughed as his tongue slithered from his mouth. Scooping up a pile of playing pieces he boasted, "Can you imagine. Two thousand years from now when it comes time to sign that blasted treaty, there won't even be humans left on this planet . . ."

"Or in the entire galaxy for that matter," the first Drago sneered with malevolent glee.

Kippy reeled at the implication. *Is the fate of the human race at risk?*

But it confirmed his suspicions these guys were up to no good.

Is Pharaoh aware? Is he in on it, alive or dead? Kippy needed to find out. He had told Richie he would help fix whatever needed fixing on the other side of time.

Hugging the wall, he made progress towards the front doors. Unlike before when he had been revered as a god, this time the people ignored him. Almost as if they were afraid to even look his way.

Kippy gathered his confidence. *I am not just a dog. I am a wonder dog.* As he embraced the notion, he increased his speed and raced across the room.

Workers were exiting the building and Kippy joined the flow of the crowd until they broke into the sunshine. Luxuriating in the taste of clean air, he was momentarily blinded by the bright light as they started down the temple steps. His view was partially blocked by a tangle of shins, calves, and legs. But what he could see was beyond anything his imagination could have conjured.

At the distant edge of the surrounding city, he saw a grassy savanna hugging a lazy river that teemed with human activity. Looking west he could see two mighty pyramids. They radiated brilliance in the afternoon light.

Each was capped with a giant jewel whose refracted rays of colored light were so intoxicating, he had to turn his gaze away.

At the bottom of the stairs stretched a long pool of cool water. *Hmmmm,* he salivated as he separated from the gaggle of workers.

From its shimmering reflection, Kippy could tell that the temple was the architectural center of the city. Resting on a knoll, it sat higher than all the nearby structures. He reviewed his surroundings in case he needed to escape or hide or find his way back to the portal.

At the far length of the pool rose one of the most beautiful buildings he had ever seen. It was constructed of layers upon layers of polished stones as white as fresh cream. There were patios draped in cool shadows and hanging flowers that swayed in the gentle breezes. In the center stood two doors of gleaming gold.

Could that be the palace? Would this be where Pharaoh would live?

Four towers anchored the building's corners, each standing ten stories tall and inlaid with jewels so expertly fashioned, that they bent the rays of light into explosions of kaleidoscopic colors and intricate patterns. They cast an ever-shifting halo about the entire building.

From the base of each tower, water basins flowed out to fountains that sent geysers high into the heavens. Their droplets caught the sun in dancing rainbows as they fell back to the Earth.

Still, for all its grandeur, Kippy knew by the presence of the hideous Dragos, it had been corrupted and turned into something ugly. Recalling the comment the dice playing Dragos had made about locking away the pesky Pharaoh, it just made sense they would seek to defile something so pure—making this thing of beauty a prison.

Leaning down to lap the cool waters, a shadow crossed over him. Without looking up, he saw in the reflection a young woman behind him.

"Poor little puppy," she said. "Are you lost?"

By her shadow he could see her reaching for him. He had to think fast. He could not afford to get caught up in a lost-doggy drama. She could ruin everything for him—for the whole world.

"Listen, sweetheart," Kippy said. "I appreciate your concern, but I didn't travel halfway across the universe to be your lapdog."

"B-b-but . . . but . . . but you ca-ca-ca-can speak," she stammered as she struggled to get her words out. Her hand shot back so fast she almost fell over.

"Bingo!" he whispered. "How do you know I'm not a god in a dog's disguise?"

She fell to her knees. "It's true!" she began to babble. "The great God Sirius has come to our land! I only sought to offer you a little kindness. Please, I mean no harm."

"Off your knees, sister. Listen to me," Kippy said, worried she might attract unwanted attention. "I need to speak with Pharaoh so that he can make the announcement that I have arrived. Can you imagine what would happen to you if Pharaoh felt you delayed me from seeing him? Or if you stole his thunder by telling others I was here before he could?"

He saw that about-to-puke look on her face.

I really do need to lighten up.

"Yes, my Lord. Yes, yes, please, I am sorry. Please, I mean no harm."

"Okay, relax, take a deep breath. Good. Now where is Pharaoh?"

Her eyes shifted to the end of the waters. An expression of concern stretched the corners of her mouth. As Kippy suspected.

"Lord, he has not been seen in weeks," she answered warily, then, almost as a second thought, she added, "His advisers have been busy preparing for the great celebration of your coming. Everyone has been working double, even triple shifts completing your buildings and finishing your plans."

"Weeks?" Thoughts of time travel flew through his head. "That palace right over there, right?"

"Yes Lord," she affirmed.

"Go," the Great Kippy commanded. "But tell no one you have seen me or the wrath of all my power will fall upon you and your family. Now go. Scat!"

Backwards she stumbled, moving as fast as a hot desert wind.

He reflected on her comment about the Pharaoh's absence.

He has not been seen in weeks. But it was only two days ago when I was here. This worried him. *Do ancient days progress differently? What if Richie comes and it's a different time?* Time travel just got a whole lot more complicated.

He needed to free Pharaoh. Recalling the young girl's concerned expression, he was sure that his people still loved and worshipped him, but . . .

Is he still alive?

Traversing beside the long shimmering pools, the crowds were thinning as he neared the palace. Up close, the building was as splendid as it was from afar. A long carpet swept up the stairway to the foot of enormous golden doors. Unfortunately, beside each were guards.

From the hideous odor, Kippy knew they were lizards. He wasn't fooled by their ridiculous headdresses.

Without a plan of what to do next, opportunity presented itself in the form of four men dressed in flowing white robes. They were making their way towards the palace. From their slouched shoulders and the hesitancy in their step, Kippy could see they were reluctant visitors.

As they ascended the stairs, the guards perfunctorily opened the doors. Kippy moved in behind the last of the men and slipped under his trailing robe—the advantage of being small.

From under the hem, he surveyed the immediate area. He could see a large limestone planter just to his left.

The dog-headed guard beckoned the men to follow. Turning right, they began down a long hall. Kippy slid out from under the fabric and ducked behind the planter that was holding a sickly palm tree.

As the sounds of footsteps receded, Kippy knew he was alone. The room had the air of decay. Planters and urns dotted the foyer, but everything inside of them was either dead or dying. The air inside the palace was greasy, hot, and humid with an unhealthy texture to it. He found it difficult to breathe.

Realizing the guards could return at any moment, Kippy raced across the greasy floors, toenails clacking as he tried to get a grip, hurrying to stay out of anyone's sight. His fur was stiff with fear—he let his imagination mushroom to the point he was convinced that they ate dogs.

Reaching the carved staircase across the great foyer, he crept to the second floor. The stench intensified with each step. At the peak of the stairs, light filtered in from windows that were high above. Depressed colors played against the grimy patterns on the floor.

"Dang it!" Kippy muttered, realizing how exposed he was. Before him lay a long corridor. At the end there were turquoise inlaid doors being guarded by two Dragos.

Could that be where Pharaoh is being kept?

Retreating below the top stair, Kippy tried to slow his heart while not sucking in big gulps of the foul air. Below he could hear two sets of feet lumbering across the lobby. They were heading for the stairs.

The guards at the end of the hall were not paying attention and halfway between them and the top of the stairs was an open door on the left. He was trapped and his options were running out quickly.

Leaping from his perch, he dashed for the open door and skidded into the room. He realized things had just gone from bad to worse.

"Well, what do we have here?" asked the huge lizard standing before him.

Kippy's heart skipped a beat

"Lord Drago," said another, "It would seem that our little annoyance need not be hunted down after all. Apparently, he has decided to come to you."

Kippy counted five stinking lizards partially shielding a bald man sitting at a desk. Though he appeared to be human, his skin had a scaly texture and seemed to sag on his body. His eyes burned with a hatred so bright it was blinding. The putrid smell from their bodies was making Kippy dizzy.

"Well, well, well," said the man, rising from his seated position. "How convenient of the gods to deliver you—and just in time for lunch. Bring the little morsel to me," he beckoned with a long scaly finger.

⚬ℳ ✦ ◆ ✦ � ✦ ● ⌇⤢ℳ

Chapter 14
Looking . . .

"I cannot believe that Squib is still grounded." Oztin said, grousing to Reshea via the halo-phone. "He's not allowed out of the house except to go to school. We have to get him ungrounded. I need to go back."

It had been over a week since they searched for Richie. If something happened while he had that bracelet on . . . Oztin was worried, and he had no way of knowing what or if anything had happened to him since they left.

"It's not going to happen," she said flatly. But Oztin was not going to take no for an answer.

"Either Squib must disobey his parents and take me back . . ." he paused to consider the practicality of the other option. "Or Squib needs to let me borrow his star slider."

"Yeah, right," Reshea said with a roll of her eyes.

"Come on, Reshea. On my next birthday I will be old enough to have my own cruiser."

She let out a long breath. "Let's discuss it after class," she said, ending the conversation. At least for the moment.

Arriving at the education center, Squib was holding court at the one place he was furloughed from his parental prison.

"Hey Squib," Oztin said maneuvering him away from the others. "I need your help." He had rehearsed his speech with a hundred variations and it was time to deliver.

"We still don't know what's happened to Richie, and you know that we are all partly responsible if he has that bracelet on and something has happened to him."

Kids were beginning to move towards the doors. Oztin was concerned that the bell would ring at any minute. He needed to close the deal. "I know you are grounded, but I'm not." Oztin paused, then asked the unaskable. "I need to borrow the cruiser."

"I don't know, Oztin," Squib replied, doubt apparent on his face.

Oztin saw his stance had stiffened and his resolve seemed firm. "I need you to trust me. Let me take the star glider back to the blue planet! And I need to do it today."

ℰℳ•◆•⊁•●⊁⊀ℳ

She's not coming, Richie conceded. *She's probably in big trouble.* Behind deep furrows he went through the motions at school. Over and over he reviewed the issues, the problems, and his limited options. An order of priority began to emerge. By the time the last bell rang, he had a loose plan of action.

Passing the tree-lined streets, Richie willed his bike to go faster until he reached Kayla's block. He hid the bike in the bushes and put on his invisibility bracelet. With a deep breath, Richie toed softly up to the back door. Heart pounding, he turned the knob and stepped into the kitchen. He could see Kayla's mother on the phone.

She turned before he could get the door closed.

"Kayla!" She stepped to the door and slammed it shut. "I've told you a thousand times to stop leaving the door open!"

Richie tried to slow his breath. Mrs. Carlyle screwed her face into a grimace and then turned back to her phone call. He eased out of the room and raced up the stairs. He found himself in a hallway of four doors, three closed and one slightly ajar. He peered through the gap.

"Kayla . . ." he whispered from behind the door. "It's me, Richie. Quick. I need to speak to you." He slipped the bracelet into his pocket. He had to try and keep his promise.

"What are you doing here?" she demanded, pulling him into the room and closing the door behind them. "Are you crazy? Did my mother let you in here?"

"She doesn't know I'm here," he replied sheepishly.

"Well if she finds out . . ."

Richie had not expected she would react like this, but it was too late now.

"Shhhhhh, I get the point," he said. "I had to sneak in because I need to talk to you. And wanted to make sure you are all right."

"And you wanted to make sure I haven't told anybody, right?" She smiled. "I keep my promises. But I know you are not telling me everything. I'd think after last night you would trust me."

He let out a deep breath, trying to relax a little. "You are right," he agreed. "It's not that I don't trust you, it's because I have made promises.

Promises to others that forbid me from telling you or anybody else about certain things."

"Ohers?"

"Let me tell you what I can when I can. Please?"

"Fair enough," she said, her disappointment showing.

Studying the various posters, he used the moment to frame his answers. *Do I tell her about the time travel? Does she really need to know? Why keep it a secret? I never promised anyone anything about the cave. She has kept her promises . . .*

"The cave does more than just let you see different times and places," he began. "It's a transporter. It can actually take us back and forth through time."

He saw the widening of her eyes, but he expected a greater reaction. *Has she already figured this out?*

"There's more."

"More!" she said this a little louder than she had meant.

"There are others who have also found out about the cave."

"The ones you made the promises to, those others?"

"I wish," he told her. Then with a serious tone, realizing how ridiculous this was going to sound he explained. "Big lizard-headed aliens. I think they may be the legendary evil referred to in my family's legend, and I think they are trying to take over our world. They are doing this by going back in time and messing with the past."

Kayla slumped down on the edge of the bed. Mouth open, he watched as her lips moved through various thoughts and the doubt spread.

"There's more. Somehow Miles Industries and the plot to take my family's land is tied into all of this."

"I want to believe you Richie, I really do. But . . . ."

"I know. It's crazy. You probably think I'm a lunatic," he said, almost laughing. But in the end, when weighing the fate of humanity over the promises he had made to his friends, he erred towards humanity.

"If you can believe this, then maybe you will believe the rest."

He took the bracelet from his pocket and clasped it to his wrist. No sooner had he dematerialized when hell's fury erupted in the form of Kayla's mother as the door was flung wide open.

"Where is he?" she bellowed. There was venom in every word. "I heard someone in here! Don't mess with me, young lady!"

"What are you talking about?" Kayla asked, scanning the room.

Mrs. Carlyle began systematically searching the room. Under the bed, through the closet, then the bathroom and even under the desk. Finally, she opened the windows and made sure the screens were in place. Nothing!

With one last look, her mother left, leaving the door open.

Kayla let out a long nerve-soaked sigh. She whispered. "Richie, where are you?"

"I'm here," said a voice. "It's part of what I can't tell you right now. Please trust me a while longer?"

"Okay, already," she giggled. "I trust you. What do you need me to do?"

"Just don't say anything about the cave. All right?"

"Okay," she smiled. "But you're too cute to stay invisible."

⟑Ⅿ•◆•)(•●)(⤢Ⅿ

With the first part of his plan complete, Richie left and used his phone to Google 'Professor Miles and M.I.'

Bartholomew Miles - founded Miles Industries. Currently it is one of the world's leading mining and aluminum manufacturing companies. Education: Princeton University, Archeology 1949.

That's an interesting twist, thought Richie.

A renowned scholar and explorer. In 1958 he discovered the lost city of Osiris in the Egyptian desert east of the Great Pyramid.

Click here for photos. Richie clicked on the link and scrolled through the photos. Most were old. But one picture caught his eye. He read the caption below the picture:

1958. Standing inside the Temple of Sirius in the Lost City of Osiris. From left to right: Bartholomew Miles, Rajiv Galib and Saba Halim.

It wasn't the people in the photo, but what was behind them that grabbed his attention. It was the painted columns in the background, they were standing in front of the Egyptian end of the time portal.

"Unbelievable," he chuckled. "It's Kippy! They have erected a giant statue of Kippy at the top of our portal!"

How much does Bart really know about my cave—and what's the connection?

There was something else in the picture that nagged him. The harder he looked, the further the feeling withdrew. He blinked his eyes and let them fall unfocused upon the screen.

What was it Kippy overheard? MI was constructing the new factory to manufacture aluminum cans, specifically for Fizz Cola.

He studied the three men posing for the photographer, rereading the caption. Bartholomew Miles, Rajiv Galib and Saba Halim.

"Fizz Cola . . ." Then it clicked and he made the connection.

Fizz Cola is at the heart of all this.

He typed in Fizzcola.com. The corporate website popped up on his screen.

Fizz Cola
Always Refreshing, All the Time.
World's Number One Soft Drink

He clicked through the site, skipping over the stock information, investor relations, corporate earnings, and press releases. And then he saw it. Management team. CEO and Chairman of the Fizz Cola Corporation—Mr. S.B. Halim.

He toggled back to the photo of Professor Miles and zoomed in on the man called Saba. Back and forth he switched between the photos. S.B. Halim. Saba. S.B. Halim. Saba. Richie felt a tingle run up his spine.

Years later maybe, but still the same.

His instincts told him that S.B. "Saba" Halim was a key piece missing from the puzzle. And so far, his instincts had not failed him. Right now, they told him he had to talk to Mr. Halim. Returning to the home page, he located the New York address of their headquarters.

"Let see what else we can find out." Once he knew what he was looking for, finding information was relatively easy on the web.

Saba B. Halim was an orphan in Cairo who came to America in 1959. He made a fortune in the stock market and took over as CEO of Fizz Cola at the age of 49. He is currently the largest stockholder . . .

ᎬᎹ ⬧ ◆ ⬧ ⋊ ⬧ ● ⋊ ⤬ Ꮇ

111

Chapter 15
Oztin's Return

Richie paced. And paced some more. 'Don't panic if I'm late,' Kippy had told him. 'I might not be back until tomorrow . . .'

The waiting was eating him alive.

Something is wrong, I can feel it. What do I do?

His mental tug-of-war continued unabated until the sound of gravel crunching in the driveway broke the spell.

Moments later there was a knock on the front door. Stepping from his bedroom, Richie glimpsed his father come out from the kitchen, flip on the porch light, and open the door.

"Robert Radcliff?" A police officer asked.

"That's right," his father replied calmly. "What can I do for you gentlemen this evening?"

"We're sorry to bother you at this late hour . . ." His voice was tinged with a trace of apology.

"Is there a problem at the store?"

"No. Everything's fine," the man stammered. "There. It's . . . well, this is kind of awkward."

"Please come in," his father offered holding the door wide. "Please call me Bob. Can I get you something to drink?"

They both shook their heads no.

"So what seems to be the problem?" he asked again, one hand under the other armpit, his second hand stroking his chin.

Richie could see his father was nervous, but they wouldn't know anything about Kippy, would they? As he listened, fear and curiosity played flip-flop with his emotions.

"I'm very sorry, sir," the second officer said, "But we have been given instructions to formally serve this upon you." And then, as if in an afterthought he added. "Fortunately, someone thought it best to get this to you tonight, before it's too late."

"What is this?"

"It's a writ of imminent domain. Your land, sir, the parcel on the other side of town. The county is going to take it from you."

This hit Richie with a thud. He wiped clammy hands on his shirt, and his lips trembled as he continued to listen.

"They can't do that!" his father stammered. "Can they?"

"They can, and they will, sir. Whoever is behind this has a lot of juice. This came from the very top.

"At least my boss . . . Well, he wanted to get this to you as soon as possible. To give you every opportunity to deal with it before it is too late."

"Deal with it? How do I deal with it? What happens next?"

"You'll need a lawyer," the officer replied.

"And quickly," chimed in the second. "They want to start clearing the land for that factory in the next couple of days."

"This just isn't right," Radcliff said under his breath.

"I'm sorry," the officer said, handing his father a pen. "Please sign here."

"What's your name?" Radcliff asked.

"Ed." He replied as they edged towards the door to leave.

"Thanks Ed. I know you're just doing your job. I appreciate the heads up."

The front door closed with a soft thump.

His father retreated to the kitchen. Richie listened, but hearing nothing more, he turned back to his room.

Two days? If we lose the land, we lose the cave. Will the Dragos win? I need to go and retrieve Kippy and we need to warn Pharaoh . . .

His mind was spinning. It felt like it was going to explode. He needed to sit and clear his head. He stared out the window. Little pins of light twinkled beyond the window. The sky was clear, and they seemed to call to him. A soft breeze rustled through the trees. A breath of warmth blanketed him in security.

. . . My little star . . . My little star . . . echoes of his mother played upon his heart.

He lost track of time, wondering, listening, thinking, plotting, dismissing, and recalculating. Focusing his will on finding solutions. In complete surrender, Richie placed his elbows on the windowsill and began praying.

It was dark and the room had grown noticeably colder. He stood to shut the window, and something caught his eye. It sparked across the sky and wobbled with an unnatural trajectory.

They're back.

"Thank you, God," he whispered, a feeling of relief filling the hollow pit in his stomach. *I need to tell these guys. Maybe they will have an idea what to do.*

He slipped on the bracelet along with his sneakers. He eased down the stairs, out the back door and hurried out into the field. He could make out the outlines of the incoming ship. But relief quickly turned to dread.

"Slow down!" he shouted, his voice crying against the palpitations of his heart. His breath was ragged as he backed away.

The ship was coming in way too fast and it was heading right for him. He started running—and no matter which juke or dodge he made, the craft was honing in on him.

Richie's feet were pumping as fast as they could go. He tripped on a rut and his body sprawled to the ground. The ship hurtled past, grazing the air just inches above his head. With a soft thud, it slammed hard on the slope of the meadow. The dew-soaked grass allowed it to slide harmlessly to a halt.

"Are you nuts?" Richie hollered. His heart was beating a million miles an hour. Moments passed before and a crack of light appeared. The doors slid open and Oztin stepped out. He looked dazed. Then a smile grew from the corners of his mouth.

$$e_T \text{m} \cdot \blacklozenge \cdot \text{H} \cdot \bullet \text{H} \nearrow \text{m}$$

"Hey Richie, not bad, eh?" His voice carried an odd sense of pride. "Man, am I glad to see you," Oztin said. He circled Squib's slider and gave it a cursory inspection.

"Are you by yourself?" Richie asked.

"It's a long story," he offered without further explanation. "But I really am glad to see you. The last time we were here Kippy was so worried about you, we searched and searched until we had to leave. Is everything okay?"

Oztin looked around but there was no Kippy.

"Don't worry," Richie said, seeing Oztin's concern. "You didn't squash him or anything. He's not here."

"Oh, good," Still, his eyes darted to and fro, as if searching for something.

"There's no Fizz Cola here either," Richie said in understanding.

There was a moment of disappointment until Oztin remembered why he had really come. "That's okay. Mostly I came here to check on you."

"Oztin, I can get you a whole month's supply of Fizz Cola. As much as you can carry. But I need to come clean on a few things along the way. Can we fly over to my dad's store? That's where the Fizz Cola is."

Oztin seemed to hesitate, more worried about another test of his landing skills than Richie's request. But the lure of successfully returning with a craft full of Fizz Cola won out.

"If you dare risk your life, how can I refuse?"

"Well, try to get us there in one piece," Richie said with a half serious tone.

"No sweat. I just crossed the fricken' galaxy, I think I can get us to the store." With an arm gesture, Oztin did a showman's bow.

"Come on in! Sit there," Oztin told him. The seat was behind Squibs' gravitron board. Oztin struggled to get his balance on the narrow slat.

"You'll have to excuse me," Oztin said, trying to get comfortable on the wave board. "I don't have this down as good as Squib."

"No kidding," Richie muttered. "Arrive alive, that's all I ask."

Richie was waiting for them to lift off, keeping bad thoughts at bay and watching Oztin closely.

What will the G-force be like? Is it like in the movies when rockets take off—face peeled back? How will he be able to keep his balance on that thing?

"What's happening?" Richie gasped. The floor beneath his feet was disappearing. Pulling his legs up he sucked in a huge gulp. They were thousands of feet above Santa Martina, and nothing stood between him and the outside.

"Don't worry about that," Oztin said, shifting his weight. "It's normal. Once we start moving, the walls and floor turn clear—it allows a 360-degree view."

With trepidation, Richie pushed his sneakers down and it was solid. Transparent, but solid. He let out a slow breath as he released the chair from clenched fists. He swiveled his head in all directions. It was like being in a giant bubble.

He could see the lights of town all the way out to the edge of the industrial section and then the dark pools that he knew were forest—the land his family owned and beyond.

Oztin brought the craft to a hover. "Where to?"

Richie took a minute to get his bearings, picked out a few familiar landmarks, then pointed left. "I'll guide you to my dad's store."

For the next few minutes they said very little. Richie was watching the buildings slide by below. Recognizing streets and houses, he offered navigational corrections as everything seemed to glide by effortlessly.

"I need to apologize to you for something." Richie fumbled for the right words. "It seems that Kippy and I might have slightly exaggerated the lack of availability of Fizz Cola."

Richie saw a shadow move over his friend's face. "You see, anybody can get the stuff. It's not so special. Really. Kippy just said that to get the voice translator from you guys—we'll get you all the Fizz Cola you can carry."

Oztin looked at him but said nothing.

Is he mad? Angry? Unable to read his expression, Richie finished what he had to say. "I'm sorry we lied to you. Really, I mean that. Please accept my apology?"

"Thank you for telling me the truth," Oztin finally said. "Apology accepted. Now which building is your father's?"

Richie pointed to the small white building that was just beyond the 24-hour sign of Donavan's Gas Station. Suggesting to Oztin that he land in the parking lot, he said a silent prayer and braced himself. Oztin's previous landing was still fresh in his mind.

"Please don't take out the side of my dad's store, please, please."

Richie was surprised that Oztin eased the craft down to the asphalt, as soft as a mother placing a baby in a crib.

"See, nothing to it," Oztin shrugged. But Richie saw relief on his face . . .

Opaqueness thickened the hull's shell into solidity and the doors slid open. Richie scanned the parking lot. Empty. Though invisible, he walked quietly to the back of the building, punched in the access code, disabled the alarm, and opened the rear doors. Oztin followed him in.

"Holy moly," Oztin whistled under his breath. "The mother lode."

Case after case of Fizz Cola was stacked neatly against the back wall. "Load em up!"

Twelve cases later, the ship was starting to get cramped. "I think that might be enough for now," Oztin said, sweat trickling down his brow. "Are you sure this is alright?"

Richie left a note for his dad explaining that he would pay for the missing soda out of his allowance. Then closed the door and reset the alarm.

"So what do you say, Richie? You want to take a little hop around the stars before you go back to bed?" Oztin asked with a wink. "You know, check out the solar system. See the rings of Saturn. Stuff like that?"

"Are you kidding?" Richie grinned, letting him show off. "That would be awesome."

I still have not told him the problem yet, this will give me some more time and . . . fricken' space!

"Okay, here we go!" We'll take a spin out past the moon, maybe whip in close to the planet you call Mars and then sling shot out around the solar system and back," Oztin suggested, a little bit of bragging in his voice.

"Cool!" Richie was now appreciating the transparency of the walls. Still, there was an unnerving sense that one should just fall. But out here which way was up, and which way was down?

"Man, it's so clear, there are so many stars." Richie said aloud. The intensity of the colors was only outdone by the beauty and magnitude of space. The sun was peeking beyond the curvature of the Earth. The stars were a billion points of light.

His breath grew long and deep, and his eyes did not blink, awed by everything around him. In an instant they were circling Mars. They moved in close to the thin atmosphere. Richie looked down upon the surface of the planet.

"What's that?" he asked, pointing to something that looked like a giant pyramid. Oztin turned the ship around and they came in close.

Oztin shrugged, as if it was unimportant. But for Richie, the notion of pyramids on Mars created a wave of curiosity. Not the least of which was the idea that at some point in history our neighboring planets had life. But more importantly it brought home the here-and-now point of Kippy, Egypt, and the Dragos. His body sagged under the weight of concern.

"Oztin, there is something important I need to discuss with you."

Oztin stayed quiet, Richie saw his muscles tense a little.

"Kippy told me when you first met, you said you guys were not supposed to be here, not supposed to be visiting Earth. Why is that?"

Earlier when staring out his bedroom window looking for answers, Richie had flushed out all the possibilities. Now it was time to explore those options.

"Where is Kippy?" Oztin asked with an intuitive flash of concern.

"That's what I need to talk to you about. Something is happening and I don't know what to do. I am hoping maybe you guys might know."

"Has something happened to Kippy? I thought you said he was okay. Where is he?"

"I know this is going to sound really weird, but he's in ancient Egypt chasing alien lizard men through time."

Richie saw the blank look that turned ashen on Oztin's face. He explained as best as he could.

"We have found a time travel cave on our property and in two days a large corporation is going to steal it from us. I have to go back in time to help Kippy stop the lizard men before M.I. destroys the time portal and most importantly, stop these Dragos before they alter history."

"Dragos!" Oztin said in alarm, nearly falling off of the wave board. The ship lurched hard to the right. He scrambled back onto the gravitron, steadying the ship until he got the vessel back under control.

"This is serious," he said still shaking. "I mean serious as in dangerous for all humans everywhere."

"You know about Dragos?" Richie asked, surprised at this unexpected comment.

The slip tumble of the craft had jettisoned them back towards the Earth's single moon. Oztin moved the craft into a stationary orbit along the edge of the dark side of its orbit. Just above the silhouette's edge, the Earth's northern hemisphere remained in view.

"Richie, what are you talking about? How do you know about the Dragos?"

"Let me start at the beginning," Richie said. His hands were trying to act as the interpreters of his unfinished thoughts.

Taking a cleansing breath, he told Oztin everything. The family's legend of the ancient Indians, the cave, his travels back in time, the Dragos . . .

With each revelation, Oztin's eyes grew wider. Richie went into detail about Professor Miles and M.I. and how they were stealing his family's land. He culminated his story with the snippets of conversation he overheard from the Dragos and what he feared were the lizard men's plans to take over the Earth.

"This is very serious," Oztin said, sinking deep into his chair. "Let me make sure I got this right. Kippy has gone back to Egypt and you haven't heard from him since . . . when?"

"Early this morning," Richie answered with a quickening pulse "I'm worried. And now, on top of everything else, I have to stop Professor Miles from seizing our land and maybe blocking that cave forever. If that happens, Kippy could be stuck back in time! Not to mention the issue of stopping the Dragos!"

"You're right, of course," Oztin agreed. "We've got to do something. And without a doubt we need to make sure this guy Professor Miles does not get control of that property. But there's more at stake here than you can possibly know."

Richie's fear was building inside of him. He tried to slow his racing heart with long slow breaths.

"You see, about three thousand years ago the humanoids, which make up a Federation of Galactic states, signed a treaty with the Dragos. They are a nasty race of creatures who want to enslave every creature in the universe. There is a fragile equilibrium in the universe between good and evil and it seems evil is about to upset that delicate balance."

Evil—that's what my mom said, what the legend mentioned. Anxiety rose another notch.

"And this is why you are not supposed to be visiting here?" Richie asked, now understanding the seriousness of his friend's infraction.

"Yes," Oztin answered a bit sheepishly, hands wringing as he cast his eyes to the floor. "But thank God we did come."

Richie swallowed the lump rising in his throat. Sitting in their little bubble in the middle of space, Richie felt small and powerless as he looked out into the endless cosmos. Below his feet, daybreak was crossing the United States.

Draped in heavy silence, he watched the sunrise streak across America towards the West Coast. As the penetrating rays reached for California, Richie saw a metallic glint rising up from his native state. He nudged Oztin.

"Look," he pointed—watching the Drago craft exit the atmosphere and dive into the cold vastness of space.

♒︎♏︎ ✦ ◆ ✦ ♒︎ ✦ ● ♒︎ ⚹ ♏︎

Chapter 16
Saba 'SB' Halim

"Yes, of course, I made it here alright. And Richie's fine. Reshea, please just call my mom and cover for me," Oztin was begging but he had to follow this through. "I'll fill you in when I get back . . . I can't discuss it now . . ."

Disconnecting the call, he saw Richie had a million questions.

"Don't you think you should tell your parents?" Richie asked, almost pleading. "I mean, isn't your dad some kind of bigwig in the Federation? Shouldn't we let him know what's going on, like right away?"

"I need to be sure of all of the facts before I bring this to him."

Oztin was worried about coming to an unauthorized planet, and he still held out hope that he might be able to resolve this without his parents finding out. But more importantly, he did not want to come home and raise an alarm until he checked on all the facts. He was going to have to tell them he was violating the rules coming here. This would lead to exposing both Reshea and Squib. He had to be sure before he got his friends into serious trouble.

"We have to protect that cave. Not only so Kippy that can come back, but if the Dragos are already in Egypt, they will have almost 5000 years to alter history. We can't let that happen."

"I agree," Oztin said as he worked out some ideas of what to do. "I will need some proof that my father can take to the Federation . . .

"You said that the factory was being built to supply the Fizz Cola company. Maybe we need to reach out to this Halim guy. He must have some pull. Maybe he can get this project cancelled, or at the least, stalled. That is, assuming he'll buy our 'Lizard men are taking over the universe' story . . ."

"Well, since you put it that way . . ." Richie grimaced, his mind raced to absorb all the what ifs.

Sitting high above Earth, Richie watched the line that divided night and day. Morning was breaking in Santa Martina. He knew his dad would be worried—again. But if even part of what Oztin said about the Dragos was true, he knew his father would want him to do the right thing.

He said he trusted me . . .

"Okay Oztin, let's roll."

Oztin turned the slider back towards Earth. "Where to?"

"New York City!" Richie said. "East—to the coast." Richie felt adrenaline fueling the courage he would need.

In an instant they accelerated, and space blurred by. They pierced the Earth's atmosphere and to Richie's surprise, they were heading west towards Japan. Traveling at the speed of sound, Richie was concerned Oztin was going the wrong way. In a blink of the eye, they leveled off.

We must be going over fifty thousand miles per hour,

Following the curvature of the Earth, they sped across the Atlantic Ocean until Richie spied the Statue of Liberty in New York Harbor, where Oztin brought the craft to a hovering stop.

"Amazing."

Richie focused on the image of a map he had pulled up on his phone when looking up Fizz Cola's offices. "North," he pointed.

Turning the craft, Richie's eyes followed a long tower-lined boulevard until he saw the park. It was like a great green carpet, hemmed in on all sides by a concrete jungle. Outside, a light rain was falling. The park was relatively empty.

"There," Richie pointed. "I think we can set it down in that open meadow."

"Do you know where to go from here?" Oztin asked.

Richie focused on the maps app—glad he had cell service.

"Their offices are only a few blocks from here."

"Alright," Oztin said. "After I drop you off, I'll hover. Don't take all day!! We've got Dragos to destroy!"

The doors opened and the ramp protruded to the soft wet earth. Invisible, Richie crossed the meadow and headed to the west side of Central Park. After a few minutes he exited and came out onto a large sidewalk. People were swarming in all directions. The sign on the far corner read Sixty-Seventh and Central Park West. He remembered the website. It said their main offices were at Fifty-Seventh and Broadway, so he turned south.

With the park on his left, he could see the sapphire craft floating above the tree line, like a huge Macy's Thanksgiving Parade balloon. Within minutes, he was at Broadway and Fifty-Ninth Street.

"What the . . .?" Richie went tumbling to the ground. He looked up to see a man standing above him, confused and bewildered. Richie scrambled backward before the man stepped on him and toppled over. He checked that no one was watching as he slipped the bracelet into his pocket and materialized.

Eventually he found himself in front of the Fizz Cola World Headquarters. He took a long deep breath. The tension of everything was draining him. Looking up, eighty-plus stories of black marble and granite rose until the very top was shrouded in mist.

How am I going to find Mr. Halim in such a huge building?

The thought was immediately followed by the obvious answer. With simple logic, he deduced where to go. Placing the bracelet back upon his wrist, he entered the lobby, passed the security desk, and looked at the various banks of elevators. Then he saw it. Floors 70-88.

The top. That's the one I want.

He stepped into the elevator and pushed the button. He was nervous, he was wet, and he didn't have a really good plan. The elevator silently raced upwards, his ears popped, acceleration stopped, and the doors opened into an ornately decorated lobby. Across the plush reception area, there were two large doors. There was a middle-aged woman behind a desk, strategically placed like a sentry. She stood between him and those doors.

"Mrs. Dangly," said the name plate on her desk. "Executive Secretary."

The elevator closed with a soft whoosh causing her to look up from her desk. Craning her neck, a frown of consternation crossed her face. She arched an eyebrow, then went back to what she was working on.

It dawned on Richie that the head of such a large corporation would probably have every minute of his day filled with meetings and appointments. Furthermore, he realized that he might not even be at the right office.

At least I am invisible.

Resolute, he slipped quietly past the big oak desk and camped out near the office door. His plan was to wait for someone to open it so he could slip in and hope this was the right door.

The seconds turned into minutes and time moved like a slug. Fatigue was setting in. He shifted his weight from one foot to the other, tempted to sit down.

"Mr. Halim's office," Mrs. Dangly said into her attached mouthpiece. "I'm sorry, he is in a meeting . . . yes, yes, okay, thank you. Hello, Mr. Halim's office. . ."

The phone never stopped ringing. With its soft chime, a steady stream of calls were professionally and politely answered. She was the gatekeeper and firmly in charge.

It's been over an hour. How much longer can they be?

He was startled when the doors opened, and two people walked out. Finally. The waiting had given his anxiety too much room to roam. Richie slipped into the office, undetected by anyone.

Wow. He swallowed a large gulp of air, marveling at the grandeur of the room. Its richness and size were something from a movie. Strategically moving to an unused corner, he took in the view from the floor-to-ceiling glass windows. Even in the drizzle, you could see for miles.

Across the room sat a short, dark-haired man behind a simple, but eloquent desk. He was not alone. Sitting across from him, was another man. Richie sighed, knowing that Oztin was waiting.

The accumulated boredom complied with the rising tension, was taking its toll. Keeping to the wall opposite of where the two men were sitting, he stopped to admire a picture here, a statue there, getting a feel for the man's taste. But one ear was always listening.

Atop a carved mahogany credenza stood a large, framed photograph of Mr. Halim. He was much younger. He was standing in front of the same statue he'd seen on the internet. However, this one was definitely clearer—Kippy! The joy of recognizing his old friend turned to worry as he wondered if his pal had made it back from Egypt.

"Okay Harrold. I appreciate you getting this wrapped up before the next board meeting." Mr. Halim came from out behind the desk and walked his visitor to the door. Richie perked up—*Maybe now . . .*

"I will take care of it, sir."

Mr. Halim closed the door and returned to his desk. "Mrs. Dangly," Halim said into the speakerphone. His voice was tempered with a natural kindness.

"Yes," came her professional reply.

"Please hold all my calls."

"The Stewarts are here for their appointment," she reminded him.

"Oh right, I almost forgot. Please let them know I will be with them in a few minutes. Thank you, Mrs. Dangly."

Mr. Halim switched off the intercom and sat back in his chair. With a long sigh he stretched his legs and rolled his shoulders. Turning his back to Richie, he stared out at the mist-shrouded city.

"It seems so long ago . . . Why me? Why that message. . ."

Richie listened as the man talked to himself.

"You knew only I could read it, and you have never been wrong, not once. Your blessings are more than any one man deserves, more than anyone would ever need." After a long silence, he reached for the phone. "I guess I've made the Stewarts wait long enough . . ."

Realizing that he must act now, Richie pulled the bracelet from his hand, materializing in an instant.

"Excuse me, sir," Richie said, startling Mr. Halim, whose finger was hovering over the intercom button. He stared wide-eyed at the boy.

"May I help you, young man?" he inquired, letting his arm fold into his lap.

"Yes sir, you can," Richie answered politely. The man seemed to relax and a kindness played over his expression.

"May I ask your name?"

"Richie Radcliff, sir."

"Do we have an appointment Mr. Radcliff?"

"No sir," Richie answered truthfully.

"And Mrs. Dangly, does she know you are in here?"

"No sir. I don't believe she saw me enter. It wasn't her fault though," he quickly added.

Richie watched as the man studied him. He seemed amused.

"Well, since you are here, how may I help you?" It was a straightforward question, delivered with an unwavering gaze.

Richie paused, nervous, eyes shifting away from the wattage of Mr. Halim's scrutiny. He knew he was only going to get one chance at this, and he was not sure how to start.

But that picture of a young Halim standing in front of Kippy's statue reaffirmed what he already suspected, he was part of this mess, and might be the solution.

"Ahem," Mr. Halim said clearing his throat, expressing impatience. "I do have another appointment waiting."

Eyeing the photo on the credenza, Richie walked over, took it off the shelf and returned to the desk and sat it down in front of Mr. Halim.

Halim looked at it but said nothing.

"Nice picture," Richie said, "Saw something similar on the internet. Where was it taken?"

"I was young, it was long ago," Halim said with a shrug of his shoulders. His voice betrayed growing irritation.

"Long ago . . ." Richie repeated. "Strange, isn't it?" he asked rhetorically. "I mean, my dog is only three years old, and you're standing in front of his statue!"

The statement was supposed to land like a bombshell, but to Richie's surprise and consternation, Halim didn't even blink. Instead, he absorbed the comment and did a little showman's roll of his left hand, queuing him to continue.

So he lobbed in the next shell, hoping for a more direct strike.

"Time travel is a tricky thing. Yesterday, a thousand years ago, five thousand years ago? My dog and I found a time portal. We have gone back and forth through time and in fact, we just returned from ancient Egypt."

There was an odd twinkle in Halim's eye, but his reaction was far less than expected. *What do I need to do to get this guy's attention?* Richie wondered. Oh well, might as well go for it.

"Miles Industries is trying to steal my family's land, which would endanger the existence of this time portal. They are doing it so they can make cans for your company. I would like your help in getting them to stop this theft before it is too late!"

At the mention of MI, Mr. Halim placed both hands on the desk, interlaced his fingers and narrowed his eyes. His expression shifted to something less friendly. His penetrating gaze was making Richie uncomfortable, draining his confidence and self-assurance away.

"My dog is in Egypt now, talking with their Pharaoh." The air became thick. Richie didn't like the feel of it.

"Son, you had me going there for a minute," Saba said, coming from out behind the desk. A grave expression hardened his wizened face.

"I almost believed you. But talking dogs, well that's a bit much, even for someone like me." He was now looming over Richie. "I'm not sure that I can help you. I think perhaps it is time for you to leave," he paused and then added. "Before I call security."

Richie relaxed. This was more in line with his original expectations. His confidence rushed back in. "Call security if you want, but you will miss a once in a lifetime opportunity," he told him. "By the time they get here, I will be gone. They can't catch what they can't see." And then, Richie disappeared.

He stepped backward to move out of arm's length.

"Yes, I can see that it would be hard to believe in talking dogs and for that matter, invisible boys," his bodiless voice continued. "But what I don't understand is why you were so ready to believe in a time travel portal and my claims to have returned from ancient Egypt?"

Saba sat down upon the edge of the desk, his right hand covering his mouth.

"Weren't you just wondering about the great mystery of your life? Well I think we are connected in some way. I've got a great mystery I'm trying to resolve. I think we might be able to help each other . . . Please, Mr. Halim, hear me out." He reached for the phone on his desk.

"Ms. Dangly, please cancel the rest of my appointments for today. Hold all calls and please ask the Stewarts if I can reschedule with them at their earliest convenience. Give them my profoundest apologies."

Then almost as an afterthought, he added. "Please instruct accounting to cut a check for one million dollars from my personal funds for The Stewart Center for Orphan Children. I would like it there before the day is out, preferably before the Stewarts even get back to their offices. Thank you, Mrs. Dangly." He punched off the intercom.

"Okay young man, you have my attention. Would you mind making yourself visible? Call me old-fashioned, but I like to see who I am talking to."

Removing the bracelet, Richie materialized. He was still winging it, but at least he had gotten this far. Mr. Halim motioned towards the couches across the office.

Oztin had left it to Richie's discretion whether he should mention his alien friends or not. The pace of events was speeding up and time was running out. Remembering the article about the endowment to the local museum, as well as his firsthand experience in witnessing the donation Mr. Halim just authorized to the orphanage, Richie made a judgment call.

"Mr. Halim. If you don't mind, I will start from the beginning."

"Please call me Saba."

Richie hit the top points. The Dragos, mankind and the Federation. As proof he told him Oztin was in his spaceship hovering over the park. He explained the writ to take his family's land and that this was forcing the clock to run out on them. "So, do you see why we need to stop MI before it is too late?"

Saba stood up, stretched his legs, and walked over to his desk, pressing the button on the intercom again.

"Ms. Dangly, please call Mort over at Miles Industries. Ask them to halt any further plans or construction on the Santa Martina Plant until we have a chance to meet. Explain that it is a personal request and that it is in our companies' mutual best interests to stop further progress at this time. Please also let Mort know that we will cover any costs that may be a result of the delays.

"And then call Gronemeyer in Legal. Bartholomew Miles is trying to steal some land from a fellow named Radcliff. Have him get an injunction signed by a local judge in their district blocking this travesty and tell him to pull out all the stops. I want this done by the end of the day out west." Saba signed off and turned back to Richie.

"Well, it won't stop him, but it should slow him down," Saba said with a little smile. "Does your dad know you are here, or about any of this?"

Richie shook his head.

"Why don't you give your father a call at least let him know you are safe? Then we will go and speak to your friend Oztin."

$e\tau \mathfrak{m} \cdot \blacklozenge \cdot \mathcal{H} \cdot \bullet \mathcal{H} \nearrow \mathfrak{m}$

Saba had ordered a car that was waiting out front. The rain had stopped, and oil-slicked rainbows glistened off the pavement. Stepping from the car next to the park entrance, he watched Richie slip on the bracelet and once again vanish.

He could not see Oztin, his craft, or Richie. He tried to squelch the rising tide of excitement. He felt like a kid again, a feeling that had been in hiding for many, many years.

"Saba, put out your hand."

Saba did as he was told. He felt fingers curl around his wrist and then, in an instant, Richie appeared at his side. Before him stood a large blue craft unlike anything he had ever seen before. He could only stare in wonder.

It's all true, he thought licking his lips in awe.

"We're going to walk up a ramp into the ship," Richie told him. "If I lose your grip, you will not be able to see a thing, so stay close to me."

Saba held tight and together they walked into the alien craft.

"Welcome." Oztin took Saba's hand and fixed a bracelet onto his wrist.

"Thank you," Saba answered trying to regain a little bit of his adult dignity.

Saba realized his hosts were just boys and yet they had admirably carried the weight of the universe on their young shoulders. He barely knew them but already had kindling feelings of pride at their courage and resourcefulness.

Saba let his body collapse on to the seat as the transparency of the walls opened the view. A wave of lightheadedness washed over him, and he squeezed his eyes tight, letting his mind catch up. He opened one eye, then the other. Below, the Earth was rushing past. His mind still churned and as he dissected Richie's story yet again.

He began to get a pretty good idea who his guardian angel had been, the one who left him that cryptic message so long ago that changed his life.

$$e_7 \mathfrak{m} \cdot \blacklozenge \cdot \rtimes \cdot \bullet \rtimes \cancel{x} \mathfrak{m}$$

Saba followed Richie's gaze as he pointed towards the woods. In the dying light, glints of light refracted from the steel, chrome and glass of the bull dozers, back hoes and dump trucks lining the side of the road leading into the property.

"How long has all that construction equipment been there?" Saba asked, wondering if Gronemeyer got that injunction yet.

"They weren't here yesterday," Richie answered, his voice a little shaky. "Do you think your calls had any effect? Is Bart going to stop?"

"My guys are pretty good, Richie," Saba replied confidently. "Remember, I just made those calls a little while ago. I'm sure this stuff was brought in earlier today." His words sounded reassuring, but inside he wasn't nearly as confident.

Oztin made three passes over the area. "It doesn't look like there are any workers around. I'm going to put us down in that hollow just over there."

They exited the craft and Saba followed Richie as he led the way towards the opening. Saba waited as Oztin was the last to enter.

"Wow," Oztin mouthed. "Time travel! They really can use this as a weapon. I need to get back home and tell my dad about this ASAP."

Seeing the dark cloud wash across Oztin's face, Saba began to understand the bigger picture. He said nothing and simply watched the two boys. Oztin was stroking the large screen as if trying to confirm it was not a mirage.

"If you can travel through time, and Kippy is already in some other realm and your bracelet functions when you travel, why haven't the Dragos just taken their superior weapons and technology back in time? They could be dominating the planet right now. What's holding them back?" Oztin wondered aloud. Then he speculated on his own question. "They would not want any proof from the future that could tip off the Federation . . ."

"Richie, after you climb into the chamber and get transported to your new location, what happens at the other end? What I mean," Saba clarified, "is you said there is a pyramid like this at the other end? What if you wanted to go elsewhere, how does that work?"

"Elsewhere? I haven't gone anywhere but Egypt, so I really don't know for sure," Richie explained. "Why?"

"It's possible this cave is like a cosmic train station," he said. "You can probably go anywhere from here, but once you get to another location, the tracks only lead back to this point."

"Why's that important?" Oztin's brows were furrowed in question.

"It means that whoever controls this end of the portal controls time travel. If I am correct in my assumption, the portal at the other end will only give you a one-way ticket back to this point in time and space."

"You think we can cut the Dragos off from here?" Richie asked excitedly. We could stop them?"

"Exactly," Saba said with satisfaction that the boy was quick to comprehend. Saba noted Oztin looking impatient, rocking back and forth from one foot to another.

"Guys, I need to get home and tell everything to my dad," Oztin said distracted. "This affects the entire Federation."

Richie cast an eye to his friend and then back to Saba. "We need to stop Miles before anything else."

"I have my guys on it," Saba said reassuringly. "I will text them again to make sure they throttle Miles until we get a better understanding of what is going on."

But there was a question etched on his face, he aired out his thought. "What we need to figure out is why he wants this spot. I saw plenty of land all around here when we flew over. It's not as if he couldn't start without your few acres."

Oztin reminded Richie of something he had told him previously that was relevant to the question posed by Saba. "A few days ago, we had visitors from a distant planet in the Federation. They informed my father, who is a high official within the Counsel, that the Dragos have learned how to morph into human form. This is extremely dangerous. I think that bald guy you said you saw is a morphed Drago. I'm guessing he works for MI. And that's why this land is important . . ."

"Of course!" Richie exclaimed, "His name is Sal O'Mander? He works for Miles Industries. Earlier this year he came by and offered to buy our property. That was a while ago."

"I met O'Mander once," Saba told them. "He was accompanying Bart at a business meeting. I remember that shiny bald head of his. There was something unsettling about it." Just the memory turned Saba's stomach.

With a serious look, Saba sat down and put his arm around Oztin's shoulder. "For this to work, our success is going to depend almost entirely on you. Here is what I think you should do . . ."

***

Chapter 17
Ancient Egypt

With the doors closing, Kippy broke to the left, darting one way and then another. A sliver of open space stood between him and the two Dragos.

Slow to respond, the nearest reptile spun his tail, throwing the thick black scales down in front of the dodging dog. Kippy tried to jump over but the Drago's powerful thrust sent him sailing—and it was only his good fortune that it was towards the door, and that it was still open. Kippy hit the floor and with nails scrabbling on the oily surface, he bolted.

"Idiots!" Lord Drago shouted. "Get him!"

He looked back to see the Dragos lunging towards him and crash into one another in the chaos, wasting precious moments as he put distance between them. Down the hall the two guards stationed by Pharaoh's room came running.

Adrenaline fueled him and fear drove him. He took the stairs two at a time, and a huge lizard appeared and blocked the bottom as the two from behind were coming up fast. He was trapped!

He bared his teeth and dived at the recoiling guard.

This was his opening! Squeezing between the sentry and the railing, Kippy went sliding across the marble floor, for once thankful for the slick sheen.

"Guards!" Kippy yelled his best impersonation of Lord Drago. "Quickly, open the doors! Open the doors, now!"

Lord Drago appeared at the top of the stairs. "Don't open those doors," he roared.

The competing orders and similar sounding voices rose to a clamor. Suddenly the doors were flung open. In his mind's eye, Kippy saw everything unfold in slow motion—the lizard men lunging, the doors opening, the collision as one was knocked unconscious and the other thrown back into a tangle of bodies . . . this all culminated in shouts and slithering tongues dripping with malice.

Kippy burst through the open door and lost himself in a crowd, running as he'd never run before. He rounded a corner and headed to the fountain at the base of the temple stairs.

I need to hide, and I need people around.

Kippy chose a vantage point that allowed an unobstructed view of the temple's entrance. There, he watched two dog-headed sentries. A group of workers were approaching. As they came near, he decided that what worked before could be tried again. He slipped under the hems of their robes to hide from the guards' prying eyes. Stepping through the doors, he stayed with them a few more yards until they began separating and going their individual ways.

Spotting a table covered with mixes of paint and an assortment of tools, Kippy hid underneath and assessed the situation. He had no plan, at least not yet. He willed his heart to slow, wishing the adrenaline to run its course. Panting, he spotted a dog-masked Drago just a few feet away, he was shielded by the table.

There's another, and yet another still. They were strategically placed throughout the building. From their relaxed posture, Kippy figured the alarm had not made its way here yet.

Leaving his cover, he moved through the workers until he found what he was hoping for. A lone Drago amid a group of Egyptian workers.

I sure hope these guys are still loyal to Pharaoh.

Kippy sank his teeth as deep as he could into the lizard's disgusting calf. "Owww!" bellowed the Drago.

"Disgusting," he said, spitting out the lizard meat. He saw that the piercing cry caused heads to turn as the Drago continued to wail.

"This man is an impostor!" Kippy shouted at the gawking workers. "They all are." He had to act quickly. "They have captured your Pharaoh and are holding him in the palace."

Kippy continued to holler. "Look under their masks. They're devils. Seize them! We have them outnumbered!"

The workers did not react as Kippy hoped, and he sensed his advantage slipping away. The other Dragos were rushing through the crowd and coming from all points of the compass. The lizard men were closing in.

Kippy shouted to an uninterested crowd as he backed up. "I am your God, and these are impostors!" he tried again, bellowing while on the move. Finally, one, then another, then another and a few more fell to their knees, bowing to the commanding canine. This only opened the way for the Dragos to move faster.

"Rise up and be worthy," he barked, trying not to sound like a god in desperation. "These men are impostors!"

It was going to be close, victory or defeat. "Seize them and remove their masks! See for yourself. They're agents of darkness! You have been tricked."

Kippy heard their murmurs and hammered home the final nail. "These men have been taking you all for fools."

Seeing the crowd spring to their feet in indignation and anger, body by body, a human mass formed a shield around him.

This stopped the Dragos, who he saw appeared stymied. They could advance no further. Momentum was no longer on their side. The stink of fear wafted from the protective confines of their costumes.

Kippy jumped up onto a scaffolding plank for a wider view. From across the room he saw a canal of humanity cleaved open as if by a mysterious wind, and the widening passage was making its way directly to where Kippy held court. It was Richie and an older man. A ton of anxiety escaped on his breath. "Thank you, thank you, thank you," he muttered quietly.

He knew that though they were invisible to the humans, the retreating Dragos could see them. But nothing they could say or do was going to change the inevitable outcome, so they hastened their withdrawal.

"Grab them," the emboldened canine god demanded. The crowd reacted with vigor.

"Seize the traitors," rose the shout from another. Soon teeming hordes closed in on the Drago guards. One by one, their masks were jerked from their heads.

"Ugh. Disgusting! Phew!" Cries of surprise and disgust rang out. One by one, the Drago guards were being pinned by the crowd. The few not yet captured had been cornered. The battle was firmly in hand.

Just as Kippy was feeling pretty darn proud of himself, without warning, the Dragos began to disappear. Suddenly all around him were gasps and wails of disbelief and he watched fear ripple throughout the crowd. All eyes turned his way. The people were beginning to panic. He had to do something, and quickly.

"Seal the door!" Kippy barked in his most commanding voice. This call to action nudged them back to his side.

"Don't be afraid," he extolled. "These beasts have cast spells upon your eyes, but I see all things. Follow my commands! Together we will capture these dark lords. We shall set Pharaoh free!"

Leaping from his perch, he ran to the closest Drago, and sunk his teeth into its leg. Gatherers rushed to the spot and slammed the creature to the ground.

He saw the tide was turning and that the Dragos were powerless. Only a cloak of invisibility stalled the inevitability. All exits were sealed. He guided the people to round up and bind the beasts. All except one . . .

Kippy spied a man he wanted to speak with. "You!" he said, pointing at a nervous young man. "What is your name?"

"Marcal, my Lord," the young man replied humbly. The gathered Egyptians retreated and left him standing alone.

"You were very clever in rounding up these hooligans." Kippy complimented. "Are you military?"

"No, your eminence," he responded.

Kippy saw his chest swell with pride at being recognized. But at the same time, a slight embarrassment was seen by the perceptive eyes of the cunning canine.

"Where are all the soldiers?" Kippy continued. "I have not seen them, and I suspect your Pharaoh would have a great army at his command."

"Gone, I mean, yes, we do have an army, but they were sent away to the south, all of them!" Many heads in the crowd bobbed up in down, as if this was familiar knowledge.

"Is that common, for the entire army to go away?" Kippy asked.

"No sir, I have never seen the city so completely abandoned by Pharaoh's guards, but he ordered it, and his will shall be done."

"I see." Kippy said noncommittally, noticing that the man fidgeted with his hands, trying to hide them. He's embarrassed, Kippy thought, and then looking closer he saw a deformity of Marcal's left hand. *That's probably why he is not in the military, he was shunned or rejected.*

"Then you shall be my new commander," Kippy told him. "Young master Marcal," Kippy proclaimed loud enough so that all those nearby would hear.

"You have shown great bravery here today. But our work has just begun. I am giving you charge to lead your people to victory. Together we will rid this land of these evil lords. As one we will free Pharaoh."

"Thank you, Lord," Marcal said with humility. "All my life I have been told I was incapable . . ." The young man stiffened his back in attention. "Your commands shall be my sole directive, oh great and powerful Sirius. What shall you have me do?"

Saba whispered quietly to Richie as he watched everything unfold. "This is your dog? Has he always had such leadership skills?"

"Marcal, clear the temple at once. Find a safe place to lock up these impostors and make absolutely sure that their hands are bound tight and they cannot assist each other. Keep them all separated, but alive!"

He nodded his agreement and understanding.

"Then gather your people together, our army per se, and wait for my further instruction." Kippy instructed.

"Very impressive," Saba said respectfully to the canine lord.

𝑒𝕸•◆•Ж•●Ж✗𝕸

Confident that the Egyptians and Dragos were cleared out of the hall, Richie made the formal introduction.

"Saba, may I present Sirius, the chow-hound of Santa Martina. Kippy, this is Mr. Saba Halim, the President of the Fizz Cola Company."

"Please, call me Saba." Looking around, he added, "Perhaps before we get too comfortable, we should do a quick search of the building and make sure there are no stragglers. "We wouldn't want your marvelous story to unravel, now would we?" He gave the dog a wink.

"Richie, you have been up for nearly a day and a half, you must be exhausted and hungry," Saba noted. "Let's take a break."

"Yea, I could use a minute to rest." Saba saw him fetch a backpack in the corner.

"I left it here before," Richie explained. He grabbed the bag and retrieved two cans of Fizz Cola and a handful of granola bars. As they drank, Richie sat down against the wall and within minutes his chin drooped to his chest and he was asleep.

"Let him rest," Saba suggested. "I'm sure he can use it.

Saba spoke as he stared about the room. "It has been a long time since I have been in this room," he began . . .

Saba watched as Kippy eyed the open can of Fizz Cola and moved the cylinder away from Richie, knocking it on its side where he proceeded to lick up every drop. Then he let out a nice long burp.

Saba gave a soft chuckle. "I haven't had this much fun since I was a kid," he told Kippy.

His memories had not dimmed with time. This place was even more beautiful and mystical than the first day he laid eyes on it so many years ago. He knew he would finally find the answers he sought for so long, but at what cost? Seeing the mural of his beloved Big Dipper, it all became crystal clear.

"You know, for sixty years, I believed a guardian angel left a message just for me. A message in my own private language that detoured destiny's road."

He chuckled at the revelation. The truth saddened him just a little bit, after all, having a guardian angel made him feel invincible all these years.

"Now I know," he whispered. "It was no angel, only a mere mortal."

He stared at the wall, a blank slate waiting for its author. Taking a hard metal pen from his jacket, he began to scratch a message on the wall, just above floor level. A place where no one would see it unless they were truly looking. He worked diligently, remembering what he had placed there before, and recalling all the great companies that have risen on Wall Street over the last fifty years.

"What are you doing?" the lip licking canine asked.

"Solving a mystery," he smiled. "This may sound a little weird, but I am leaving a message for me to see in the future, when I am just a little boy."

"Okay . . ." Kippy chuckled. "Can I ask you something?"

"I'll answer your question, but you must answer one of mine. Agreed?"

Kippy's wagging tail confirmed acceptance. "Tell me what you wrote!"

"Okay." Saba said, realizing he had never shared this with another individual, ever. "When I was a boy, I created a language of my own. Don't ask me why, but I did. Anyway, when I was nine-years old, we had just discovered this building, it had been sealed for five thousand years.

"First, I found a metallic can like one I'd never seen, then I saw a message written in my personal language. It pretty much sealed my fate then and there. It reads:

'Saba, the Professor is going to fire you. Go to the docks and climb aboard the Mystic Princess, a steam ship bound for America. Put yourself through school, study very hard, and save every dollar. When you have a chance, buy stock in Microsoft, Wal-Mart, Apple, Yahoo, Google, Amazon, and Fizz Cola. Every last dollar you invest will grow beyond your wildest imagination. When you take a job at Fizz Cola, work hard, be honest and remain humble. Always help others when you can. Most importantly, always remain true to yourself. Your goodness will be rewarded.'

"That's how you became rich!"

"I was blessed," Saba responded with humility. He now felt fulfilled. Warmth flowed into a part of himself he never knew was empty. Saba never had the luxury of a pet. He had, in fact, never had much of a childhood, always trying to simply survive.

"Kippy, will you answer one of man's oldest questions?" Saba's mouth turned into a crooked grin. Kippy shrugged.

"Why is it dogs like to sniff each other's butts?"

Kippy had a simple answer. "It's our way of checking if we have similar ancestors. You know, like, are we related?" Kippy explained. "Humans send in samples of their DNA to find out where they come from. Who their relatives are and things like that. We do the same thing, but differently. We sniff each other's butts to see if we are related. Do we have similar relatives and if so, from where and how many generations back. Remember, as puppies, once we leave our mother we almost never see our siblings again." Kippy continued. "You smell the butt, you know from where you came."

Saba had never considered that most dogs are separated from their brothers and sisters at such a young age. It gave him a moment of pause.

"There's a lot you can learn from dogs." Kippy answered with a simper of mischief.

"Oh? Do tell," Saba urged.

"Well . . . For instance, when loved ones come home, always run to greet them, and no matter how often you're scolded, don't buy into the guilt thing and pout. Run right back and make friends."

Saba liked his sound wisdom.

"Avoid biting when a simple growl will do. On warm days, stop to lie on your back in the grass. I think it would help a lot. You worry too much."

Saba envisioned himself walking out of his office in a suit and tie and rolling in the grass of Central Park. Smiling, he declared that he would try it.

"When someone is having a bad day, simply sit close by, remain silent, and nuzzle them gently on occasion. There's nothing better in the world. Oh, and always be loyal."

"You are a wise one, my friend," Saba said with a smile of genuine affection. He put his arm gently around Kippy's neck and scratched him behind his ear.

☞ℳ ◆ ⊁ ● ⊁ ⇗ℳ

Chapter 18
Turning the Tide

Kayla's concern for Richie pounded its way into a headache. She had not seen nor heard from him in two days, nobody had.

I've got to do something! She thought. Maybe I should go out to the cave. Maybe he's hurt.

The growing dread was only made worse by sitting around fretting. Wheeling her bike out of the garage, she felt a shiver run down her spine. Someone was watching her. She could feel it.

"It's no one," she whispered to herself. "Just nerves." Hopping on the bike, she coasted down the driveway and banked into the turn.

The warm sun beat upon her shoulders as Kayla headed towards the woods. The clammy feeling in her stomach remained. With trickles of sweat running down her forehead, she arrived at her destination and lowered the bike into the grass.

Looking into the cloudless sky she saw nothing and heard nothing. No birds, no insects, nothing at all. Her breathing seemed to amplify the open spaces. When she reached the spot where she was to enter the woods, a fresh rash of goose bumps blistered across her forearms. The silence gave her the creeps, and her courage waned with each step.

"Maybe this isn't such a good idea . . ."

Suddenly, the sunlight dissolved into shadows as a mottled darkness grew around her. Larger and larger it became until a sweeping band voided the sunlight's warmth.

Have the birds returned?

She lifted her chin skyward but there was nothing there. Her senses moved to high alert. She heard something in the woods, and strained to listen, but the pounding of her heartbeat filled her ears.

Snap. There it was again, dried twigs underfoot, breaking. It's coming from the direction of the cave. There was a rustling noise, heavy footsteps.

"Richie, is that you?" she inquired meekly. Her instincts screamed, *Get out! Leave as fast as you can!* But her heart clung to an irrational hope that it was Richie. The internal cry raged until finally, it was too much to ignore. She whirled about and took off running. Her heart raced on gulps of breath.

Inside the forest's edge she could hear snapping twigs. Heavy footfalls were tracking her, gaining ground. She needed to move away from the trees. Her bike lay just a few yards ahead.

Arriving breathless and shaking, she yanked her bike up and froze. She stared in disbelief. Both tires were flat.

"You should see the look on your face, Kayla!" Chucky laughed, calling from behind a rock. "Priceless!"

"Chucky, it's not funny," Kayla screamed. "There's something in those woods and it's after me! I've . . . we've got to get out of here! There is some kind of monster back there!"

Then she felt the touch of cold clammy hands seize her. Panic welled up as an unseen creature locked her arms at her side and started to drag her away.

"Chucky! Help me!" she screamed. "Do something!"

Kayla continued to struggle against the invisible horror. It was dragging her up a ramp when suddenly a sharp pain was followed by darkness.

𝒆ꞛℳ◆✦ℋ◆●ℋ⤢ℳ

"Mom, Dad, I'm sorry," Oztin said as he rushed through the front door. "Reshea called, right? Said that I would be late?"

But their body language had the universal pose. Arms crossed, stone faced and unyielding. Ticked-off parents. Normally, Oztin knew there was no excuse for his behavior, but he also knew these were special circumstances.

Even though he had arrived home more than a day late, he needed to get his parents past this obstacle and quickly. Time had taken on new meaning. Minutes mattered.

"She called . . ." The slow deep baritone of his father's voice amplified his displeasure.

"Dad, I know you are mad, and when I am done explaining it might even be worse," he began. His hands were fidgeting. "I mean, bad as in a galactic scale disaster."

"What is . . . What's happened?"

Oztin could tell his father's anger was replaced by worry.

"Let's go into my study and discuss it."

Following his dad across the living room, Oztin felt safe. He knew his parents loved him. Enoch opened the curtains to allow the moons' light in. Sitting down into his favorite chair, he let out a long sigh. "Okay son, start from the beginning."

Oztin had rehearsed his explanation a hundred times on the journey home. He knew it was still going to sound lame at first.

"Dad, we visited the blue planet, the one that is off limits. We met a boy and his dog . . . And Dragos are there and my friends are in danger. We need to do something . . ." Oztin touched on the cave.

"The Dragos are using this cave to go back in time. I think they want to rewrite history. Dad, they have morphing abilities. What if they are able to go back in time, long before they ever entered into any treaty with us. How would we ever know?"

He waited for his father to say something, feeling the silence pull at every molecule in the room. His father turned to look out the window. Oztin looked past him to the shifting shadows on the lawn. It was a beautiful night. One would never suspect that harmony in the universe was coming unglued.

"Do you remember when we discussed non-interference, causes and effect?" His father asked, turning to look at his son.

"Yes, father," Oztin replied, looking down at his feet.

"Well, sometimes the universe has its own plans. It would seem that your ventures may have been part of a greater plan, a natural balancing perhaps, or maybe even divine influence. How can I punish you for that?

"Son, the blue planet is called Earth. Throughout the history of the universe, Earth has always held a special place in the cosmic makeup. It is actually a much older planet than the population can recall. The planet has seen great civilizations rise and fall and rise again.

"We have been protecting the Earth from the Dragos for thousands of years. That was one of the core objectives of getting them to sign the Diageo Treaty. And now, I fear they have not only discovered Earth's location, but they just might also succeed in stealing it."

As the desk lamp cleaved at shadows in the corner, the faint glow exposed the furrows of worry growing deep into his father's brow.

"Dad, what is so important about Earth? I mean, don't get me wrong, I do not want any harm to come to my friends. Or for the Dragos to get control. But, I mean, it's out of the way and really quite small by most comparisons. Now you're telling me an entire galactic treaty was engineered to create a layer of protection just for them?"

Enoch rose to his feet. He drew his hand across his face, rubbing the stubble on his chin.

"It is a complex question with a complex answer. I need your patience so that I can get the ball rolling through the halls of bureaucracy."

"Sure," Oztin agreed, "But before you call them, there is one more thing."

"More?"

"Yes sir," he answered. "You see, it's the cave. I told you the Dragos were using it to go back and forth across the eons, but what I failed to mention was that my friends have gone back in time and are trying to disrupt the Dragos.

"And there are more Dragos waiting just beyond the Earth's biosphere. They are parked behind the Earth's moon. I caught a glimpse of them when I was returning from my last trip. I don't think they saw me. I get the feeling that whatever they are waiting for is rapidly approaching.

"Can you convince the Federation to make sure that those Dragos are not allowed to interfere? We need to block them and make sure they do not get control of the cave from this side of time."

His father remained silent as he squeezed his eyes shut.

"The cave is the key, Dad," Oztin said, "The man we picked up—Saba, he thinks it is the departure terminal, the origination point. Control the cave and you control who goes where and when. And it is my job to make sure that they cannot get control of it."

"Let me make those calls. As soon as I'm finished, we'll discuss what needs to be done next. "I am proud of you. Very, very proud."

After a spell, Richie stood and rubbed the sleep from his eyes. He awoke to a nagging thought. *What's in the boxes . . .?*

"You feel better?" Saba asked as Kippy came over and sat at his master's feet.

"A little." He walked over to the nearest crate and ran his hands along the edge of the top. He found an indent in the lid.

"Saba—can you help me, I want to get the top off."

Saba gripped the other end and together removed the heavy top. Inside was another box, it gleamed like polished metal and was cool to the touch. There was a panel of three buttons on the front center.

Richie pushed a green button and with a *Pffffffitt* the lid rose smoothly and efficiently. He stepped back to even his breath and relish the small victory.

"Wow!" Kippy said, sticking his snout into the fray. The box was filled with bundles of documents and drawings. Undecipherable, but clearly building plans.

"Sets sixty through seventy," Kippy mumbled.

"You can read that?" Saba asked.

"It's a side benefit of the voice translator, I can understand almost any language, whether verbal or written, and apparently, it includes these lizard-butts as well."

"Lucky break for us."

Taking one of the rolled bundles from the box, Richie unfurled it onto the crate next to where Kippy was standing.

"Looks like blueprints," Saba said, appraising the open roll. "Kippy, are they planning to build something?"

Kippy had Richie flip the various pages back and forth. He studied the drawings. They were rife with hand notations at various junctures.

"I don't like the looks of this," he finally told them.

"What is it?" Saba had concern growing over his face.

"I don't think they were opening these crates," he said with a frown. "I think they've completed whatever it is that they were building, and these crates were on their way back to the safety of their spaceship."

"Hmmm," Saba sighed. "But plans for what?"

"It's hard to tell, some kind of structure. It seems very complex!"

They pulled out more rolls and unfurled them on the floor. Kippy showed Richie and Saba that each bundle was numbered on the side which allowed them to be viewed in order.

"Tunnels," he told them. "It's a system of tunnels."

Saba grimaced. "Can you tell where the passageways are?"

"Not really." Kippy said with a tilt of the head. "I have no reference points. Perhaps if we go through the rest of these boxes I may learn more."

They opened crate after crate. With each opening, Richie was sure that Kippy was right.

"What's this?" Richie asked, leaning over the last remaining box. He lifted out a small metal case and laid it on one of the discarded lids. The case was lined in protective padding. Inside were three rows of four metallic objects.

"Stars, crescent moons and well, these look like comets. What do you think they are?" Richie pulled one of the stars from the container. It was about the size of a walnut, fitting easily into his palm.

"Weird, right? Feels cold to the touch, and, well, it sort of feels like it has a current pulsing through it. Here take one."

Saba took out a crescent moon. "You're right, they are kind of tingly."

"Could they be weapons?" Kippy asked.

Richie hefted the weight of the star. "Whatever they are, they certainly didn't want them getting scratched or broken."

"Anything else in the box?"

"Just one more large bundle." Richie dropped the star into his pocket and he and Saba lifted the last roll onto the floor. Using their feet, they pushed it open. "It's a map."

"Look here," Saba said putting his finger at various spots on the parchment. "This must be the Nile River. If that's the case, these plans cover miles and miles, maybe more. And here, here, and here . . . Do these marks look familiar?"

"Stars, crescent moons and . . ." tracing his finger along a yellow line, Richie saw the final piece. "Comet symbols!"

"What's the connection?"

"That's the million-dollar question!" Saba said. "I suggest we take these little buggers along with us, just in case."

"If those lines are tunnels, why the different colors? And look how far these things fan out. It could be for miles."

"Well, at least we have a map," Saba reminded. "We might be able to figure out what they are up to. Or where their entrances might be."

Richie studied the huge map. "Look there, at the Pyramids. Could that mark be an opening?"

"There's only one way to find out," Saba said. "Shall we go and see?"

Ꮛℳ•◆•⽱•●⽱⤢ℳ

Do you guys mind?" Kippy asked stepping onto a plank. "I mean, they will expect a grand entrance. After all, I am a god." His expression was serious, but the twinkle in his eye showed humor.

The two humans looked at one another and rolled their eyes. "All right," Richie said, grabbing his backpack.

"Right, but first things first." Saba unfurled the first set of plans, the smaller set. He laid them face down on the Lord's magical board. "We might need these later, so no accidents."

"All aboard, oh great pompous one." Richie bowed in mock reverence.

Reattaching their bracelets, the two invisible friends lifted the board above their heads and proceeded out the front door. It was early afternoon and the bright light of the Egyptian sun caused Kippy to squint as he peered out over the expansive plaza.

"Look at the size of the crowd." Richie whispered.

"It appears Marcal has succeeded at getting the message out that Lord Sirius has arrived," Saba agreed, with a hushed tone.

Kippy didn't care why they had come, he sat up on his hind haunches and waved, like a boxer in triumph. The crowd roared with approval.

"Greetings, my lieges," he barked at the top of his lungs.

"Lieges?" Richie whispered. "Where does he come up with this stuff?"

Marcal ascended the temple stairs and bowed. This was picked up by the crowd and a wave of demurral rolled as far back as he could see.

"Loyal subjects of Pharaoh," Kippy bellowed, enjoying the moment. "I am Lord Sirius, Master of the Dog Star in the heavens of Orion."

The crowd hushed and Kippy's voice boomed out over the human tide. "I have come to warn you of great peril . . ."

Letting his voice drop, stilling the massive crowd, he set the hook. "Your Pharaoh needs you. He is being held captive by the forces of darkness led by these treacherous Dragos."

"No!" Boos and exclamations rose from the crowd. Kippy held up his paw and the crowd quieted.

"I have given full authority to young master Marcal standing here before me, together we shall overcome. Together we shall set Pharaoh free!" The crowd burst into applause, he had them eating from his paws.

Kippy turned to his Captain. "Marcal, does the Pharaoh have dogs? Hunting dogs or any other royal canines?"

"Yes, of course," he replied. "There are many."

"Have some men go and gather them up, all of them. And bring them to me as fast as you can," Kippy ordered.

"We will be ready, my Lord," he said confidently.

Kippy turned and faced the crowd below. "Citizens," he boomed. "Those that claim to be the Pharaoh's overseers have deceived us. They are foul creatures who seek to take over our homeland. But together, as one, we will stop them."

Kippy noted that the people had become more energized and were now pressing forward as Marcal called each of his handpicked captains to come forth.

One by one they ascended the stairs and bowed. By the time the last had stepped back, a loud commotion erupted in the rear.

With yelping, barking and intermittent snarls, a pack of leashed dogs numbering fifty of more, made their way towards Kippy. There were various breeds of all sizes, shapes and colors straining at their tethers. This heightened the general chaos of the excitable crowd.

"Marcal," Kippy commanded. "Clear an area for presentation. I will review these hounds and give instructions."

Kippy realized the issue of the Dragos' invisibility was going to be a problem, but being the all-knowing lord that he was, he divined that using the dogs as hunters was a solution that just might work.

They proceeded down the stairs to an open square at the side of the temple landing where he confronted the pack of dogs.

"Release them from their leashes," Kippy told the men. As soon as they did some of the dogs started to run.

"Stop, now!" Kippy barked with absolute authority. "I am the alpha male here and you will follow my commands or pay the price." With satisfaction he saw the dogs turn, and some began to whimper in fear. All but one.

"Who made you King?" said the Royal Dane, challenging Kippy's authority before the gathered pack.

Completely unfazed, Kippy looked him up and down and proceeded to humble this troublemaker. "Not King. I am a God. Get used to it."

"You are no God," retorted the large silver haired dog, saliva dripping from his exposed fangs. He stood and flexed his well-honed muscles. His ears were now pinned back.

"You may have fooled the humans, but I am the Alpha here. Submit or I will eat you alive!"

His words ended in a low menacing snarl. Most dogs would have cowered, Kippy simply looked him in the eye and whispered so low, that even with great canine hearing the big dog was forced to lean forward to catch his words. "You had your chance."

"Marcal," Kippy commanded. "Take this mutt away. He is not worthy of battle."

Before the Great Dane could react, two burly men snapped a leash on his collar and yanked him backwards, dragging him away until he was lost in the crowd.

Satisfied, Kippy called each dog to approach and lay down before him. He was the new alpha-male of this pack. He then dismissed the handlers. Once they were gone he instructed the dogs to form a circle around him. There was a natural pecking order. As Kippy studied the forming circles, he was able to ascertain each dog's role in the group.

"How would you like fresh meat and long afternoons running free instead of being cooped up in pens all day?" This was greeted by a chorus of wagging tales and panting breaths.

"Well, I think it's about time that dogs get a little more respect around here. If we are successful, you are all going to be revered. Are you with me?"

They howled in unison.

With promises of rewards, he had their loyalty and thus proceeded to tell them about the Dragos, their invisibility to humans, and the fact that they were most likely hiding throughout the city.

"You will go out in pairs with the men and search every room, alley and gutter for these hideous beasts. You will track their scent and follow your instinct. You will be in charge. You will lead the men, not the other way around."

There was a waggle of tails, and Kippy smiled. "When you find the trail of these beasts, lead the men to them. You are their eyes. They will not be able to see them. If they try to hide, bite them until they are captured. Do this and I promise you, you will be treated like royalty to the end of your lives."

When Kippy was sure that they were ready and that they knew exactly what they were supposed to do, it was time to execute the plans that Richie, Saba and he had discussed.

"Marcal, please come."

"Yes, Lord?"

"Split your men into twenty-four groups of six—each group takes two dogs. The hounds are your eyes, ears, and most importantly, snouts. They can pick up the scent of these foul creatures. Let the dogs lead your men."

Marcal nodded his understanding.

"Have your teams fan out through the city and search for any Dragos who have not been able to seek safety inside the main palace. If they are out there, our canine friends will find them. And your men will seize them."

Kippy barked out something only the dogs could understand, and in pairs, they began to move forward. As Marcal readied to leave, Kippy had one more thing to say. "Trust them. Once the city is secure, we will free the Pharaoh."

Kippy ascended the temple stairs and looked out at his people. It was clear he had the crowd's full support. Already they were breaking up into smaller, more manageable groups.

"How long do you think it will take the dogs and men to clear out the city?" Richie asked.

"I would think a few hours, at least?" Saba answered. "Why?"

"At some point we are going to have to confront the Dragos at the palace," Richie said hesitantly. "And we still don't know if they have weapons."

Ꮛᛏᛟ • ◆ • ᚻ • ● ᚻ ⤬ᛏᛟ

Chapter 19
Hunting Dragos

Kayla regained consciousness but a hazy fog of fear dulled the details of how she had arrived in this nightmare. She remembered being dragged through a door, and eight hideous creatures staring down at her. Lizard-men with darting tongues and oily skin.

Her eyes roamed the room, suppressing her growing dread. She fought the wave of panic welling up within her. The noxious smell of her prison was overpowering. She vomited all over the floor.

Kayla had always been a strong independent type, but here, now . . . She searched the room for any hope of escape, a fighting chance. *I can't just wait here for whatever . . .*

There was a faint slit in the wall. *A door? Escape?*

Then her thoughts shifted to her captors.

These are the creatures Richie was so worried about. Can he really take on these monsters and win? Even trapped, his courage gave her some hope.

She watched in panic as the wall parted and three serpentine men entered. They grabbed her and bound her arms and legs. She tried to resist, but she was no match for their size and strength. Another beast entered pushing a gurney.

Fear filled her with knots so tight she couldn't even scream. They strapped her to the cold, hard table. She felt a skull cap being screwed into her head. Wincing as they tightened the screws, she tried again to scream, but nothing came out. The pain was becoming unbearable, then it stopped. It was replaced by a flowing sensation, like some sort of current was floating over her brain. It created a sensation of disembodiment like she was a spectator in her own movie.

How did you find the cave? floated the thought across her brain. *How long have you known about it? Who else knows?* The questions were unending, surging through her at a torrid pace.

Kayla wanted her mind to have its desire fulfilled, its questions answered. It was natural for questions to evoke memories that would unfold as scenes inside her head. It seemed that as soon as a thought popped into her head, it was plucked out and they knew what she was thinking.

Even from her hazy distance, Kayla realized what was happening. *They're sucking out every one of my thoughts.*

Directly in front of her, the wall went translucent to form a window. She could see they were in deep space. The Earth's surface was a blue marble sinking amongst the stars. It was psychological torture. She was being shown that all hope of escape was gone.

The questions continued over and over and over. She tried to resist them, consciously scrambling her brain, thinking random ridiculous thoughts.

A Drago entered the room, limping. There was malice in his step. The others snapped to attention. Though fearful, Kayla refused to acknowledge him.

He ran his cold clammy hands along her face and down her shoulders. Her revulsion grew, fueling a flickering light of resistance.

"What is this?" he demanded, fingering the leather rawhide around her neck.

Why can I understand what he is saying?

"Because I let you understand," he snarled, reading her thoughts.

The bittersweet moment Richie gave her the amulet before they explored the cave flashed through her mind.

The lizard stole her memory and yanked the amulet from her neck. He muttered his guttural language to the others and left the room. The others followed, leaving her alone.

The window became opaque and the light was extinguished, and with it she slipped into defeat. But there she found no solace. Inside her head, her brain remained under assault. Their questions hammered at her again and again and again. She could not shut them out. Her every thought, memory, and fear were being exploited by the band of serpents.

She tried to move, but nothing would work. Her arms, fingers, eyelids, lips . . . nothing would respond. The questions continued. Kayla realized she would not survive this. And worse still, she knew that with each question, her subliminal answers doomed Richie. And maybe, all of mankind.

ⴹℳ•◆•℣•●℣✗ℳ

Hours later, the limping lizard returned to the cave and slipped unnoticed through the temple's security to make it back to the palace. He gazed at the growing size and temperament of the crowd outside. He did not voice his concern openly, but for the first time, he had doubts.

"We have scanned her brain," he reported to Lord Drago. "She does not know about the talking dog. She has no idea what the Federation is. And she does not know much about the power of the cave. She is of little use. Shall I dispose of her?" Planting the suggestion, he started licking his lips imaging how tasty she would be.

"You will do no such thing! She may be useful," he hissed. "There is more here than meets the eye. The humans are too well-organized. The Federation must be involved!"

The limping lizard watched as Lord Drago lashed out his tongue and licked an eyelid. He knew his plans were collapsing, and that failure was not an option.

"We searched for centuries to find this measly planet," he hissed . . .

ⴹℳ•◆•℣•●℣✗ℳ

"Nothing," Kippy muttered in frustration. They had scoured half the city. But as hard as they tried, they could not align the blueprint markings against any structures in the city.

"It only makes sense that a reptilian race would design tunnels. Somewhere in this city they have got to have openings. It's not like the lizards can walk through walls."

They stopped two blocks short of the palace. Its beauty was marred by the growing impatience of an encircling mob. Opening the plans onto a stone banister, Richie studied them for the umpteenth time.

"You know," he said aloud. "What if they didn't build anything on this side of the river? Maybe just one or two small passages under the city?"

Saba studied the blueprints.

"Look at these two lines here," Richie pointed. "They intersect and then shoot across this wavy line until they reach this point. Remember the other plans, could these be the pyramids?"

Saba considered this. "Maybe the Dragos did not want to take a chance that the people in the city would find out. Or maybe the Nile blocked them, so they built them on the other side. Either way, it might be prudent for us to cross the river and take a look."

"Lord Sirius," Marcal announced upon his arrival. "We have rounded up all the stray Dragos that we could find. I believe some managed to escape, and we will keep searching. We have surrounded the palace and are waiting for your instructions."

"How many are there?" Kippy asked. "Including those you rounded up at the temple."

"Fifty," he said, his eyes downcast, suggesting that he was leaving something out.

"What else?" Kippy demanded with his god-like omniscience. Marcal hesitated, shuffling his feet before replying.

"Yes, Lord. I am sorry to report there was an incident back at the temple." The young Egyptian bowed his head.

"We had guards stationed at both the front and back entrances. At one point the doors opened, then closed again but no one was there. We did not have a canine sentry with us. I fear that more of these creatures may have been hiding inside the temple and escaped."

This was exactly what Kippy had feared. He exchanged looks with Saba and Richie. He knew the wounded Drago had been able to escape to the future. Had he returned? Hopefully not with an army of reinforcements.

"Marcal," Kippy said, trying to mitigate any future losses. "Post additional guards around the entire temple. Be sure that the doors remain closed and post dogs as sentries. We need to capture every last Drago—it's a matter of life and death. And not just for the Pharaoh." Marcal bowed in obedience.

"We need to confront Sal O'Mander," Kippy said after the man had departed. "Once he realizes his plans have been exposed to the Federation, they would have to surrender. Right? What choice would he have? Richie and I need to enter the palace and see if Pharaoh is still alive before it is too late."

"Okay," Saba conceded. "I will wait outside for the two of you to return. But you realize that if the people think anything has happened to their Dog God, their support could unravel in a minute. We've only got one chance."

When Sirius stepped to the front of the palace doors, a great hush fell over the crowd.

"Lord Drago," Kippy called out. "We must speak before harm befalls all of us. Open the doors. It will be just me and my shadow, no one else." Kippy kept his nerves in check.

A slit opened between the two doors allowing just enough room for both Kippy and his invisible master to enter before they quickly slammed shut again.

Saba wedged himself in a place where he could monitor the situation without getting trampled.

Inside, two Dragos flanked them as they crossed the foyer and climbed the stairs.

"Is that where Pharaoh is being held?" Richie gagged. The foul air made him want to hurl.

"Silence!" snarled the Drago guard. They came to the middle of the long corridor and entered the room.

Richie had mentally prepared for this confrontation, but he was expecting the bald-headed O'Mander. Instead, towering over him, was a gigantic lizard that reminded Richie of a raptor from prehistoric times.

The Drago's eyes burned with hate as his powerful tail muscles quivered under its leathery skin. Richie fought to keep his knees from buckling.

"How dare you enter my kingdom and threaten my guards," the leader bellowed. Staring down at Kippy he extended sharp clawed fingers. One at a time, until all eight gleamed dangerously close to Richie's not-so-invisible body. His breath was indescribably rank.

"Seize this pitiful creature."

Richie had never been so scared in all his life. If he failed now, they would be finished. Straightening his back, he stepped forward before the guards made their move. His bluster was running on fumes of fear and adrenaline.

"Your reinforcements are not coming." The words sounded hollow, but he pressed his one and only chance.

"They have been blocked by Federation battle cruisers. Your ships, parked behind the dark side of the moon are now in the custody of the Federation. You have only one chance—and that is to surrender."

Richie had gambled. He wanted Lord Drago to wonder, how could this puny human know of my ships? How could he have contacted the Federation?

It worked. From the crestfallen shoulders, Richie knew he had scored a direct hit.

"Of course, you miserable humans could have never pulled off such a coup . . ."

Richie needed him to feel threatened by the Federation if there was any chance in freeing the Pharaoh.

"You and your men have ten minutes to surrender and release Pharaoh."

The room was deathly quiet. But Lord Drago did not move. Minutes piled up, one upon another. Finally, the silence was broken, "You have captured many of my soldiers," Lord Drago responded in a low measured tone.

"Bring them to me, all of them, here to the palace, and I will return your Pharaoh."

"Why?" Richie asked with more bravado than he felt. Richie knew the people would not be willing to give up their captors that easily.

"If I fail, then my men and I shall die together, as one."

"That is not possible."

"Then Pharaoh will die—I will eat him myself," he said with a menacing growl. His slithering tongue moved in and out of his hideous mouth.

"I may be young, but I am not foolish, bringing you the entire army would only be suicide for me. I refuse. You must bow to my terms." Richie insisted, his insides twisting in knots.

"I promise you on everything you hold dear, Pharaoh will die, and it will be a most unpleasant death!" His words were now sure, and throaty. Richie had no doubt he meant it.

Richie stopped—he was at a crossroads. But he had no doubt Lord Drago would not back down.

If we lose Pharaoh will the people still follow Kippy? Or worse, will it alter history? They had come this far and were too close to success to let him get away now.

As the two paths fought to be heard inside his head, he found himself gaining confidence and with it, he tried to negotiate with the lizard king.

"If you surrender, peacefully, without incident, you will have our assurances that your lives will be spared. You will live."

"I have no plans to surrender, boy," the offended Lizard Lord replied with a snarl. "You want your Pharaoh. I want my men. Take it or leave it!"

Richie knew they were on shaky ground. It was only a matter of time before the Drago hostages managed to make themselves invisible again, or worse.

Oztin, don't let us down now buddy! He silently prayed.

"You have ten minutes," Drago said, mocking Richie's earlier decree. Standing to his full height, Lord Drago flexed his muscles, pointed his clawed arm at the door and bellowed, "Now go!"

Richie needed no further prompting. Following Kippy, he scrambled through the door and out into the hallway. Kippy was way beyond controlling the stream of gas that trailed from his tail pipe and wasn't sure if it made the room smell better or worse. Holding his breath, Richie hurried down the stairs, across the room and out the front door.

When Kippy emerged, the uneasy crowd erupted into cheers.

Richie gulped large quantities of fresh air, clearing his fear.

Eyeing the crowd below, Richie saw Saba ease down from the adjacent portico. "Well, how'd it go?" he asked with a concerned look on his face.

Before he could answer, Marcal rushed up the stairs to his lord's side, almost colliding with Saba who forgot he was invisible.

"Marcal, listen to me and do not question anything I am about to say. Understand?" Richie realized they were invisible and that Kippy did not want to reveal their presence.

"Yes, my Lord."

"I am not alone. I have two invisible spirit guides that I counsel with. I need to speak with them, now, at this moment. And I need you to listen to what is being said without question or interruption. Is that understood?" Marcal nodded his obedience.

After affirmative eye contact with Richie, Kippy proceeded to explain the situation, mostly for Saba's benefit. "If we don't release our captives, he will kill Pharaoh. Surely he cannot be trusted!"

Saba asked a more strategic question. "Were you able to gauge how many other Dragos are within?

"Perhaps fifteen, maybe twenty," Richie said.

"Do they have weapons?"

"None that I could see."

"Marcal? What do you think?"

"Me?" he asked worriedly, as the spirit questioned him.

"Yes. He is your Pharaoh, what do you think?"

"It is not even a question, oh great spirit. He is our King. We must free him. And besides . . ." he said with a wide sweep of his arms, "We have them bottled up in here, they have nowhere to go. Let us free our Pharaoh and then finish off these beasts once and for all."

"Okay Marcal, bring the prisoners here. We have ten minutes," the canine God commanded.

Marcal turned and raced down the stairs. Richie wasn't sure if it was the pressing deadline or his desire to get away from the invisible spirits, but he had to admire the man's haste.

"What if he is dead already?" Richie asked as his anxiety boiled on adrenaline, fear, and worry. Then from the back of the crowd, he spotted Marcal followed by a parade of bound Dragos flanked on both sides by an overwhelming number of citizens. They cleaved a path through the revolted crowd. The dark sheen of the Dragos glistened in the afternoon sun, and from the vantage point of the palace steps, it looked like a long black snake slithering its way toward them. Even in the hottest part of the day, a shiver ran through Richie.

Kippy moved closer to his master, shielding himself from the evil.

"Go get Drago," Richie told his friend.

Walking to the top of the stairs, Kippy called out to his young master.

"Wait! We must have proof that Pharaoh is alive." He turned to the door and barked over and over again. "Open these doors and show us Pharaoh." After several attempts, the doors opened inward, and the bright sun of afternoon framed the entrance in deep shadows.

Richie peered into the room, and what he saw revolted him. Swinging, like a tire hung from a tree, a pallid man in soiled clothing was dangling upside down from the top of the staircase.

"He's still breathing," Richie said. His body tensed at Pharaoh's condition.

"Barely," Saba whispered back.

Lord Drago grabbed the swaying mass and squeezed it tightly against his massive body. "Your time has run out," he hissed at them, and then took one of the dangling arms, slit the bindings with a razor-sharp claw and jammed the human hand into his mouth, as if it were a French fry, ready to be devoured.

Richie saw the fear in Pharaoh's eyes as he struggled.

"Wait," Kippy screamed. "We have your men, see, look, look down there!"

"There, is not here!" the lizard king replied, spitting the hand from his lips.

"Just wait!" Richie said. "Kippy, get one of the prisoners." He needed to act quickly, and this was the first thing he could think of. It bought them some time.

Kippy ran to the edge of the landing. "Marcal, quickly, bring the prisoners here."

The train of glistening bodies began moving again, gathering momentum as they crested the stairs. Stepping to the side, they counted each Drago they could see inside, as well as the added battalion of prisoners. Once the final detainee had crossed the threshold, Lord Drago gave the Pharaoh a huge heave, sending him twirling and spinning at the end of his rope.

He glared at the two humans. "I do not know how you became involved with the Federation, and it pains me the amount of trouble you have caused, but you will not stop us."

"What about Pharaoh?" Saba demanded.

"What about him?"

"You said we were exchanging hostages, well how about it?"

"He's yours," Drago said, "Take him!" Kippy turned to call for help but Lord Drago snapped at him. "Not them. You – you get him down."

"Kippy, stay here!" Richie demanded. "Saba, come with me." He raced up the stairs two at a time. Richie untied the rope from above. "Saba, hold on, he's coming free."

Richie unwound the rope from the railing and strained every muscle as he lowered the Pharaoh into Saba's arms.

Richie raced down the stairs, oblivious to anything else. Grabbing Pharaoh by the feet as Saba lifted him under the arms, they dragged him out onto the landing, into the fresh air and sunshine. No sooner had they left the palace when the doors slammed with a loud thud.

Marcal untied Pharaoh and called out. "Quickly, bring the sedan."

Richie knew he was too weak to walk, and thanks to this young commander's planning the Pharaoh's luxurious sedan was standing ready to carry him to safety and comfort.

"I beg your leave, my Lord," Marcal said with formality, "We must prepare to take these intruders before they are allowed to cause us any more harm."

"Carry on!" Kippy barked.

ꜩ𝔐 ✦ ✧ ● Ж 𝔐

Richie felt the pressure of a racing clock. Now that they had played their only card with the Dragos, his arsenal was depleted.

I hope Oztin comes through. His comments on the Federation had in part been a bluff. *Come on buddy . . .*

Still, Richie was impressed with the ragtag militia Marcal had pulled together. Kippy had made a wise choice. Once the building had been adequately surrounded and sealed, a large battering ram was wheeled with tack and pulley up to the top of the stairs.

He watched the action unfold from the balcony of a nearby administration building. From that vantage point he could see the front of the palace, the spectacular fountains, the temple in the near distance, the Nile River and two of the Great Pyramids of Egypt.

"Come on guys," he willed under his breath. The feeling that the weight of humanity confronted them created the anxious feeling that had him tapping his feet in worry and hope. *Come on, get in there.*

Once the ramming apparatus was properly buttressed, two dozen men began hammering the door.

Bam! Bam! The ramming could be heard across the open plaza. Richie looked out at the two garrisons of poorly armed men, ready to rush the doors with spears and swords.

"Such beautiful doors," Saba mused as the gold-plated wood began to splinter.

"There is no other way," Richie lamented above the thumping sounds of the soldiers' efforts and the beating of his heart.

With one final shove, the resistance gave way, and the doors were flung inward. The first wave of troops pushed the buttressed ram into the large hall, using it as a shield.

Richie knew the plan was to enter the foul-smelling chamber, fan out, and confront the enemy. Next, the second assault group rushed forward, zipping up the stairs while the third, fourth, and fifth filed in behind them.

From the balcony, the three friends watched the commanders, their tunics distinguishable by their red sashes, exit the palace doors and confer with Marcal. From the slouch of their bodies, the waving of arms and the look of confusion, Richie knew something was wrong.

"We better go see," Saba told them.

"No sir, they are nowhere to be seen . . ." he heard as they arrived at the top of the stairs. "Yes, we have checked the entire building, yes, the basements too," said the second man standing by his side.

Kippy looked to Richie. "What's happened?"

That would explain their body language, Richie thought. It was clear from their conversation that the building was empty. Somehow the Dragos had escaped.

"I have let my Lord and Pharaoh down," Marcal said.

"I believe that if you search the basements more closely, you will find a tunnel," Richie suggested, still in his invisible form.

"Tunnels?" Marcal straightened at the possibility.

"Yes, I believe they have developed a network of tunnels," Kippy echoed, reinforcing the idea. "And if I am correct, they are using them to escape out into the desert as we speak."

"Tunnels, to where? The desert is large." Marcal squinted in confusion.

"We need chariots," demanded the invisible consort. "We must get to the pyramids on the other side of the river as soon as possible. And we'll need soldiers, we may be able to head these creatures off if we move quickly."

"Yes, of course," Marcal replied. "I will prepare chariots and a regiment."

"There is no time," replied the same voice from the beyond. "Show us to the stables, have your men meet us at the base of the pyramid. Let's move!"

Chapter 20
Into the Desert

Richie removed his bracelet as did Saba before confronting the young lad who led them to the royal stables.

With some assistance he opened the huge doors that protected the royal chariots from the hot sun. Inside, under cool shadows, were row upon row of hunting chariots. They were two-wheeled open-backed vehicles, made for speed and agility more than for warfare. The chariots were fast, and that was what they needed right now. Grooms brought out two horses and quickly hooked them up to a readied wagon.

Saba inspected the harnesses.

"Do you know how to drive one of these things?" Richie asked, feeling a little uneasy about the open back.

"When I was a child, I had the opportunity to try my hand at many things," Saba responded. "Necessity, they say, is the mother of invention."

"So you have driven these before?" Richie affirmed with relief in his voice.

"Well . . . I never exactly drove a chariot per se," he said. And then lowering his voice he added, "It was more like a garbage wagon pulled by a donkey . . . but I imagine it's based on the same principle. Still, better hold tight."

Kippy jumped into the cart and wedged himself against the bowed front. Richie knew he would be unable to see what was coming up, but it was the safest spot.

"Don't worry buddy, you can keep an eye out the back, make sure we are not being followed."

Wrapping the reins tightly around his hands, Saba gave a shout and a flick of the leads and the horses lurched forward. Richie grabbed hold of the chariot's railing and held on for dear life.

Saba wheeled the chariot in a circle and made for the front gate. A soldier appeared before them, gasping for breath.

"I have news from Marcal!" the warrior shouted. "He is sending the first regiment of charioteers, you should wait."

"We have no time," Saba said. Slapping the reins upon the backs of the two stallions, the cart leapt forward and soon a trail of dust obscured the gate behind as they made haste to the river's edge.

The town was a blur, but the smooth roads allowed for a relatively stable ride. Richie lifted Kippy so he could see the grandeur unfold and smiled as his buddy pressed his face into the wind.

Coming down from a hill, the river loomed near, the taste of moisture scented the air, and cool fingers caressed Richie's skin as they drew close to the water's edge.

"Barge master," Kippy called out, hailing a stout mountain of a man working a nearby ferry.

The muscled man lowered his head in reverence. Bringing the flat-bottomed transport to the edge of the stone quay, he expertly docked it.

Kippy jumped from the chariot and took time to lap some of the sweet river water as the man stepped from his boat and bowed down.

"May I have the honor of ferrying you to the other side, my Lord?" he asked.

"If you would take me and my servants across the river near the pyramids, it would serve my pleasure," Kippy told the humbled man.

"Yes, oh great and wise Sirius," he affirmed. "I knew that you would come, that you would free us of the curse of these underworld dwellers."

"Underworld dwellers?" Saba shot Kippy a quizzical look.

"Please tell me, why you would call these false gods underworld dwellers?" Kippy asked.

The man gave scant pause before answering with his layman simplicity. "Because, I have seen them, coming up from out of the ground."

"When?" Kippy prodded. "When did you see them?"

"Always very late at night, when they thought no one was around they would come up out of the ground, do strange incantations, and using their fire sticks, they would make their signs."

"Fire sticks?" Richie mouthed. A frown belayed his concerns. *Could these be weapons?*

"You say they came up out of the ground. Near here?"

"Near Little Bell," he replied letting his gaze cross the river in the direction of the pyramids.

"Little Bell?"

"The infant pyramid," he said with a hint of pride. "It is almost complete."

"You say you have seen the creatures at the small pyramid. Did I understand you that they were using some type of fire stick and that at the small pyramid, they have left behind strange markings?"

"Yes," he said.

"What kind of markings?"

"Signs from the heavens," he said, his eyes wandering upwards.

Fishing into his pockets, Saba pulled out the walnut-sized metal locket that he pulled from the foam packed case. "Like these?" he asked, holding his hand out for the man to see. Inside lay a star and a crescent moon.

"Yes, yes like those," he nodded in recognition.

"Have you seen any other marks that they might have made?"

Richie sensed excitement in Saba's voice as he followed his reasoning.

"Yes, carved into the rocks at the base of the cliffs to the west, beyond the great sentinels of our city."

"Which way?"

He turned and pointed towards the lowering sun, beyond the river, past the pyramids and out into the desert.

"Then we must go see these markings now," Saba said.

"Take us to see them," Kippy declared.

"Of course, my Lord. Please have your slave move the chariot onto the barge. Unhook the horses and tie them to the lateen rail," he explained.

No one moved, so the bargemen took the horse by the reins, maneuvered the cart onto the boat and unhitched the horses.

"If the boat tips over, or the chariot breaks free, it will not drag the horses under and drown them," he explained, while he finished securing everything.

Once this was complete, the bargemen set course for the other side of the river. Even here, at a fairly narrow point, Richie could see it was over two hundred yards to the other side.

Standing at the front of the boat, Richie let the fresh breeze waft over him. Holding Kippy in his arms, the three of them gazed across the lazy Nile. The Great Pyramid shone with a blazing brilliance.

"Look how different the Great Sphinx is compared to its present form," Richie pointed out, as the boat drew closer to the shore.

Surrounding the Sphinx was a sparkling reflection pool, giving the statue the status of an island unto itself. Completing the symmetry of the compound, each of the pyramids were encased in brilliant white marble and had long reflecting pools leading up to them. They were intertwined as part of a greater complex.

Nothing in any book Richie had ever seen described the tremendous power that pulsed from this place. As they drew close, his skin tingled as if washed in ozone. He could imagine that these pyramidal structures acted as some sort of cosmic generator or vortex that amplified the harmonic frequencies of heaven and earth.

"Look at the top!" Richie exclaimed. The light of the sun refracted from the tips of the great stone sentinels. Each was capped with what looked like a giant diamond. "I bet these can be seen from space."

"I think they call those capstones," Saba told them. "Legend has it that the top of the pyramids were capped with great crystalline structures that were used as transmitters to the gods. Maybe it is not such a myth after all."

Arriving at a quayside dock, the barge master unloaded their chariots.

"Sir," Saba asked. "Can you tell us where you saw the underground dwellers use their fire sticks?"

The man stood up, placed his hands on his hips, and studied the compound. Then, pointing to the third pyramid, the one under construction, he said, "If you look to the far corner, away from the dying sun, about two stones above the ground, you will see a star has been carved into the rock.

"But look carefully, it is not much larger than a pomegranate. That is where I saw them. Would you like me to show you, my Lord?" he asked.

"No, thank you," Saba said.

"Then I must leave you," the barge master said with a bow. "Others will be gathering on the far shore in need of my services."

As the boatman pushed back into the meandering river, Richie paused to take stock of the situation. After a few silent minutes, an acclamation period to absorb such awesome beauty and engineering, Saba gave a light slap of the reins.

"Let's go find those marks."

𐌄ᴛ𐌌 ◆ 𐌇 ● 𐌇ꓘ𐌌

The ride was not as smooth as in the city. The road had turned rocky and caused the chariot to lurch. They pushed through a giant shadow cast by the Great Pyramid and rounded the corner of Little Bell.

"He said it was around here," Saba told them, and he set about searching for the spot where the bargemaster had told them to look.

"Here," Richie said triumphantly. He placed his fingertip on a thin indent of a five-pointed star. As sweat trickled down his forehead, Richie looked far out into the desert. There was nothing but sand, rock, and more sand.

Saba studied the sophisticated markings and pulled a matching locket from his collection. "Stand back," he said. "Further . . . Just in case."

He tried placing it into the carved slot, but it would not work. Reaching for Richie's backpack, he took the other two and tried these as well. Still nothing.

"I was sure these would work," he said, deflated.

Richie could see his frustration. Saba had explained that as a youth he had removed a star from the door that was discovered, and it had activated its opening . . .

Have we gotten this all wrong? He slumped his shoulders in worry. He thought they had gained an edge. Richie wiped the sweat from his hands onto his pant leg. Brushing against something, he recalled putting one of the stars in his pocket.

"Try this one," he offered, fishing it out.

It effortlessly fell into place and Richie heard the click behind them.

"Whoa . . ." wailed an unexpected cry. He turned just as his buddy dropped out of sight.

"Kippy!" Richie shouted. He rushed over to see sand pouring into an opening in the earth. "Kippy, are you okay?"

There was a rectangular opening in the ground. The rock hung like a trap door on a hinge. It had been totally invisible.

Richie looked into the hole. Splayed on a floor deep below, it appeared only his canine friend's pride was hurt.

"What are you guys looking at?" Kippy whined with indignation.

Richie studied the pit and looked at the wall. He saw cuts in the rocks that were clearly used as a ladder. "I'm coming down, buddy," Richie said as he let out a sigh of relief.

"You alright? Anything broken?" Richie sat and gently lifted Kippy into his lap.

"No. Just scared the crap out me, but I'm okay."

Richie gave him a once over, running his hands over Kippy's fur as Saba stepped from the bottom groove. Seeing that Kippy was no worse for the wear, Richie lifted him off his lap.

"You were right," Kippy said. "The star opened the door?"

Saba sat down with a sigh. Richie could see he was weary. He retold the story of his discovery of the extra star in the temple's colossal doors, segueing into the idea that that technology may have been reminiscent of something the ancient Egyptians had gleaned from the Dragos.

"Anyway," Saba said in a tone of finalization. "It would appear that those metal lockets we found are site specific, so we now know that the stars are for opening doors."

"What about the moon and comet?" Kippy asked. "What do you think those are for?"

Saba shrugged.

They stood in a rectangular shaft of light, only darkness lay beyond. Richie took off the backpack and fished out his flashlight. "Let's take a look around?"

He waved its beam and began to explore the tunnel. It was about twenty feet wide, maybe fifteen feet from floor to ceiling. The walls were smooth, almost glassy. There was a slight pitch to the floor, which ran off into an inky darkness.

"Do you think this runs back to the city?" Kippy asked. "Could the Dragos have already passed us?"

Pointing the flashlight into the impenetrable dark, Richie calculated aloud. "I would assume that this way runs back toward the river. If they came from the palace, they would have to get across the Nile somehow. If they have the technology to build these, I doubt a shallow river would have stopped them."

"This tunnel really is quite impressive," Saba said stepping next to Richie. "We were riding at a pretty brisk pace and did not take a lot of time. I would think seventy to eighty Dragos that are walking would not have passed this way yet, if at all. They would need to be running at a pretty fast clip to have beaten us here."

"Assuming they are walking," Richie said, thinking these tunnels were large enough for chariots if they had them. He realized how little they really knew about their adversary. Lacking any real intelligence, they were hopelessly unprepared.

"I'm going to go back and pull the star out of the slot, then we should do a little bit of exploring."

As Saba climbed up the footholds, Richie explored the tunnel. Following the general direction that led out into the desert, he hoped to find some additional signs or symbols. After a few minutes, he found something. Almost lost in the shadows was a thin sliver of a crescent moon. Richie aimed his beam on the mark. He moved the light in widening circles. He could see no opening or hidden seams or anything like that.

Still searching, Richie heard the pitter patter sound of nails clicking on the stone floor. Shining the light ahead, Kippy's trotting body wavered in and out of the beam.

"Find anything?" his dog asked, tongue panting.

"I found a moon indent," he answered. "Is Saba back?"

"He's looking over the blueprints. I think he wants to see if he can locate some additional stars."

More doorways, Richie thought.

He returned to the rectangular light cast from above and saw Saba scrutinizing the Drago drawings. "Anything?"

"Maybe. Look here, I think this wavy line might be the river. And here," placing his finger at a point on the page, "It's a star. This could be us."

Saba let his finger drift along the map-line towards the river. "And there is a third symbol, the comet. If this is to scale, then the comet symbol here is roughly a quarter mile that way. And if these wavy lines are what we think they are, it's another mile or so to the river.

"Look how the line splits on the other side of the river," Saba continued. "Once you enter the city it makes a 'Y' and then there are only two corridors. One heads towards where the palace is and the other angles towards the temple."

Richie studied the map and looked back to where they were standing represented by the star. He noticed that nearby there was a crescent moon symbol, and placed a finger on it for Saba to see.

"We know that a star is a doorway," Richie said. "Should we go find out what the moons represent?"

"Perhaps later," Saba said. "We need to figure out what we are going to do if the Dragos come up from the river and we are still in here."

"They might have escaped out of the palace and worked their way back to the time portal," Kippy said wistfully.

We should be so lucky. Still, the idea that they may no longer be a threat to them was all Richie needed to convince himself to explore a little bit more. He knew that whatever was going to happen, these tunnels would be key. The more they knew about them, the more prepared they could be.

"Let's go find that third symbol and see if any of our pieces fit." Without waiting for a reply, he slipped on his pack and looked to Kippy. He saw his grimace and then led them down the corridor with his beam aimed ahead.

They walked in silence, Saba lagging a little behind. Richie heard him counting off the number of paces as they moved forward. He also noticed that the ceiling was slowly restricting, making the space feel more and more claustrophobic. Richie stopped, and peered into the darkness ahead. Ahead were some irregular shapes.

"They're boxes," Kippy said to his master, using his canine eyesight.
"Boxes?"

"Up there, along the wall." Kippy answered. He sprinted ahead to get a better look. "There are eight of them, about six to eight feet long, and four feet wide. All made of wood . . ." he described them as the two humans approached.

Richie noted they were similar to the wood crates they had opened back in the temple. All stacked randomly on the right side of the tunnel.

This worried him. It meant the Dragos were using this place for more than just transport, possibly storing weapons or worse.

"Let's see what's inside." Richie used his fingers to work one of the tops loose.

"Shhhhhh . . ." Kippy whispered with alarm.

Richie froze. As did Saba.

"They're coming. Quick, we need to get out of here."

As the sound of shuffling of feet grew stronger, Richie realized they were very close.

"Inside the boxes," Saba ordered. "Put out that light."

With an adrenaline rush, Richie yanked away the top of one crate while Saba pried at another.

Grabbing his dog, Richie climbed into the large open box and managed to get the lid down just as he heard the chattering Dragos crest the bend.

The last thing he saw was Saba struggle to cleave aside whatever was in the box before the lid would close flush.

Richie slipped on his bracelet and saw the Dragos appear. He had a slivered view of the parade and counted the lizard men as they passed. He noted that they marched in an orderly pace, and in no way appeared defeated. After counting a total of seventy-seven, Richie waited for a few more minutes. Only after the sound of footfalls had receded into the distance, did he dare climb out.

"They're gone," he whispered. Kippy jumped to the floor as Richie got out.

"That was uncomfortable," he mumbled wondering what on earth he had been laying on. He took his flashlight and aimed it inside. The beam sprayed onto some cloth, then something white . . .

Stifling a screech, Richie dropped the flashlight, which hit the floor with a clatter.

Saba flinched at the sound. "We left the trap door open," he said. "They'll know we are in here! We've got to go. Richie, come on!" Saba grabbed the light and shone it on the boy's ashen face. "What is it?"

"Bones," Richie said in horror. "Look!"

Saba shone the beam into the box. It was full of human remains!

ℰℳ•◆•⋇•●⋇⤢ℳ

Chapter 21
Santa Martina, California

Chucky knew the town was in an uproar by the police cars cruising the city streets; he had already counted five times they had passed their house. Everyone was looking for the missing Carlyle girl, and a lot of fingers were being pointed at the Radcliff family.

Torn by guilt, fear, and self-loathing, Chucky had told nobody about what had happened. And the longer he waited, the more difficult it became to ever say a thing.

I'm a coward. What a creep. God, will you ever forgive me?

All his life he had used his larger size to get attention, and it never worked out right. *I need to do something—but what? What can I do?*

Then he heard the door open downstairs, followed by an angry slam. *Dad's home.*

"No work is going to be done out at the jobsite until Kayla Carlyle is found," his father groused to his wife. "Bite me! That's what I say."

Chucky heard his dad open the refrigerator. He knew he was starting on the beer, which only made his anger worse.

God help me!

"That guy O'Mander had a guy pay me a thousand bucks to wire that property with dynamite. I guess he plans to blow the damn place to hell and back. Well, good riddance."

Chucky fought his conscience. *What would I tell them?* he rationalized. *That invisible demons from Hell hauled Kayla up into a hole in the sky?*

But his conscience would not let it go. Deep inside, Chucky felt that he had to do something. Downstairs he could hear his father speaking harshly with his mother as he opened the fridge for the third time.

"If this sheriff thinks he can keep M.I. from building that factory, he's got another thing coming. And now this stupid girl is missing. They should lock Radcliff up," his father continued, his words starting to slur.

Chucky did not like to be around his father when he got drunk. His anger boiled over and he struck out at anyone in shouting distance . . . And it was becoming more and more common.

"I bet that poor girl's mother must be at her wit's end," Chucky's mom said vacantly, even though Chucky could imagine his father wasn't even listening.

"Well tonight, I'm going go out there and earn my keep," he rambled on. And then paused long enough to let out a loud belch.

"Yes siree, Bob. Got me a truckload of dy-no-mite. I'm going to wire that place so tight that an ant hill couldn't survive. Hired, wired and fired. Kaboom!" he chuckled at his own joke.

eₜm • ◆ •)(• ●)(↗ m

The Niles Edge

On the other side of the river, Marcal had gathered forty war chariots, each carrying a driver and two spearmen. It was slow to get them across to the other bank, but they were almost done.

Marcal listened as the boatman informed him of his conversations with the Lord and his two friends.

"They were headed out towards Little Bell," he pointed.

"Two men?"

"Yeah, an older man and a young boy."

When the boats finished unloading the last of the charioteers, Marcal ordered his men to head towards Little Bell.

eₜm • ◆ •)(• ●)(↗ m

Beneath the Desert Sands

"My God!" Saba gasped. Fingering a spear inside the box, he examined the skeletal remains, conscious that at any moment the Dragos would be returning. Though most of the meat, flesh, and organs were long gone, the bones were still dressed in their clothing.

Saba rummaged around and came across another spear. "These were soldiers," he said aghast at the piles of bones.

Richie's first thought was about the Pharaoh's army, the one supposedly sent south. But there was no time to dwell on it, he heard footsteps returning their way along with angry words. They had been found out.

"Quick, take a spear and let's get out of here," Saba hastened. "Towards the river. We'll have to cross over and find an exit." They took off as he labored under a heavy breath and tried to keep up. "Don't stop! Keep going even if I fall behind."

Saba saw Richie freeze in his tracks. And then he saw why. They were blocked by a large Drago.

"It's the one I bit back at the temple," Kippy cried out, seeing the pronounced limp.

They were trapped. Behind them, the urgency of running feet grew in volume. Ahead, stood an angry reptile with revenge on his lips. There was nowhere to run to and nowhere to hide. *Does it all end here, Saba thought?*

Kippy lunged at the crotch of the foul beast and sank his fangs in as far and deep as they would go.

"Yoooooooooooooowwwwww!" screeched the wounded lizard, as he reeled back clutching at the embedded dog. The footsteps behind them grew louder, more pronounced.

The howling Drago grabbed Kippy by the neck and squeezed his head like it was a ripe melon. Saba gasped in helplessness as the Drago raised the object of his pain in fury, preparing to slam this foul mutt's body onto the stone floor and crush his skull.

It was all unfolding so fast, Saba felt almost as if he was in a trance as he held his breath and watched Richie draw back the spear and hurl it at the exposed chest of the hideous beast. It sailed across the space between them and exploded into the Drago.

This broke the spell Saba had fallen under, the paralysis of fear eviscerated as the wind heaved out of the mouth of the lizard and an oily stain spread across the serpent's chest. Kippy leapt free as the Drago dropped his hands and clutched at the spear, choking as he tried to spit out his dying words.

"Y-y-your princess y-y-you will never see . . ." but he never finished the sentence. With a final agonizing wail, he keeled forward and died.

"What? What Princess, damn you, what princess?" Richie screamed into the face of the cold reptile.

"Over here, quick. It's the comet," Saba said, looking to refocus their attention on getting out of there.

Richie rummaged through his pack and took out the metal comets. With a quick eye, he grabbed the one that looked like it would fit and handed it to Saba.

"Lord," he said.

Kippy cocked his head. "Not you, the real one. Please God, help us!" And he pushed the comet's flame into place.

From far, far down the tunnel there was a muffled rumble, almost like distant thunder, followed by a series of detonations. Saba heard the running feet behind them stop. Then, just as quickly, he heard them retreating. And it seemed with an even greater sense of urgency. He looked at Kippy, who he sensed had heard them too.

From the bowels of the tunnel a breeze stirred, blowing cool across his face. Within seconds it had turned into a wind. And it continued to grow in strength.

"What's happened?" Richie yelled as Saba's mind raced through the probabilities.

Kippy stood, nose in the air, with tongue tipped lips. "Water!" he replied.

"The river, the comet, is a sign of destruction," Saba said in horror. "We've blown the coffers and the river is flooding into the tunnel. That's what's pushing the wind. If we stay here, we're gonna drown."

Richie could feel the moisture-driven wind racing through the tunnel. Soon the sound was deafening. Drops of water carried up by the rushing air pelted them like rain.

Richie steeled his resolve. He swallowed his panic and with adrenaline ignited he fought for a solution.

"The pressure of the Nile is pushing everything forward," he cried above the noise. "A wall of water is gushing this way. If we don't get out of here we will drown."

"Quickly, back to the boxes," Saba yelled above the screaming maelstrom. Dump out the bones and climb in, fasten the lid as best as you can. Hurry! Run!"

Richie looked towards the direction of the ladder but already water was rising around them. They would never make it. With his options down to one, he grabbed his pal and began dumping out the dead soldiers and righting the boxes.

"Jump in Richie, I'll tamp down the lid."

Richie climbed in and tucked Kippy between his cramped legs and pushed the fear from his mind.

"What about you?"

"I'll be fine," Saba said under ragged breath. "Quickly, in the box."

There was no time to argue. Already, water was above their knees. The last thing Richie saw was Saba's worried face as he pounded the lid in place.

In mere moments, the box was slammed hard by a fast-moving wave. No longer stationary, water seeped in from the lid, but it held. It was pitch black, and Kippy was letting out a low whine and his stink bombs amplified their fear. Faster and faster they careened, spinning, banging up, down, sideways, end over end. Richie felt like laundry tossed in a dryer.

Anxiety at being trapped in a lightless box, spinning around and around in a tunnel deep below the desert sands created a deep claustrophobia that was clawing at him, but he was too afraid to open the lid, fearing they would drown.

Faster and faster they turned. He was sure that any second now the box would split open, but then, it began to slow.

Is it safe? Is the tunnel full? What will happen if I open the top?

Kippy let out a long silent stream so gross that it forced Richie to take a chance. Richie popped the top and sat up.

Behind him, he could see the light from the open trap door. But ahead—it made no sense . . .

Before, there was a tunnel, but now? He logged the info. Before the tunnel had extended farther . . . Now there is a wall.

The water had run out of places to go. Now it was a only matter of minutes before the tunnel was completely flooded.

Grabbing Kippy, he rolled out of the box and made his way against the dying current back to the ladder. It was difficult swimming and holding Kippy, so he stuffed him under his shirt with his head wedged though the neck hole as he breast-stroked the last twenty yards.

Grabbing a handhold, he was surprised to see a familiar face staring down at him.

"Marcal, I need help," Richie called out. But Marcal just gawked, dumbfounded. Richie realized he had never actually seen him before, and now was not the time for proper introductions. "Lord Sirius needs you."

This triggered an immediate reaction, and two men dove into the water and retrieved the dog and the freshly materialized boy.

"In one of the boxes, that way," Richie said pointing away from the river. "There is another man, he is an advisor to Sirius. You must find him. Quickly!"

As Richie was being pulled from the hole, exhausted, wet, and emotionally spent, he heard a cry waft up from below.

"We have him!"

ᛖᛘ•◆•ᚼ•●ᚼ⚹ᛘ

Chapter 22
Chasing Dragos

Richie sat quietly as Marcal took a saddle blanket from one of the horses and wrapped it around the water-soaked man.

"Thank you," Saba said. Richie noted he patted his hand against his pocket, probably making sure the bracelet was still there.

"These are my friends and protectors," Kippy said to Marcal who had a questioning look on his face.

"My name is Saba, and this is Richie." Saba extended his hand in greeting and hesitantly, the young commander grasped it.

"Tunnels?" he said, more as a statement than a question. "We did not find anything back at the palace, but you were right. How did you know?"

"We came across one of their writings. I did not understand it, but Lord Sirius, he truly knows all." Saba paused and looked at the shaken canine.

Richie saw where this was going and stepped in to protect Kippy's status as God and therefore, their faith in him. "He is able to understand all things."

After an awkward moment, Kippy looked to his Captain and in an increasingly commanding voice, started giving out orders. "Wheel that cart over here." Two men pushed it over and Kippy jumped up on to the back.

"Marcal, how is Pharaoh?"

"He is recuperating quickly, my Lord."

"Good. My two counselors are to be shown the same respect and treatment you would show me. If they tell you to do something or ask for something, you are to comply."

"Yes, my Lord," he said without question.

"Sometimes you may see them, and other times you may not . . ."

Kippy looked to Richie and gave a slight nod of the head. Richie understood what he wanted and fished the bracelet from his pocket.

"Notice my young counselor here."

Richie waited until everyone was directing their attention upon him and then he vanished, and then reappeared again. The men flinched and as expected, a cloud of fear passed amongst them, but they stood their ground, albeit warily.

"Now, we must continue our quest to capture these beasts."

Richie saw their sense of duty and pride at the mention of the Dragos.

"Yes, Lord," Marcal said and bowed to one knee. The soldiers followed suit.

"Thank you," Richie breathed under his breath, looking skyward into the deep blue. Because of Saba's wisdom and Kippy's command performance, his pal's godhead was righted, back where it belonged.

Saba unfurled the map onto the cart next to their canine god, and Marcal and two of his lieutenants joined to look at it.

"This is the only map we have of their tunnels," Saba told them. "We do not know how they made them or how far they run, but we believe the Dragos are heading west and that if we act fast, there is a chance we can still catch them."

"How?" One of the lieutenants spoke up.

"First we will need the barge master. Send someone to find him."

Marcal barked out some orders and the next moment a lieutenant was slapping reins on two chariot horses and took off in a quick trot.

"What is out here, west of the pyramids?" Saba asked.

"Down here is a high-ridged plateau. Sheer walls rise up two hundred feet from the desert floor. It is mostly arid land, of little use for grazing. There are some old gold and silver mines, but mostly these have been abandoned."

Richie watched as the man drew his finger along a squiggle of wavy inverted 'V' lines. *Mountains. Didn't the bargeman also say there were old mines out here? Could they have tied them into the tunnels?*

Richie stayed silent as the men discussed various options, all the while stroking Kippy's back trying to calm his pal's racing heart—and his own.

"From the chart, the tunnels appear to lay deep inside the walls of the plateau," Saba articulated to Marcal and his two underlings. "I am beginning to understand some of their topography symbols. Here is the river's edge, these are geographical markers, not the actual tunnel route . . ."

"I am not sure what the two symbols are side by side. See here, a comet and a star. Do you know this place?" Saba asked one of the soldiers who seemed most informed.

Richie watched intently as the man studied the map, looked west, and then studied it further. "I believe so. The walls of the plateau are generally quite straight, but at one point, about five clicks away, it juts out like the bow of a ship. It is called El Kasaad. I believe that is the place."

"What are these symbols, the star, the comet, and here farther to the west is another one, and also a crescent moon?" the man inquired.

Richie had been thinking about this. He had nagged for explanation why an unseen wall had appeared during the flooding of the tunnel. Then he had an idea.

"The stars represent doors," Richie told the man. The comet's tail represents destruction. They must have built in explosives or traps in case their defenses were ever breached. And speaking of defenses, the slivered moons are keys that add fortifications or walls."

He noted the recognition spreading over his two companions' faces as he continued.

"That is why the water stopped flowing. Remember I told you I saw this moon etched into the wall, but the tunnel continued well beyond it. Now there is a solid wall there, as if it has always been there. If I had not seen the mark, we would just have assumed the wall ended there and still be wondering how the Dragos had escaped yet again."

"So there is a door and a detonator at El Kasaad?" Marcal asked, his expression somewhere between doubt and wonder.

"Yes," Saba replied with renewed energy. "And that is where the barge master comes in. He has seen some of these symbols in the rocks and can show us where they are."

Marcal's fingers traced various lines on the map. Richie watched as the man studied the plans, and then followed the main line as it continued to the edge of the page. Turning it over, he saw the man place a finger on each of the marked spots of stars, comets, and moon symbols. Especially one clump that were all bunched in one spot.

"Here," his finger lingered. "This is the Palace of Cadiz. It is the holiest of the hallowed grounds. The burial place of the legendary kings of old, the well of souls. There was an extended rock outcropping called El Shan-non, and it was not that far from El Kasaad.

"I believe this is where they are heading. If we move quickly we might be able to catch them.

"I agree," Saba concurred. Richie followed his gaze out into the desert, watching the rising dust coming from the direction of the pyramids.

"Hopefully, that is the barge master," he said, but the words dropped to the ground as he saw a cloud of worry grow and spread over Saba's face.

"What is it?"

"It's the weapons thing that is still bothering me. If they can make tunnels like that," he pointed down into the nearby hole. "How are we going to stop them with spears and arrows?"

Richie was appreciative of Kippy's silence since whatever speculation he might make would be deemed truth as their Lord. And the truth was, they did not know.

"They didn't have them in the tunnel, and we didn't see any when they were in control of the palace . . ." Richie mumbled as he stroked his chin.

Saba leaned over the plans and studied them. Richie followed his finger to the spot on the map where they were standing, and then the symbols at El Kasaad. He could almost hear the gears grinding in his head. A plan was forming.

"Richie, look here," Saba told him. "Notice that at El Kasaad there appears to be a small tunnel that leads into the Earth and then connects with the main tunnel. Also notice what lies just inside the main tunnel."

"A comet's tail," he answered.

"Correct. What if we were able to trap the lizards inside the mountain by blowing it up? We would not have to be concerned about the possibility of them having weapons."

"Better yet," Marcal added, "Look here, on the other side, this is the juggernaut of El Shan-non, at the Palace of Cadiz. Notice how abundant the fortress signs are. This may be their main retreat. What if we brought our chariots into the tunnel here at El Kasaad, trapped the fleeing Dragos, and then followed the tunnel west as part of a two-pronged attack on their fortresses?

"Of course we would need to make haste, so we could get in and move far enough down the tunnel that we do not get caught in the explosion."

It was risky, but Richie could see Saba considered it their best option. Like Marcal, he also thought that with all those symbols bunched around the conjunction of tunnels and caves, Cadiz Palace was probably their stronghold.

"Marcal, bring all the men in close," Kippy said authoritatively. "If we are going to rush out and confront the Dragos, I need to make sure they understand the challenges we face."

Marcal gave orders to four nearby men and they hurried out to the perimeter and his soldiers fell in quickly. "The men are all here, Great Lord."

"Good . . . good." Kippy cleared his throat and turned to the army before him. "Men of Egypt!" he began. "The beasts who held your Pharaoh hostage are trying to make a last stand out here in the desert. They are heading for a fortress buried in the sand. We must catch them before they reach safety."

Richie was impressed with how well he understood human nature as he waited for their murmurs to die down. They had been fooled once back at the palace and he saw that they wanted revenge.

"They may have great weapons, weapons that could make our vastly superior numbers obsolete.

"We need to stop them before they are able to get to their weapons." And then raising his voice to a fever pitch, he shouted to his army, "If we trap them at El Kasaad, we will secure victory, avenge Pharaoh, and protect your homeland!"

Richie smiled inwardly at his little pal. He truly was a wonder dog. Once again, his presence caused a loud roar from the crowd as eager soldiers moved to their chariots and mobilized for war.

"Mount up and move out," Marcal ordered.

Richie held his dog and let his face point into the wind. Soon the pyramids were falling behind them in a trail of dust and he could see the towering red cliffs ahead as they rose from the desert floor.

"We only have a couple of hours of daylight left," he said to the man next to him. "This plan isn't going to do us much good if we don't get to El Kasaad first," Richie yelled above the clacking of metal-banded wheels on stony ground.

The driver goaded the horses faster with a snap of the leads, which caused whipping sand to sting his cheeks and water his eyes.

"There," the barge master said, pointing to a towering outcropping. His chariot was alongside, in hailing distance.

Richie imagined the prow of a large ship the way it sloped up and out. The driver turned towards the direction of the barge master's outstretched arm.

Chapter 23
El Cadiz

Richie saw that they had raced way out in front of the other carts, so he instructed the driver to come to a halt in the shadow of the rock juggernaut.

As they arrived and pulled alongside, Richie watched the men wipe the sweat from their brows and saw the steam rising from the horses' flanks.

The barge master climbed down from his chariot and gave a brief bow to Kippy. "If you will follow me, my Lord, along this path is where I spotted what you asked about. I have come here often with my sons; it is where I took them hunting."

"Yes, yes, here it is," he said with pride. He stood and rested his finger on a small star etched into the red tinted rock, almost imperceptible to anyone who did not know where to look.

Richie dug through his backpack as Marcal and a few of his soldiers arrived. "This looks like the one," he said, pushing the piece into the fitted slot.

Nothing happened. He was sure he had the right piece. He tried it again, and again, but nothing. "Why doesn't it work?" he said in an agitated voice, clearly frustrated.

Have we miscalculated what these medallions do? He thought back to the other time and couldn't think of anything they did that was different.

"Maybe when they got wet it shorted them out or something," Kippy suggested. But Richie didn't buy that. This technology was too sophisticated to be that fragile.

"No, it's something else." He rubbed the star on his pants and tried putting it in a second time.

"Over here, over here," rose a cry of triumph. Richie looked to his right towards the cry and saw that further down the red rock wall, a door had swung inward. One of the soldiers had apparently been standing there relieving himself when it opened.

He raced to the opening along with Kippy, Saba, and Marcal. One by one they stepped into the darkness. The opening was as large as a barn door. Inside, a thirty-foot-wide passage ran directly into the side of the cliff.

"It must be the spar on the map that hooks up with the main tunnel," Marcal recalled aloud. "I don't think you should go any farther, let my men go forward and look around first."

"I appreciate that," Richie said with genuine thanks, "But I want to find that comet's tail and make sure we have a match first."

Kippy settled it. "Marcal, bring in a small team of men and let their chariots do a little scouting."

"Yes, my Lord," he said, and turned to gather his team.

Flipping on the flashlight, Richie was surprised that it still worked. He entered the tunnel, Saba and Kippy followed him. After a bit of a hike they came to the junction where the main tunnel intersected, forming a tee.

"Here it is," Richie pronounced. He rummaged through the remaining lockets and was about to try putting it in just to be sure.

"Don't do that," Saba said, grabbing his wrist.

"Oops, you're right!" he said on a rush of breath. "Dang, we would have been blown to pieces! Thanks, Saba." He wiped his brow and tried slowing the thud, thud, thud of his pounding heart.

Instead, he held the locket close to the wall. It appeared to be a perfect fit. He was interrupted by a loud racket of wheels on stone and turned to see eight war chariots rolling their way.

"Lord Sirius, have you found what we need?" asked one of the young lieutenants.

Shining the light on the comet, Richie handed the locket to the soldier who hesitated. His eyes were transfixed on the beam flowing from the cylinder.

"Is this fire stick what the gods use?" he asked in wonder.

"Yes," Richie replied, eager to move forward. "Once you put this in here . . ." He shone the light on the indent. "You get out of here as fast as you can."

"Because it will explode, right?" he asked for clarification.

It was a pivotal moment. If the Dragos did have weapons at their fortress, their lives depended on success. Richie knew what they were up against. Turning, he spoke to his friends in hushed whispers about what to do, specifically about the risks they were going to place these soldiers in. They all understood and accepted what needed to be done.

From the corner of his eye he noted the officer name Lieutenant Furan politely tried to ignore his hurried whispers, but he could tell from the man's face he knew a great decision was being made.

"Lieutenant, I think you will need these," he said, offering both his flashlight as well as the remaining star, comets, and moons. Then, fishing a tattered piece of paper and pencil from the near empty pack, Richie made a crude duplicate of the chart. Saba had insisted they not part with the original.

Most importantly, he focused the young soldier's attention on the outlines of the Dragos' probable stronghold.

"Remember, stars equal doors, moons are fortifications, and comets, well," he paused as he thought back to the river rage through the tunnel that almost killed them all, "with these, be careful."

The soldier took the proffered items and Richie hoped the clear sense of pride that swelled his spirit was not rewarded by their death.

"Would you like us to take you back to the entrance, my Lords?"

"No, we will walk," Richie told him. "Good luck."

When they exited, Richie could tell the men were spoiling for a fight. The nervous energy was palpable. He accepted a water skin from Marcal and cupped his hands for Kippy to drink. Then, hoisting the water, he took a long swallow of the tepid liquid.

As he passed the skin to Saba, he had to steady himself as the ground beneath his feet trembled, slowly at first, and then low groans began shaking the earth.

"Quickly, move to the open desert," Marcal ordered his men.

Richie reached for Kippy as Marcal's voice was lost in the din and rumble. Everywhere he looked, rocks began falling from above, and soon entire sections of cliff face sheared away, crashing along the ridgeline.

"Get in the cart," Saba yelled, pushing them forward. Richie stumbled as the shaking intensified. The horses were growing nervous, and he had to avoid one that was rearing up, trying to bolt out to freedom.

Saba grabbed Richie by the arm, gently tossing Kippy into the chariot and pulled the boy in behind them. Richie scrambled to find his footing as the horse lurched, almost losing their riders as they fled the trembling mountain.

Richie tore his pants pocket clambering into the cart. Dangling from the hole was his bracelet. His heart stuck in his throat as a flood of what ifs washed over him. Anxiety blossomed along the worst-case scenarios.

If I couldn't see the Dragos . . . He quickly secured it to his wrist and vanished. Saba did the same.

As they pulled farther from the high cliff face, Richie's mouth hung open in awe as the panorama of the ridgeline grew wider, and the scope of what they had unleashed became apparent. To their right, for over two miles, the mountain was caving in on itself. Millions of rocks were collapsing.

"Nothing could survive that," Saba commented under his breath.

"Let's head out to the other side of El Kasaad, see if it is also collapsing," Richie called out. He found himself fearfully focused on the fate of Lieutenant Furan and his men. This only amplified as they moved out into the unfurled desert. What he saw beyond the jutting juggernaut startled them.

"Look!" Richie said as Saba slowed the chariot.

"What-what?" Kippy was eager to see.

From a gaping hole in the side of the mountain, fearsome reptilians were fleeing into the desert. With great leaps and bounds, they moved swiftly away from the towering walls.

"These guys are fast," Richie said in trepidation, surprised at how much ground they could cover with each hurdle. They continued to pour from the collapsing tunnel, their order disintegrating into survivalist chaos.

Saba raced the horses forward. "We know where they are headed," he said barely audible above the clattering chariot. "Let's see if we can't get ahead of them."

Richie's adrenaline had fueled his emotions, fear, confusion and worry as they tried to keep their distance from the gaggle of reptiles. He was close enough to see their expressions and what he saw sent a shudder down his spine. Their faces were enraged.

"Arrack," bellowed the guttural call. He could tell each was alerting the next by the sounds and reactions. Like a school of fish, as one changed direction, they all did. Then they shifted their angle of attack, forming a pincer move which would prevent their chariot from retreating.

"Hold on!" Saba yelled. He tugged hard on the leads and the horses veered left, plunging into a stony wash. Richie gripped the sides, his knuckles white, his teeth jarred with every rock and rut. He looked over his shoulder, but they were gaining.

Saba slapped the reins, urging the horses to run faster.

"They're separating!" Richie cried out as he watched the Dragos fan out and take an intersecting bead on their trajectory. Some began hurling huge stones. Richie could not believe their accuracy, it took a strength that could not be matched by humans. Soon grapefruit-size rocks pelted the chariot, one just missing the right side of the stallion's head.

He regripped the side as the horses dangerously veered away, crashing into each other. One of the wheels rose up off the ground and the cart teetered on the abyss of being out of control. Another rock bounced off the chariot. For a moment they shimmied and swerved, and Richie thought for sure the chariot would spill over.

Another rock arced toward Saba. There was nowhere to dodge. Instinctively Richie threw up his arm. The rock struck his forearm with a glancing blow and fell harmlessly to the floor of the chariot.

"Dang it," Richie gritted his teeth, as pain shot down his arm.

Richie could see a huge beast running to intercept. At his speed and angle, he was sure to catch them. And to make matters worse, a cluster of boulders ahead cut off any chance of escaping on the right. Richie glanced between the alternatives, his mind racing. The rock rattled against his feet.

The Drago lunged towards the horses with such a force that he was flying through the air. Richie grabbed the rock from his feet and with all his strength, hurled it at the closing reptile. The projectile found its mark and slammed into the shoulder of the flying beast. Not enough to stop him, but it knocked him off his trajectory. He landed hard, rolling against the scrabbled earth.

Richie exhaled a sigh of relief, followed by a deep gulp of dusty air.

At the same time, Saba was able to get the chariot out of the gully wash onto more level ground. Richie saw him snap the reins, urging the horses to run as if their lives depended on it. With their speed increasing, they were able to pull ahead, putting distance between them and the following Dragos.

Richie relaxed his grip when he saw the Dragos would be unable to catch them and saw them turn and head back toward the red cliffs, resuming their westward trek.

ꝇℳ •◆• �️Ж •●Ж ⤢ℳ

"Where is Lord Sirius, and the other two?" Marcal barked to those closest to him. All around them was pandemonium. Over half the carts lay crushed by falling stone. Others were being dragged by panicked horses.

One of his lieutenants stepped up with a report. "Sir, they took a cart and were last seeing heading out beyond El Kasaad."

Marcal surveyed the scene around him and began making commands to restore order. "Lieutenant, gather two chariots and capable men and send them to find our Lord. Have Kreul and Rames determine how many men are hurt, how many chariots have been destroyed and how many chariots have vanished. Then send men after the horses and get them under control. We are going to need everything we've got."

It was clear that the destruction had taken a heavy toll. Twenty-two dead, half the chariots destroyed, and half the horses were being chased all over kingdom come. And worst of all, he had no doubt that his wife's brother, the lieutenant he had charged with investigating the tunnels, had surely perished with his men.

Poor Furan, Marcal thought. Staring at the life-giving sun, he prayed for his brother-in-law's soul. A tear streaked down his grimy face as he considered what he would have to say to his dear wife.

With great fortitude and courage, the young commander marshaled his troops. "Gentleman," he addressed them from the top of a splintered chariot.

"We know where they are headed, it is as I feared all along. Their main fortress is at the Palace of Cadiz."

The soldiers said nothing, but Marcal felt as they all did. The blasphemy of these beasts was stirring a rage that now burned bright and hot. But he was tempered by his childhood stories about the well of souls.

"We are down to sixteen working carts, and five of these we will need to help transport the wounded back to the city. But I have already sent our fastest rider back to the garrison and expect to have additional war wagons and siege vehicles here before the moon drops below the horizon. We are going to need courage and strength. Cadiz will be their final stand—I promise you!"

☌ℳ◆✠●✠⤢ℳ

"They're gone," Richie said, standing aside the resting horses, winded as they tried to catch their breath. The ground was littered with tracks funneling to the outcropping of stone ahead. Leaving the horses behind, they let them recover from the hard desert running.

"What do you think, Kip? Can you smell where they went?" Richie was thankful they had all survived, but he did not think they were out of the woods yet.

Kippy put his nose to the ground and cautiously followed the scent of the Dragos. As the alien tracks got closer to the wall, Richie felt goose bumps tingle the back of his neck. He stopped, sure they were being watched.

He scanned the cliffs above. High atop the outcropping sat a squat, rectangular building. Its sandstone walls sloped to a pointed roof. Too tall to scale. They could see only one entrance. It was flanked by slits cut in the stone, no doubt for firing some sort of weapons.

"A lookout tower?" Richie whispered.

"We are too close to the wall to be seen, unless they are looking straight down," Saba assessed. "It looks impenetrable."

"Do you think the Dragos are inside?" Richie already knew the answer.

"Some for sure," Saba replied, pulling out the map.

Richie stretched his aching muscles. It had been a long day. With the light fading and darkness not far off, he scanned the horizon. In the distance he could see plumes of dust.

"I hope it's Marcal," he said, both weary and worried.

ᘓ‍ᛗ•◆•ᚻ•●ᚻ✗ᛗ

Lieutenant Bentham Furan assessed their situation as he choked on air thick with dust and debris. They had survived the explosion and his men were all still alive. But they were deep inside the excavated plateau and behind them, their route no longer existed.

He calculated they had traveled about a thousand clicks down the tunnel when all hell had broken loose. Now the tunnel was gone, returned to its natural state of an immovable mountain. Forward was their only option.

He set forth under a false belief that they had succeeded in either trapping or killing the fleeing Dragos. Now the second part of their mission was to penetrate the fortress at Cadiz, and he and his men were eager to avenge Pharaoh.

The deep darkness was made worse by the still air and stifling dust. The men had to tear the bottoms of their tunics to make masks to cover the snouts of the horses as well as their own faces.

"We have only a league to go," Furan said confidently to his men. The sound of the metal-banned wheels clacking on the stone floor droned a steady beat as they got closer. The texture of the air grew fetid, and soon the dust was replaced by a growing stink, too noxious to ignore.

"It smells like death," one of the men complained. The soldiers clutched and re-clutched their spears and bows, nerves honed—ready to engage the enemy.

ᘓ‍ᛗ•◆•ᚻ•●ᚻ✗ᛗ

Night falls quickly in the desert. Soon the crimson sky was replaced by an inky blackness, and Saba worried about the army's visibility. Taking a chance that the dusty plume was in fact the advancing army, he guided the chariot toward the ever-growing clatter of wheels.

"Commander Marcal," Kippy said, addressing the lead chariot. "How are your men?"

Saba noted the man's face was tinged in sorrow.

"We took a heavy blow, my Lord," he said with a bowed head and slumping shoulders.

As he proceeded with his report, Saba paled at the loss, worried how they would proceed. When Marcal paused, Saba shared with him what scant info he felt relevant. "There is a lookout tower just ahead," he told him.

"Did you see any of the beasts?" Marcal asked.

"Only their tracks."

Marcal seemed to hesitate, giving weight to the statement. With a swift recounting of everything that had happened up to this point, Saba saw that it was as if the weight of the world had fallen on their young commander's shoulders.

"And Cadiz, were you able to scout the face of the kings?" the young commander asked.

"The face of the kings?" Richie asked questioningly.

"Beyond the last outcropping of El Shan-non, tucked behind the red cliffs, is the Palace of Cadiz. It is the burial home of the legendary kings of old. Those of the First Time," Marcal said with great awe and reverence.

"It will be better if we move south, farther out into the desert and then circle back," Marcal explained. "Away from the eyes of their sentries. We have heavy armaments and substantial reinforcements on the way. I will send a rider back to check on them, make sure they know to stay well south of the plateau. They should arrive later tonight. We will ride ahead, make camp and perhaps, allow ourselves a little rest."

Soon the night grew cold and by the time the thin sliver of the gibbous moon reached its apex, the sky was an explosion of stars and twinkling lights. After tending to their horses, Saba pulled the blankets from their backs and put it down for bedding. It was only a matter of minutes before he heard the soft rhythm of sleep overtake the young boy and his dog.

He lay there, staring into the night sky. Memories transported him back to his childhood, the days in the desert, working for Professor Miles. Each day had been an adventure, each day bringing promise and hope. It now felt like a million miles away.

"I'm getting old," he whispered, and then his eyes drooped, and he slipped away into a world of a deep, dreamless sleep.

ᏋᎢᎷ•◆•Ж•●Ж⤢ᏵᎷ

Chucky heard the old pickup truck pull out of the driveway. He stopped chewing. His mind began to race.

"There is something I can do," he mumbled, coming to grips with his decision. He slipped on his shoes, slid the bedroom window open and quietly eased down to the front yard, found his bike, and walked it to the street. Once there, he began pedaling out to the Radcliff's woods.

At this hour cars were few and far between, but every time he saw headlights, he would quickly hide until the car passed. *Dad's still so pissed,* he thought as a police cruiser passed by. *But I've got to stop him.*

The unfamiliar sense of righteousness was a strange comfort. As he labored under the cloudless sky, drawing closer and closer to the spot where Kayla had vanished, he saw that his father's truck was already there.

Seeing nobody nearby, he pulled back the tarp of the truck bed. The dynamite and blasting caps were gone.

Dad wasn't kidding, he really is going to wire this place up tonight.

⚜ ✦ ❋ ✦ ● ❋ ⚜

Chapter 24
Preparing for War

Richie woke and his mouth tasted like desert. His lips were chapped, and his throat was parched from the arid landscape. Next to the bedding somebody had left him a water skin. He drank a long gulp and saw that during the night reinforcements had arrived.

"Wow," he admired, wiping droplets from his lips. What had been desert when he went to sleep was now an array of tents and encampments filled with hundreds of additional men. And more importantly, huge wooden catapults and battering rams had arrived.

Somewhere across the plain, Richie could hear barking. *They brought the dogs, good—we'll need them.*

Checking that his bracelet was secure in his other pocket, he began thinking about the difficulties Marcal's men would have battling an invisible army.

Kippy's plan worked out the first time—I guess he already knew they were going to need the dogs again.

He set out to find out where his two companions had gone. As he plunged deeper into the camp, he could sense both anticipation and apprehension. With each passing minute, dawn was slowly unveiling the panorama around him.

"Richie, over here," came a familiar voice. He saw his two friends in deep discussion with Marcal and a few of his lieutenants. Just beyond them, the obvious focal point of their conversation—El Cadiz.

"Ohhhhhhhhhh man," Richie exclaimed in wonder. With its top tinged in the pink light of dawn, it revealed a mighty cathedral carved into the face of the cliffs where parts were still draped in shadows.

"Like Petra, it's just so beautiful," Saba said. Richie just nodded, unable to take his eyes from the grandeur. It was like a fairy tale castle. El Cadiz rose over a hundred feet straight up. The cliff face had become a canvas for ancient artisans. Its grandeur gave the Great Pyramid a run for its money. It wasn't the size and scope—it was the intricacy and craftsmanship on such a grand scale.

"It's awesome," he said. "I mean who could have created such beauty out of a cliff?"

A lieutenant answered his question, "It is ancient," he began. "It pre-dates the great flood. This was the city of the gods. They lived here during the first time, when men and gods interacted on a daily basis, it was our golden age."

"What happened?" Richie asked.

"Demons," Marcal said. "Throughout history there have been stories of evil spirits hovering here ever since the great flood washed over the Earth."

Richie's insides churned as he recalled the tunnels they had been in. "What about the Dragos," he mustered. "Could these spirits, or demons or ghosts, whatever they are, still be living in there? Do they enter flesh and take over one's body?"

No one answered the question, but the way their bodies flinched at his question, he was sure this was weighing heavily on their minds.

"Like we don't have enough problems," Kippy whined.

"What we know is that our enemy is real and holed up in this city," Marcal reminded them. "And if we do not deal with them now, we will no doubt have to deal with them later. I believe that destiny dictates we confront these beasts today and the sooner the better."

"What is your plan?" Saba asked.

"We need to get inside those walls," Marcal began. "Unfortunately, there is no record of what lies beyond, or how deep their tunnels run, so time is to their advantage. While we sit out here in the rising heat of day, they are safely ensconced within, preparing, and we have no idea for what."

Saba slumped under the weight of worry as dawn pushed away the shadows. The light of day soon revealed the entire structure. From its base down along the ground, to its top, so high above one had to look straight up to see it. The facade extended well out from the mountain wall meaning that at least that amount of cliff face had been chiseled away. Saba marveled that thousands of tons of rock had been removed and any quarry trailing had vanished long ago.

He marveled at how the artisans had used the natural red rock and polished the cathedral face to a high sheen, articulating the swirling white seams and veins of alternate stone in the mountain's face. The base of the structure measured at least two football fields long, with minor indents of sealed doors evenly placed from each end. In the center were colossal doors.

Carved into the cliff, between the doors, were twelve statues. He knew from his childhood they were the ancient gods known as the Watchers.

Above this, etched deep into the rock and accented by colored stones or possibly even semi-precious jewels, appeared an ancient map of the night sky. Perhaps the earliest example of the zodiac ever seen.

Set against the symbols and swirls of the twelve signs of the zodiac were arcane symbols. Each symbol had a matching god and was carved into the base of each of the statues. The place was both mysterious and beautiful, but at the same time, it radiated a foreboding.

"I don't think we are meant to go into this place," Kippy said. The fur on the back of his neck stood stiff with fear.

Richie squatted to one knee, stroking the nape of his dog. Like his friend Saba who stood beyond gazing at the Palace, he was worried. The grip of trepidation was unsettling. He could not articulate it, but it went beyond the Dragos, or even the possibility of death itself. Instinctively, Richie knew they were entering a realm of gods and demons, angels and devils, a battleground that was not the dominion of mere mortals.

"We need to get inside." Marcal set forth and explained how the battering rams and catapults would be used to breach the doors and how he would pair his archers and swordsmen with the dogs brought in during the night.

Richie listened intently, but in reality, battle and warfare was beyond his practical comprehension. By now he trusted Marcal and silently prayed his plan would work.

"Daylight is burning," he suggested, politely letting them know he had to get started.

"Carry on," Kippy managed. Marcal turned, followed by his men, and prepared for war.

"I don't like any of this," Richie confided in his furry friend as they ambled back to their wagon.

"Well, my boy," Saba interjected as he rejoined them. "In for a dime, in for a dollar. Let's get our gear together and move out far enough to get a good vantage point for all the action. No use getting in anyone's way now, is there?"

𝑒ᴛℳ ∙ ◆ ∙)(∙ ●)(↗ ℳ

With their chariot now far out into the desert just beyond the extended point of the Cadizian ridge, Richie noted that the outcropping was devoid of any signs of life. Behind them was endless desert, and to the west, the plateau of El Cadiz was swallowed in the distance.

Richie watched the heat shimmer across the sands. Shadows were gone, and the hard edge of daylight showed a cadre of war wagons closing in on the target.

"Still no sign of the Dragos," Richie said. And then he heard Marcal's voice ring across the plain.

"Fire!" In an instant, catapults the size of semi-trucks hurled great stones. One after another, the projectiles raced across the open space to destroy what had survived for eons.

Crash! Slam!

Richie watched in wonder as the sounds of crashing boulders created a resonating wave that came roaring back against the encampment. Men fell to their knees, trying to cover their ears from the aural assault. Richie heard horses whine and then saw them bolt.

"My God," Richie groaned, putting his hands to his face. They watched as the catapults and wagons closest to the source began to splinter. Like the biblical bugle tearing down the walls of Jericho, the sound had been turned against the gathered army and was destroying them.

He watched in horror as the wave grew and expanded, decimating everything in its way. Richie saw an array of colored light where the boulders had struck. Taking his bracelet from his pocket, he slipped it on and saw ripples of kinetic energy from the flying boulders siphoned off in all directions.

"They have a force field." he yelled above the din.

"I see it," Saba shouted.

The pulse was whipping up the sand into a maelstrom. Richie helped Saba as he struggled to keep the horses in check, one was trying to rear up as the other pushed back against the onslaught of the gathering sand squall.

"Oh my God," Saba said with dread. Richie and Kippy followed his stare.

Marcal had amassed the remaining line of siege vehicles and was commencing a new wave of assault.

"No," Richie shouted at the top of his lungs. But it was swallowed up by the growing roar.

"Hold on," Saba shouted. He yanked the reins to the left, slapping the horses hard, trying to break through their fear and driving them out into desert as far away as they could get.

Richie held Kippy under his arm as he clawed the side of the fast-moving chariot. Behind them there was another crash. This was instantly followed by the *wa-wa-wa-wa-wa* reverberations of the force field. Richie turned to see the deafening sound had turned into an angry cloud of sand, and debris that raced forward, destroying everything in its way. Marcal's army was being routed by their own aggression.

"Behind the ridge," Riche yelled at the top of his lungs. "It's our only hope or we will get swept away . . ."

Saba jerked the reins to the left and angled to the leeward side of the juggernaut before they became consumed by the growing hurricane.

Pushed by the expanding force, sand filled Richie's eyes as rocks slammed into their chariot.

"Duck!" Saba shouted.

The wind whistled above them, howling like banshees, all but drowning out the screams of fear emitted by the crazed beasts. But they ran on, driven by panicked instinct.

Richie squeezed his dog tight and thought of the torment these poor horses were being subjected to, but he dared not try look over the top.

One of the horses stumbled, and the wagon tipped precariously to one side. They were going to be hurled from their protective cocoon.

"Hang on," Saba shouted.

Richie held his breath, ready to roll from the careening cart, but it jerked back upright, and Saba pulled hard on the reins to bring the horses to a stop.

Daring to poke his head above the chariot rim, Richie stared into the back face of El Shan-non. Protected by the rocky outcropping, he could see out beyond into the desert that the wind was still screaming as it picked up every lose grain of sand, rock, and debris along its path.

Saba got out to check the horses. Kippy and Richie stood inside the chariot. Shock and adrenaline fatigue was receding from his body. Behind them, with ever decreasing force, the winds began to die. Eventually ending in an unnerving silence, a hush akin to ghosts and death.

𝑒ᴛ𝕸 ⋅ ◆ ⋅)(⋅ ●)(⤢ 𝕸

"The smell is going to kill us before we ever encounter those wicked beasts," the young soldier said to Furan.

It's true, Furan thought, while saying nothing to his men. His bravery shrank with each passing step. The smell of death was so strong that each gulp of air seemed to bring him and his men one step closer to their maker.

"We have to be close," he replied. "Let's take a break while I consult the map the gods entrusted us with."

Opening the rough sketch, he knew that if he did not get his men out from this tunnel soon, one by one they would begin to fall. Ill soldiers will be of no help to those fighting outside.

I wonder if they have engaged the enemy yet, he thought. *Are we winning, could it be over?* His instincts told him it was far from being over, victorious thoughts were just a flight of fancy.

Looking at the chart, he homed in on the symbolic star. He recalled that these represented doorways to the outside. The hand-drawn map was confusing because of all the other symbols in proximity to the one star he sought. He studied the cluster of moons and comet tails. None of this is to scale, he worried.

"Somewhere, etched into these rocks you should find a carving of a small star . . ." Furan told his troops. "Find that star and we can get out of here!"

Working in tandem with his men, he felt his way along the smooth walls of the warren, using his hands as eyes in the dim damnable tunnel.

In moments, success was achieved. "Over here, I found it," shouted a soldier.

Furan's heart skipped a beat, the dry taste of anticipation filled his mouth as he moved towards the man.

"Keep your finger there, we will come to you. Don't lose it," Furan sidled up to the man, shining the light. "Good work," he told him. It was exactly what they were looking for. Reaching into the pack, he felt around until he plucked the star from the bottom. With a deep breath, his men fell in around him.

"Be ready, men." He placed the star into the etching. It fit perfectly. For a moment, nothing happened, and then, to his utter amazement, sunlight spilled into the gloomy darkness. With a newfound energy, Furan guided his men to freedom.

ℰ𝕸 ◆ ◆ ⋇ ◆ ● ⋇ ⤢ 𝕸

"We need to go check on Marcal," Saba said. His voice rang loud in the stunning silence. In truth, he feared what they would see.

"You're right, Saba," Richie said, in a tone draped in defeat.

"Wait," Kippy said, "I hear someone coming." He jumped off the open rear end of the chariot. Saba followed his gaze and saw that far behind them, where the extended juggernaut joined the long line of the east-west plateau, the walls were opening. He could see a mass of moving life but was not sure who, or what—they were

"Quickly, back into the cart," Saba warned with his eyes firmly fixed on the growing breach at the base of the Cadizian Ridge.

Saba was worried that the horses were at the end of their limit but pushed this concern from his mind. Grabbing the reins, he snapped the right horse. Its sand-covered, sweat-soaked back glistened as tiny droplets slurred under the force of the reins.

"They're alive. All of them," he said with a speck of hope in his voice.

He now could hear the trumpet shout of triumph and joy as it rolled across the gulf between them. The approaching men snapped their reins and closed the gap in full gallop.

"Greetings, my Lord," Furan said, pulling adjacent to their cart. There was no room to bow, but each man lowered his head.

"What is the good word?" he asked.

Saba sensed a sense of jocularity. Like he should never have doubted his God. But he said nothing, and the joy fled as quickly as it had arrived.

"What is it? Where is Marcal, the army?"

Saba filled him in on all that had happened. From the Dragos bounding out of the hillside, to the impenetrable shield of deathly sound protecting their fortress.

"Then we must ride quickly," Furan announced. "We must assist our squadrons."

"Yes," Saba concurred. "I will go with you, leave your men here with Lord Sirius and Master Richie. We will survey the situation and then return."

Saba saw that Richie was about to object and gave the boy a sharp stare.

"My bag. Do you still have it?" Richie asked looking scorned.

Reaching to the chariot floor, Furan handed over Richie's backpack.

"We'll be back," Saba said, and then stepped from his chariot onto Furan's.

"Tend to the horses," Furan ordered one of his men, and then they were gone.

Richie immediately picked up on the soldiers' nervousness at being around their God, unsure of how to act, whether to address him or avoid him. Richie tried asking them some questions, but it was awkward. They answered with perfunctory precision, but it was clear they preferred to keep their distance.

Taking the map from his pocket, Richie unfurled it next to Kippy.

"Obviously, this is the doorway here," Richie said laying his finger on the map. "This doorway will give us a good reference point, maybe help us find the other symbols. Notice how many are clustered about the same place.

"Two crescent moons, which we know represent keys to fortifications and two comet tails . . ."

"Yeah, more boom," Kippy answered.

"What if one of these moons disengages the force field?" Richie's mind was whizzing with possibility. "I mean, that's what it is, right, some form of fortification."

"This is the only place on all of the maps that we have seen pairs of the same symbols rest side by side. It just might be," Kippy said in agreement.

"Let's go!" Richie said.

"Now? Alone?" Kippy balked. "We should wait for Saba."

"Look, the symbols may be just inside that doorway, and since he has left the star in its slot, and we do not know how long these portals stay open before they may close automatically . . ." he paused as he thought out loud. "If we don't go now, we may lose our only chance. We don't have any more stars."

Kippy walked over to the nearest soldier as four teams of charioteers scrambled back into their wagons and lined up before their Lord.

"You may ride with me," the young liege in charge said. Richie hefted his backpack and they climbed aboard.

"What is your name, soldier?" Kippy asked.

"Syed, my Lord."

"Syed, tell your men to break up into two groups. One group will remain just outside the tunnel, and the other will go forth and advise Master Saba and Lieutenant Furan of what we are doing. Also have one man wait there, at the bow of the rocky protrusion. Explain that we are trying to close down the wall of sound. If we are successful, we will be able to penetrate El Cadiz."

The man nodded as Kippy continued. "Once we locate our target, we will send one of these men back out of the tunnel. When you see him exit, send the man you station at the bow's end running like the wind to advise the leading group we have commenced."

Richie found himself nodding along with the soldier, fully understanding and respecting Kippy's plan to try and save every conceivable second they could muster.

eⲅ𝕞 • ◆ •)(• ●)(⤢ 𝕞

Stepping into the cool cavernous tunnel, a shiver quaked along Richie's spine. *Are there really spirits and demons in here?* He worried, thinking about what the soldiers had said earlier about the tunnels being haunted. The idea creeped him out.

He kept a wary eye for any unusual anomaly, but instinctively understood that all of their special powers would not help them in this otherworldly realm.

"Show me where the star was placed," Richie said to the soldier. He felt Kippy's unease staring hard into the thickening darkness. He fought to stay focused, pushing fear into a corner of his mind.

"Over here," the man said, stopping the cart.

Richie and Kippy jumped down. Richie focused his flashlight on the wall in front of them. There it was. He took the map and placed his thumb and forefinger on the nearby symbols. He mentally calculated direction and distance.

"This way," he said, following the wall deeper into the tunnel.

After twenty steps, the wall began to bend. The soldier kept pace while remaining in the chariot. The soft clopping of the horses' feet broke the silence.

"The smell is not as bad as before, eh Samuel," one of the soldiers whispered to another.

"It probably wafted out through the opening," said his compatriot.

"Dang," the soldier called out as they made the turn where the smell smacked them head on.

"We should have waited for Saba," Kippy mumbled miserably.

But Richie ignored him as he continued his quest. Kippy stuck to his side.

"It should be here somewhere," Richie calculated. The patterned sound of the horses' hooves started to change. Richie flashed the beam, piercing what should have been extended darkness. Instead it struck a wall in front of them.

"This should not be here," The soldier said with dismay. "It wasn't here before."

"It must be another fortress," Richie told him, thinking of the wall the Dragos had closed off during the flood back at the pyramid. Shining the light, he grew concerned that perhaps the crescent slot was on the other side. Or worse, it wouldn't deactivate the force field.

"It's a dead end," the Lieutenant cried out in defeat.

"It's not a dead end!" Richie told him, partly trying to convince himself. "I'm sure of it!"

The thick gloom made it difficult to see anything specific without the aid of the flashlight. For the next few minutes Richie covered every inch of wall from the floor up to the top of his head.

"Nothing," he growled with growing frustration. Hoisting himself onto the back of the chariot, he sat down and reeled through the possibilities, absentmindedly rolling the flashlight beam back and forth.

As a distraction, he watched in amusement as the soldiers gawked at his godly powers to cast light from the end of his fingers. Mesmerized, they followed every twitch, roll and slither of the beam as it aimlessly tracked against the stone.

"Lord," said one of the soldiers. "The signs, I saw one."

"You did! Where?" Richie's heart began to beat faster as he sucked short gulps of air. Anticipation tingled throughout his body.

"Right there, but higher. Maybe a stone's length off the floor."

Richie was not sure what a 'stone's length' measured to, but slowly moved the beam up the wall. At first, he saw nothing, then he reversed course and aimed a foot higher.

"There," the man exclaimed. The beam washed over a crescent moon.

"Syed, can you back up the chariot? I need to stand on it to reach."

While he was doing this, an idea occurred to Richie. If the map showed two symbols, perhaps one was for this wall but there was another for the force field beyond. With that in mind, he returned scanning the light back and forth.

"Watch out, sir," the charioteer warned.

Stepping aside he allowed the man a wide berth but kept searching for a second symbol.

"There," he exclaimed with satisfaction. The beam was steadied on a second crescent moon. He retrieved the two remaining moons from his pack. They weighed almost nothing, yet probably contained the fate of all humanity.

"Let's try this one first."

He hopped onto the back of the wagon as the horses let out a nervous nay.

"Syed, keep them still."

Richie climbed upon the rail, bracing one hand on the wall in front of him, the other reaching upwards. He tried to slip the moon into its slot, but his fingers came up short. Standing precariously on tip toes, he tried again, but it would not go.

"Come on, come on," he said with his arms stretched as far as they would go.

It's not the one. Please he mumbled in a soft prayer, please let me be right! He took the second moon from his pocket and tried once more.

"Got it!" he said in triumph.

A quiver shook the walls. It was a single rumble and then nothing.

"Syed, run and send the signal."

𝑒𝜏𝍼 • ◆ • 𝈷 • ● 𝈷 ⤢𝍼

Saba stared in horror at the devastation strewn across the desert plain. Men, horses, and wagons were toppled, crippled, and scattered from the temple walls to far out into the desert. The war wagons had been obliterated. Men were tending to the wounded, others were gathering up the horses, and yet others still trying to collect the howling dogs running scared throughout the encampment.

Saba watched as three soldiers approached, covered in sand and blood. He recognized defeat as they slowed their horses to a walk.

"What happened?" he asked as they came to a halt.

"The ghosts, they sent their devil winds. Picking us up and tossing us like dolls while conjuring the sands into gnashing teeth. We were flung from the sacred city. El Cadiz does not want us here," he said, and dropped his eyes swollen with superstitious fear.

Though they were battered and bruised, Saba was relieved to see them alive. He turned his gaze back to the field of destruction. With a brief glance to the rear, he saw the raised dust of a hard-riding chariot coming around the bend of El Shan-non. Immediately, feared gripped his throat. Had something happened to Richie and Kippy? Anxiety clawed with panic that wanted to take over.

"Furan, wait. Look." Within minutes, the panting horses slowed and came alongside one another.

"They have entered the tunnels sir," the soldier said between gasps of breath. "They said that they may have disarmed the wall of sound. Our great Sirius has used his powers to aid us."

Saba followed his gaze as the soldiers looked in dismay at the field of fallen comrades.

"We must find Marcal," Furan strongly urged.

Saba nodded, and in a flash, the horses were galloping to the center of the melee. Drawing closer to the walls of El Cadiz, the stark light of day magnified its majesty.

Near the base, where the catapults had been staged, Saba saw Marcal marshalling his troops, organizing for a new assault. His charisma and courage were visible even from a distance, and wherever he went, his men took strength.

"We'll be alright," Saba whispered thankfully. Kippy made a great choice in this young man.

Picking a path through the bramble of war, Saba called out. "Look who I found. Your brother-in-law!" He knew a respite of good news was needed.

"Furan!" Marcal exclaimed, jumping from his horse. "The gods have spared you. I was sure you were dead when that mountain collapsed."

Saba considered this a gift from God as he watched the two embrace in an unabashed hug of reunion.

"What of the others?" Marcal asked, releasing his relative with a fresh worry painted on his face.

"Everyone is safe," Saba said reassuringly. "Furan can fill you in. I must tend to something for my Lord. I shall return in a few minutes."

Saba eased the horses forward and picked his way through the clusters of men. As he drew closer to the point of the Dragos' defenses, he stepped from the chariot, bent over, and retrieved a few small rocks.

Could they really have pulled it off? He eased forward, one worried step at a time. Slipping on the bracelet, he worried about the deafening sounds caused before. He took the smallest rock he could find and hurled it, bracing for the repercussions. It fell with a soft tinkle to the ground.

"They did it!" he shouted. "They did it!"

He had not realized he had been holding his breath. There was a buzzing sound, as the flow of excitement caused a rushing sound in his ears. Still, he advanced warily, and side-armed a second rock. Again, the same result. After doing this two more times, he was at the very base of El Cadiz.

With hope, his eyes roamed over the details where they eventually focused on the center doors. He turned and approached, all the time worried that at any moment the Dragos would shoot him down or worse, seize him. Sweat trickled down his neck as the sun rose higher into the sky. There was no sound, no wind, not even the incessant cloying of the desert flies. Nothing.

Reaching the front doors, he noticed a zodiac motif carved with astronomical inlays of mosaic tiles covered the facade of the building. As each constellation followed the other, the tail of an old familiar friend culminated along the frame of the ornate doors.

"My maiden," he whispered in soft reverie. Like the doors from his youth, there was one extra star in the handle of the Big Dipper.

Chapter 25
El Cadiz and the Gods of Old

Richie stepped aside as Syed and the remaining charioteers brought their wagons in. He counted a total of seven.

"Gentleman," he began, as he placed Kippy up on the edge of a chariot. "Beyond this wall lies the heart of our enemy. When it opens we will face a force like you have never seen before."

He was trying to bolster their flagging courage, but he could sense apprehension. He slipped on his bracelet and was rewarded by a stifled gasp. He needed to remind them that they had their Gods to protect them.

"You will not be able to see the enemy, but we will be your eyes. We will place the wagons in front of us, wall to wall. The archers will form a line and aim into the opening. If anything tries to get through, we will instruct you on when and where to fire. Lastly, your spearmen will keep your points held at throat level, ready in case our defenses break down."

"When do we move?" Syed asked.

"We wait," Richie told him, noting his uneasiness at the invisible voice. "We wait until word comes from the other side of El Shan-non. We need to know that we have succeeded, and they are preparing. We are only going to get one chance at this, and we must have faith." He eyed the other sign and felt the last medallion in his pocket. And prayed.

As he expected, the men looked to Kippy, who tried to act regal. But Richie knew that since the discussion of ancient gods and demons, he wasn't sure that the real gods were going to be pleased with his impersonation.

$$e\tau\text{m} \cdot \blacklozenge \cdot \text{℧} \cdot \bullet \text{℧} \nearrow \text{m}$$

"Look! See . . . our great and mighty God has opened the way." Saba shouted with embellished reverence, trying to instill a renewed sense of courage and bravery into their battered psyches. His words were having the desired effect. The drooping shoulders of the gathered men straightened, and a gleam returned to their eyes.

"Our war wagons are destroyed. How will we open the doors?" Marcal asked.

"I will open the doors," Saba said with unfettered confidence. "We must prepare to storm the cathedral."

As they turned their backs to the gathering men, Saba spoke to Furan.

"Send your fastest men back to Lord Sirius, let them know they have succeeded, and we are preparing to attack.

$$e_T\text{M} \cdot \blacklozenge \cdot)(\cdot \bullet)(\nearrow \text{M}$$

"What has happened to our defenses?" Lord Drago bellowed in rage. His underlings had no answers. Now all was about to be lost. He knew what had to be done. They still had the comfort of eternity, and the original fundamentals of their plan were still intact.

"The plan can still succeed," he snarled, his tongue darting in and out. "One last deception, and if they buy it, victory will be ours!"

He looked over his Drago warriors. All one hundred had been handpicked for this galactic mission. Each trained until human morphing was second nature. He gathered them for the final act of his greatest trick.

Once finished explaining his plan, the men broke into their respective positions. Some would be sacrificed, some would vanish, and in the end, the great empire of Drago would succeed. It was time.

$$e_T\text{M} \cdot \blacklozenge \cdot)(\cdot \bullet)(\nearrow \text{M}$$

"Look!" Syed pointed, breaking the tension of waiting.

Richie saw the lone chariot rounding the bend and heading at a full galloping speed towards the cavernous opening. He was alone but his face glowed with confidence.

"It's working," Kippy said in recognition. The rider was still too far away for Richie's humanized sight, but the unmistakable confidence in Kippy's words was received like a reprieve given to a condemned man.

Syed exited the tunnel, waving down the hard-pressed charioteer.

"It worked," the rider said in exalted breath. "Lord Sirius, you've succeeded in destroying their defenses. Your counselor said they are preparing to attack, that the star on the door shall open the way."

"Okay men, the time is now," Richie bellowed in excitement as the men fell into position. Retrieving the last lockets, Richie prepared for the final assault.

I hope this works. Please, just one more time.

eᴛ℔ ✦◆✦〉〈✦●〉〈⤢℔

When Saba pulled the star from the door mantel, a cheer arose as the colossal gates opened into the very bowels of hell itself. When the doors had fully opened, he directed the shower of fleeing arrows that raced into the darkened interior.

He listened as the withering sound of feathers followed one after another after another, then another. He was torn at the sounds of anguish and pain being returned to sender but felt satisfaction that some had found their mark.

"First and second team, advance," shouted the command from the forward lines.

Saba stayed back as they rushed into the room and fanned out, letting off another volley. He knew the archers could not see their targets, but the sounds of the scrambling cries receded farther and farther into the great foyer.

"Bring in the dogs," cried Marcal.

Saba entered as the archers moved deeper into the hall. He saw the torch bearers and lance men at their rear. The flames revealed a room of gigantic proportions including furniture built for giants.

Saba gazed in amazement at the sheer proportion. Even the Dragos would not have made accoutrements this large. *Had giants really roamed the Earth? Could the biblical stories of David and Goliath have been true?*

But his reverie was brief, fleeing deep in the recessed portion of the Cathedral, he spotted the largest of the Dragos, the Lord himself. With a small band of beasts, he escaped into the shadows of the tunnels behind.

He looked around and counted at least twenty Dragos down and dying, the dogs had others pinned while the lancers parried the spears. Hit and miss, striking the poorly armed beasts, the dogs were doing a magnificent job guiding their handlers.

"Marcal," Saba called out. "To the rear, they are escaping."

ᴇᴛᴍ ⬦ ◆ ⬦)(⬦ ●)(⤬ ᴍ

Richie thrust the sliver of metal into its matching receptacle as the men around him sparked flint and lit their makeshift torches. The flickering glow cast eerie shadows against the wall that began to sink into the floor. There was a hiss as air raced through the opening, blowing smoke back into their faces.

Richie almost hurled at the stench. The smell of death was so overpowering, and men all around him began vomiting.

"Oh my God! It's a slaughterhouse!" Syed cried out.

Richie saw hundreds of men dead or dying men chained to the floor. Row after row, descending deep into the tunnel as far as the torch light would carry. Most were barely alive, and many had been intentionally maimed. Richie's nostrils flared in anger and his spiking adrenaline sought confrontation and revenge.

"It's Pharaoh's army, they're caged like pigs," a soldier wailed.

Richie was revolted, but wary. "Find a way to release these men, we need to get them out of here."

"Shhhhhh!" Kippy commanded.

Richie listened through the pounding anger. Farther down the corridor he heard a commotion. Though there was light on this side of the tunnel, it was dim at best.

"I hear voices," Kippy said.

"Fire the rest of the torches," Syed called out.

Richie watched the receding shadows as each man lit their bundled reeds from their comrade's flame. As the firelight pushed deeper into the room, movement at the far end of the hall unveiled an approaching battle.

"The Dragos are being pushed backwards," Richie called with urgency. "Prepare to engage . . ."

Spilling into the hall of prisoners, Richie watched as a band of Dragos raced towards them. "Archers advance," Richie ordered.

The archers advanced on foot as fast as they could run. Richie saw that some of the Dragos were breaking ranks, some continuing to flee, but he kept his focus on those looking to confront the unexpected visitors.

"To the right," Richie directed the archers. A flurry of arrows hurled into the air and with satisfaction the boy-turned-commander saw them piercing the advancing horde. As the first wave reached their marks, Richie could see that one of the cadets found a lever that released a row of manacles.

"Find the others, each row has a release," he shouted. "Help the prisoners able to walk get to the exit." This added to the confusion, but he needed to get them out of the way.

He turned his attention back to the rear battle. Dogs were chasing after the fleeing Dragos and hand-to-hand combat was confusing when most of the enemy was invisible. Chaos on every side, Richie took a deep breath and tried to assess the situation.

As his eyes adjusted, he could make out things in the flickering torch light, horrible things. Lining the wall he made out the shapes of grotesque machines. Human body parts were laying all over the floor with blood and gore festering. Were they experimenting on humans? What if they were stealing their identities? Did they need humans for morphing? Had these soldiers been abducted for their identities, their humanity? Cocooned within the maelstrom, an awful thought occurred to him.

What if the stories about alien abductions on the covers of the grocery store tabloids are true? Could this somehow be related?

Across the fire-lit room, Richie felt the presence of his nemesis, Lord Drago. Chasing away errant thoughts, he scanned the back of the room, his breath caught in his throat.

"I knew it," he said, spying the huge upright lizard.

Lord Drago stopped at the far wall, his face glaring pure hatred. "You shall die!" He taunted, as he held up both palms and a vicious smile creased his lipless mouth.

"No!" Richie shouted.

He saw nestled in those raised palms two lightning bolt shaped comet tails. The Lord of the lizards moved to the closest wall, placed the keys of destruction into their slots, and gave a sinister wave.

"Goodbye."

He fled around the corner where Richie assumed he was retreating deep into the mountainside. Already a soft breeze was wafting from the bowels of the earth. Recalling the explosions that had flooded the tunnel before, Richie knew they had precious little time.

"Everyone get out, now! It's going to blow. Hurry!"

He shouted again and again until the urgency of his voice cut through the chaos. Only when the fury of battle receded into a retreat of survival did he stop yelling. Like wildfire, his message spread as men began fleeing to get out.

Marcal was yelling. "You and you," he singled out. "Gather the weakest and move them towards safety."

Everything was unfolding in chaos. Richie saw the regiment of bedraggled men in various states of dress and health converging on the lone exit that led into the desert.

Deep within the mountain, he felt a low growl vibrate up through the passage. What set his nerves on end were the screams and wails, like banshees wallowed up from the darkened abyss. This only heightened the sense of urgency vibrating down the corridor toward freedom.

He saw Kippy freeze. "We must go! Now!" Richie hollered. He grabbed two injured soldiers, which slowed him, but he was determined.

"Hurry Richie!" Kippy returned the warning, but his voice was being drowned out by the raising shrieks emanating from deep within the Earth.

Richie tried to block out the sounds. They were unnatural, like the wails of demons, and it was unnerving him. *Push, dang it—keep pushing.* He saw that freedom was close.

The growls grew as the first wave of explosions rocked them from deep inside the Earth. The sonic pressure loosened rocks and tore debris from the walls and ceiling. Richie saw huge cracks opening in the floors as the walls started to buckle.

Suddenly a huge explosion from behind blew him over. As he fell to the ground, Richie saw Kippy thrown off his feet as the concussive wave of wind and sound raced past. All around him the tunnel was crumbling.

"Get up, Richie," Kippy cried out.

Richie lay sprawled, his hands were bleeding, and he was cut all over. As he came to his knees, a rotund man raced up from behind and intentionally pushed him back to the floor, driving his face into the stone.

As gaggles of legs ran by, Richie caught a glimpse of the receding head that had been uncannily accurate in driving his face into the floor.

It can't be . . .

Richie jumped to his feet, whisked his dog under his arm and raced for their very lives. Just ahead, streaked rays of sunlight shone through the haze of dust and falling stone. Small rocks pelted him as he scrambled over loose debris.

"We're almost there," he yelled, squeezing Kippy tight under one arm. Then, a tangle of feet, loose rock, and debris sent a wave of people cascading head over heels. With presence of mind, and the grace of an opening, Richie flung his dog to safety before the human avalanche collapsed upon him.

Scrambling out of the thicket of legs, arms and bodies, Richie got to his feet, and extended his arm to help the man below him, but he forgot he was invisible. Slipping the bracelet into his pocket, he bent forward as something crashed onto his back and he winced in pain.

Large parts of the ceiling collapsed onto the back of his head until he collapsed. The last thing he saw were feeble rays of sunlight being choked off as the entire mountain caved in around him.

erℿ ♦ ◆ ♦ ⑂ ♦ ● ⑂ ⫞ ℿ

Chapter 26
The Final Stand

Saba watched as soldiers poured from the mouth of Cadiz. Bellowing dust belied what he knew—inside, the Earth was being torn asunder. The mountain was collapsing. From deep within, explosions continued, one after another, after another.

He was startled from his worry when Furan, along with Marcal, grabbed him by the arm and pulled him into their moving chariot.

My bracelet? It must have come off in the cave, he thought, barely caring at that point.

"The mountain is imploding," Marcal shouted above the din, pointing. "There will be no more Dragos . . ."

"And no more Cadiz," Saba said under his breath. He watched the receding landscape as they moved out into the desert. The crumbling mountain was causing the red rocks of Cadiz to collapse under the towering weight of the very cliff itself.

The outward rush of air was whipping up the sand. He felt the sting against his face as he listened to the shrieks of grinding stone and the groans of a dying mountain.

He was incredibly anxious with worry about his two friends. He had seen them heading for the other exit, and he could only pray that they made their escape.

"Furan, please turn the wagon around. I must see if Lord Sirius and young Master Richie have escaped."

He knew this might be a problem. Everything had collapsed into the desert. All references points were reduced to a single plain of silted sand, soil, and death.

"Yes, my Lord," he nodded, but his expression lacked conviction.

Saba was having trouble seeing very far ahead. The desert was fogged by dust and sand. The tornado-like winds were slacking along with the diminished rumbles of the earth. The violent shaking and aftershocks seemed to be lessening.

An eerie calm descended upon the hazy plain. Saba stared as they passed small hillocks of wind-tossed sand and mountainside piles of debris that continued to waft down to the desert floor. As the air cleared, Saba cocked his ear for sounds of life.

"Hear that," Saba said. "Turn the wagon and follow the sound."

Furan turned towards the east, and they moved slowly through the desert.

Saba saw that behind chariot wheels left a trail as they cut through the accumulated silt. Above, signs of death were carried by the sight of carrion birds circling in the distance.

"Look—there!" Marcal exclaimed. Saba saw tears forming at the edge of the young Lieutenant's eyes as he swept over the wide swath of desert where there were clusters of men, many injured and lying down, amongst toppled chariots and wagons.

A lone flag hung limply in the still air. "Head there," Saba said. Thinking this would announce where a Pharaoh was encamped.

God, I hope Kippy and Richie are alright.

Sorrow and anxiety mixed, as he looked to the men, and recalled the horrors they had witnessed inside the Drago prison. *War is evil,* he thought, as he considered the daunting tasks that lay ahead.

Anxiety formed a tight knot in his throat—Kippy and Richie were nowhere to be seen. Moving toward the masses, Saba could see that many of Pharaoh's freed army huddled together. The able were giving assistance while the newly conscripted soldiers created a sense of order.

What few horses had survived were gathered off to one side, and a few dogs lay huddled a little farther away.

Is this what victory looks like? There was no reason for celebration, there was so, so much lost this day.

Saba saw the now legendary Dog God. His eyes flew wide and with his shoulders pulled back in relief, he had a new bearing. *Oh thank God,* he mouthed.

"Kippy, you little rascal," Saba exclaimed with joy.

The dog ran from the huddled group of men and jumped up into Saba's open arms and began to lick the sand-covered face of his friend.

For just a moment, Saba savored the answer to his prayers. "Where's Richie?"

Saba felt the little body tighten and knew in an instant something was wrong.

"He's over there . . . Unconscious."

Saba gulped as he looked to the cluster of men. Suddenly he had a dry metallic taste in his mouth. Fear. "No God. Please!" He cried out. Setting Kippy on the ground, he hastened to see Richie. He pushed his way through the circle of men to see the battered and bloodied body of his young friend.

Saba was stricken with grief. A lump formed in his belly and suddenly all the years caught up to him and he slumped like an old man. Despair washed down on him like a heavy rain.

"Water, someone give me some water." Saba demanded. One of the soldiers handed Saba a skin. He poured it into his hand and eased it into Richie's mouth. His tongue instinctively moved against his lips, but he lay motionless.

"Thank God, he is still alive."

Using his forefinger, Saba began washing away the grime from Richie's mouth and eyes. After a few more minutes, Saba worked the moist fingers along the back of the injured head.

"Owww!" Richie shuddered in a wail of pain. He tried to rise up.

"Richie, Richie, oh my God, you're alive. Thank you, thank you," he stammered. Words came tangled spilling out on a river of thick emotion.

Kippy started licking his master's face. Saba saw the look on the gathered men and improvised.

"He is transferring some of the life force of the universe," he said with authority and noted the reverence sweep over their faces.

The atmosphere of renewed optimism attracted a crowd and soon the circle of men became thick with curious onlookers.

Richie sat up and scanned the crowd as he rubbed his hand gingerly across the back of his scalp. He watched as one of the soldiers was pushed aside. A man from behind was rudely gaping down at him.

"You!" Richie cried out, struggling to stand. His agitated eyes stared guiltily at the intruder.

"What! I didn't do anything." The man recoiled in alarm.

The man had a sweat-glistened bald head and momentarily Richie thought it was O'Mander. The last he had seen of him was when he crushed his face into the floor and ran out of the cave with the others.

He's escaped. The thought fueled him with anger.

"I need to get up," he insisted, and gently moved Saba's arm aside. He reached into his pocket, found the bracelet, and slipped it on and vanished before the gaping crowd. He needed to be sure there were no Dragos lingering. Though he knew Kippy would have seen them, he had a gut feeling Lord Drago was hanging around.

"I can no longer see you," Saba said, holding up his bare wrist, implying he had lost his bracelet.

Richie slipped his back off. "I'm sorry."

"I don't need it anymore," Saba said with a forced smile that could not mask his weariness.

He stood up on partially cooperating legs. "Sal O'Mander has escaped. I saw him sneaking out with the crowd. He is dressed as one of Pharaoh's guards. We must find him, before he can escape and cause more damage." Richie slipped the bracelet back on.

"Kippy, come with me, we need to round up the dogs and find him. I am sure he is still here. He'll be trying to blend in."

A hundred yards away, Sal watched, and he cursed his fate once again. His plan was to blend in all the way back to the city. He could not risk morphing into his lizard self, there were too many dogs. From a distance, he was safe as long as he remained Sal O'Mander, but he was not immune from closer inspections.

Sal turned and made his way towards the few remaining horses. He moved slowly, careful to attract little or no attention. He was planning his escape to destroy that portal once and for all.

If they can't return, it doesn't really matter what they may or may not know.

He moved from group to group, stopping, blending in, and trying to stay away from the dogs. Bolting toward the horses, Sal slipped in behind them, grabbed the reins of the four remaining animals, and untied them. Hiding between two of large beasts, Sal saw that he had not been noticed by the dog or human. He eased onto the back of the largest and fastest horse. Taking the other reins in his hand, he started moving, keeping his head turned away.

At that same instant, Sal O'Mander lifted his head ever so slightly, to see if he had been spotted. Like lasers, his eyes locked on Richie's.

Damn it, he's seen me.

"Aya!" Sal screamed, kicking his mount, slapping the reins hard down on to the other horses. He was hitting them so hard that they wailed under the leather. Sal continued beating them, driving them faster and faster, farther out of the camp and into the desert.

"It's him!" Richie yelled . . .

At full run, his head was pounding. He raced towards the chariot that Saba had rode in on and jumped up onto the wheelhouse.

"Sal O'Mander grabbed the horses and is making for the portal. I'm going after him. If we can't stop him, he could trap us here forever."

Richie saw his comments had elicited a response from Furan and Marcal as they shaded their eyes and into the receding distance to see the silhouette of a man riding a horse as he drove the others out into the desert.

Richie did not wait for them to respond. He reared the horses and sped for the open desert. He could see Sal's plume of dust far ahead and this spurred him to urge the horses on. He hadn't given thought to his actions, it was instinct, and the stakes were permanent residence in this ancient past.

Gaining speed, the wheels turned and churned, throwing up sand, rock, and gravel. Beads of perspiration flowed down his brow, into his eyes. He was soon plastered in a soft coat of grit.

Just ahead were two of the horses Sal had taken, Richie took notice, but did not slow. Obviously, he let them go. They're too far away from the soldiers to be of any use.

Bouncing across the rock-strewn plain, it was hard to keep both wheels on the ground. The chariot hit a rut, throwing him up into the air. Clutching the reins, he held on, fortune smiled, and he landed back upright in the flying wagon.

Richie continued to eat away chunks of desert but failed to close the gap on his adversary. The horses were panting hard, sweat dripped from their glistening bodies. Richie did not know how long or how hard he could push them. Lord Drago seemed to be getting farther ahead.

The distant sentinels of antiquity rose before him. He was passing beneath the shadows of the great pyramids. He could feel cool fingers of air coming from the river bottom. At the top of the hill, the Great Sphinx cast him in shadow as he stopped to scan the river below.

Sal O'Mander had beaten him. Inconspicuously nestled amongst a few other passengers he sat at the front of the ferry closing in on the distant shore.

He slowed the horses to wait the ferry's return. *I know where he's heading.*

Watering the horses at rivers edge, time moved like molasses. Finally, the barge master was in shouting distance. Removing his bracelet, Richie waved and shouted and was relieved that the man recognized him. Within moments, he boarded, and the ferry turned back to the city.

As soon as he touched shore, he pushed the horses into the shallow lapping water and raced up the slope towards the city. At the top of the hill he saw Sal's riderless horse stymied by a throng of people.

Maybe this is a break.

Richie scanned the crowd, realizing that trying to go against this tide was impossible. A young girl bumped into him and smiled.

"Praise God, Pharaoh has returned. He is now in the house of kings, hallelujah."

A celebration? Maybe Sal hasn't been so lucky after all. Richie continued to study the stream of people. Picking through gaps and seams in the crowd, Richie kept a vigilant eye out for his prey as he moved steadily towards the temple. He was making exceptional time, people seemed to positively respond to courtesy, and magically seams would open for great stretches.

"Gotcha," Richie exclaimed, spotting the head of Sal O'Mander. He was passing under the overhang of the great hall. Richie redoubled his effort to slip through the human tide.

If he gets to the other side, I am sure he has a plan to shut down the portal and I can't let that happen!

Sal shoved aside a young woman, she reached out to break her fall, and grabbed at the bald man's tunic. It flew open, and Richie stumbled, stopped, and sucked at the air, his breath coming in short gasps. As Sal slipped back into the sea of bodies, the image inside that tunic was indelibly frozen onto Richie's mind.

"The amulet! He's wearing Kayla's amulet?" The sight pierced him like a dagger. He fought to shake it from his head. "If he gets away . . . what has he done with Kayla?"

Fresh adrenaline surged through his body, his arms and legs moving him forth as if a crowd was not even there. But Sal had also broken free and now was racing up the stairs. Richie saw that there were no guards surrounding the temple—they probably had joined the celebratory revelry.

Richie broke free from the final throng and bounded up the steps two at a time. Hardly breaking stride, he yanked the doors open. Once inside, the noise and chaos from the square disappeared behind the soft whoosh of the closing door. Only the thump, thump, thump of racing feet could be heard.

Blindly passing pillars, Richie hurried towards the back of the temple. Its beauty, grandeur, and fine craftsmanship a blur, his focus radiated solely on catching Sal before he could activate the transport. The portal room was just ahead.

A nova flashed before him, then dissipated. He was too late.

"I'm coming for you," he wailed with reckless courage.

Racing up the stairs, he jumped into the tub. He tore off his shirt and threw it down to the pyramid floor. Sweat was pouring off his body. A beacon for my friends. Then Richie launched himself across the eons.

🗿 🗿 ◆ 🕀 ● 🕀 🗿

Chapter 27
The Cave – The Present

The commander of the Drago craft hovered at the outskirts of Santa Martina, near the Radcliff woods. He ignored the armada of tractors, trailers, trucks, and heavy construction equipment that sat motionless and unmanned. Just above the tree line, he waited and waited. Prepared to evacuate.

"There, exiting the mouth," announced the navigator standing beside his leathery body. He zoomed in the monitor, enhancing the rocks that surrounded the portal entrance. Outside the cave's mouth, the human form of Lord Drago, Sal O'Mander, was frantically searching for something.

"Lower," growled the seasoned commander. He was a Salamanderan warrior from one of the outer planets. He saw the form of Sal continue to search, moving farther from the mouth, as he was turning over rocks and brush, hunting for something.

"What is he doing? I know he sees us." The commander seethed as ripples rolled across his muscled spine. Irritation blossomed chameleon splotches upon his massive chest.

"He's running the wrong way." Instead of making his way to the agreed upon clearing, Lord Drago was scrambling up the hillside. "Flip on the audio," the commander ordered.

"No one gets the better of me," the voice of Lord Drago droned through the craft's audio sensors. The commander could hear the hot sting of vengeance that burned deep within him.

"I paid that dung heap to wire this place. I am going to trap that kid and his measly mutt forever." He cursed.

The Drago ship's commander prepared to land, but he was unhappy with Lord Drago.

"If he has failed, I will personally see that he is sacrificed." He had no love for his commanders. This was all about self, he thought with a slithering satisfaction. He could not take his eyes off of the events transpiring below.

"Just where I told him to leave it," he hissed. "Goodbye, menace." He pressed the demolition ignition button.

◆ ◆)(◆ ●

Lord Drago grew angry. "Nothing's happening!"

There was no explosion. "Blow up!" he demanded. And he pressed the button again and again—to no avail.

"Looking for these?" Chucky questioned, stepping out from behind a tree. In his hand he held a tangle of wires. "There aren't going to be any explosions today, you creep!"

"Imbecile!" Lord Drago roared in disbelief. He lost his cool and, in his anger, Sal O'Mander reverted back to his non-cloaked self, his alien presence, slipping into invisibility.

He glared at the boy who foolishly stood his ground, albeit with a tad bit less bravery.

"You fool!" Lord Drago shouted, his breath driving the human backwards until his knees gave way. "Give me those wires."

Lord Drago barely registered the flying blur before he was bludgeoned by that insufferable Radcliff kid's flying tackle.

"You!" he bellowed, taken by surprise that this measly piece of human dung had knocked him off his feet.

With superior size and strength, Lord Drago disentangled himself and rose to his full ten feet, towering over the boy. He eyed the landing vessel as a slew of warriors swooped out of the ship's belly.

"Get back," Lord Drago snarled. "He's mine." One by one, he flicked open his yellowed nails, their edges more menacing than the fabled teeth of a great white shark. His eyes were laser focused on Richie who was sprawled amongst the pine needles, rocks, and leaves.

"Your luck has come to an end, and with it, humanity," he said with rage.

Lord Drago felt he was being cheated. He expected whimpering, pleas for mercy, and all that crap that humans puke upon each other. Instead, this stupid kid looked unflinchingly into the eye of his executioner, with a disarming smile.

℮ℳ ◆ ◆ ◆)(◆ ●)(↗ ℳ

"Where's Richie?" Kippy asked anxiously, standing at the base of the stairs of the portal where he had been sure he would be. He ran around the pyramid structure, frustrated. No Richie.

What's he going to do if he catches that beast?

Saba trudged the portal stairs. "Up here," he cried. "His shirt, it's laying on the floor." He waved it so Kippy could see.

Kippy suddenly noticed that Saba looked old. The worry had aged him.

"Kippy, perhaps we should we go back home? I think Richie made it to the other side. He's followed Sal O'Mander there. I'm sure he left this as a clue."

"Maybe Oztin will be there," Kippy said, his tail thumping on the stone at the one hope he still clung to.

"Let's go find out."

ℯ𝕿𝕸 ⬧ ◆ ⬧ ✠ ⬧ ● ✠ ↗𝕸

"Look, father," Oztin said touching the viewtron. He was sitting in a Federation battle cruiser just beyond the Earth's atmosphere. "Exiting the cave, it's Richie."

"And there is Lord Drago himself," Enoch said astonished.

Oztin saw his face pale.

It must be extra important if the leader of the Dragos is here.

"Commander, prepare the pods. We are going down. I want their ships quarantined, their lunar base embargoed, make sure that our firepower is apparent."

Oztin was aboard the first shuttle pod as they entered the atmosphere and saw that their appearance froze Lord Drago in his tracks.

The humongous lizard cried a piercing scream of frustration. He looked torn between killing Richie and self-preservation.

"Where is she? Where's Kayla?" Richie could be heard yelling.

"I bet she's a tasty little morsel," he sneered. Panic was spreading across the boy's face.

"My lieutenant brought me that lovely little artifact from around her silky white neck. And now, she is safely tucked away where neither you nor your Federation friends are ever going to find her." Lord Drago's voice dripped with malice. It was clear to Oztin, who was monitoring the entire scene, that Lord Drago was enjoying Richie's discomfort.

"How about a trade?" Lord Drago suggested. "My freedom for your girlfriend?" The words slithered like maggots from the foul slit of his mouth.

"Where is she? How do I know you'll let her go?" Richie demanded.

Oztin let out a sigh of relief as the other pod emptied dozens of Federation soldiers. But he noted the lizard leader wasn't even fazed. He stood ready to die. *Does he have another card to play?*

"Oh, she's safe alright. I was saving her for myself. Come with me. I'll take you to her." He laughed.

He's stalling, Oztin thought, willing the craft to land. His anxiety amped at full throttle. When the doors finally opened, Oztin rushed past the soldiers.

"Richie! Are you alright? Where's Kippy and Saba? Are they okay?"

Before Richie could answer the torrent of questions, an older man came up next to Oztin. "Richie, this is my father."

He kept one eye on the Dragos, thankful that they made no attempt to move. He could see they were taking their cue from their leader.

It concerned him that Lord Drago was still confident.

"Sir, it is Kayla—they have her. He has her!" Richie said pointing at the Lord of the lizards. "Please, I need your help."

No one said anything and Oztin could feel the tension rising in the studied silence. He watched as his father cued his men, who raised their weapons and the Dragos formed battle positions in an outward-facing circle.

"What do you want, Lord Drago?" Enoch demanded. There was no pretense of formality, it was a hostile question.

"Why, Sir Enoch," the Drago leader responded. "What brings a council member here to this puny little world? I know you didn't come just to see me."

Enoch did not respond.

"It is quite simple, really. You let me go, follow in your battle cruiser, and I will return the girl to you. But I must have your word that you will not try and capture me after she has been returned," he offered with a cavalier 'nothing to lose,' tone and posture.

"And you, once she is safely returned, you assure us that you and all the others will depart this quadrant of Orion with no further hostile attempts against the Federation?"

"For now, Enoch, only for now," Drago replied dryly.

"Commander, station guards here and block the entrance to that cave. Do not let anybody in or out until we return. Richie, Oztin, you come with me."

Lord Drago smiled. He had changed the odds. Like the chameleon he was, he always adapted to his situation. He knew his ship was no match for the battle cruiser that had to be somewhere above, but that didn't mean he couldn't play another card that he had maneuvered to the top of the deck.

He had counted on the human weaknesses of concerns for others. And knew this measly runt was not going to let his little precious be forfeited as a spoil of war. With the die cast, there was still one chance left to win the game.

Chapter 28
Rescuing Kayla

Richie was filled with competing emotions as the pod returned to the main cruiser. To distract from his fears for Kayla, he watched through the port window as they docked. The battle cruiser was everything he could imagine and more.

His palms were sweating, and he had the taste of bile on his lips. Richie attributed this to his overwhelming concern for Kayla, but there was something else as well.

Oztin led him into the main salon where a video monitor showed Lord Drago loading his crew onto their craft. He recoiled at the nonchalance of the Drago leader. He knew him well enough by now to know that he still had not surrendered.

"What am I missing?" He toiled through every angle he could imagine as the pit in his stomach grew. Biting his lip, his mouth quivered with worry.

He watched the lizard craft come to altitude and couple with their mother ship. Black—it seemed to suck in the light and appeared as nothing more than a hole in space. It was sinister, pure evil, he thought.

The lizard appeared on the communications screen. "Enoch, follow me to the edge of the solar system, near that passing comet. We will talk again when we are ready to perform docking protocols." The screen went blank.

When they started moving, Richie watched space fly by. He was trying to digest the emotional roller coaster he was on. *This seems so familiar,* he thought. *Like I've been here before.*

Enoch entered and started with a long list of questions which Richie tried to answer through his distraction.

"Dad, give him a break," Oztin interjected on Richie's behalf. Richie smiled appreciatively.

"We're coming up on target, sir," said a voice over the intercom.

Kayla Carlyle had all but given up hope. She had summoned unknown reserves of strength but even these were losing steam.

I am not going down without a fight, she vowed. But her body was draped in defeat. Like she was being suffocated by a giant wet blanket. She assumed she would never see her home or family ever again.

"I will not cry," she muttered under her breath, not willing to give them the satisfaction. Her limbs were shaky, but she was no longer strapped to the gurney.

Her heart was racing, and she fought desperately against the despair of no longer caring. Time seemed to lose meaning and she found herself hypersensitive to her surroundings. She heard footsteps clopping her way and with a hiss of pressurized air, the walls parted like a pair of elevator doors.

"Come with us," said the leading lizard.

She noted his scowl and worried. *Now what?*

"Where are you taking me?" she mustered with false bravado. He said nothing as another fell in behind her, forcing her to keep pace with the one who was leading her.

She noted that the corridor was coated in an oily texture and that the air was greasy with a putrid stink. Like a solvent, it began to dissolve her resolve and she fought panic welling up. It would not abate and rolled in one wave bigger than the next. Her legs wobbled and she was about to collapse, no longer to fight the inevitable when . . .

The wall before her opened and a miracle arrived.

𝑒ᴛ𝔪 ⬩◆⬩𝓗⬩●𝓗↗𝔪

"Richie," she cried out tearfully. Two Federation soldiers took her from the Dragos who quickly turned as the transfer doors closed.

Richie was relieved at her spirit. And surprised when she pulled free from the soldier and threw her arms around his neck.

"Kayla—are you okay?" He had expected so much worse. He realized she had endured the unendurable and survived. Actually, more than that, had beaten back their attempts to break her.

Embarrassed, but happy, Richie introduced Kayla to Oztin and his father.

"There is so much to tell you," he said. "Where do I start?"

"Uh hum," Enoch coughed lightly. "Why don't you two come sit up in the front of the battle cruiser? We need to circle back behind the sun before we can get you home."

Richie still had that pit in his stomach and his mind was torn between relief, the warm feeling of Kayla's presence and something else.

It was the something else that he was picking at like a scab on a wound. His mind would not let it go.

"Sir," the First Lieutenant asked. "The Drago craft has not made any attempt to leave. What do you want us to do?"

Richie and Kayla took seats side by side as they gazed at the 360-degree perimeter monitors.

"We had better keep an eye on them," his commander replied. "At least until they are out of the quadrant."

He saw that Enoch nodded his agreement and felt the Federation cruiser back away. It began a turn to move away from the trailing path of debris jettisoned by the departing comet when Richie had that feeling again.

Déjà vu? *What is it?* He asked himself. The warning sensation, the one he got in his gut when something was wrong, went haywire. Caution bells were ringing in his head. He could not put his finger on it. *What, what, what?* He kept asking himself.

"No!" Richie yelled. In an instant it became clear. He had this very dream a week ago. "Stop the ship!" he shouted. "Now, now, now! Stop the ship!"

Enoch gave him a startled stare.

"Sir, behind that next ice flow, there are two Drago cruisers waiting to ambush us." Richie said, not a doubt in his mind.

"Captain, take preemptive action," Enoch commanded accepting the truth of his comment.

"Fire torpedoes 1-3-5-7," the Captain ordered. "Aim for the center of the ice cluster. "Fire at will."

Richie watched as four tubes of light shot from the front of the ship. In an instant, the ice vaporized followed by two large explosions.

A cloud of metallic debris left no doubt as to the accuracy of Richie's hunch. The waiting ambush had been obliterated.

From their heads-up monitor, it was apparent that Lord Drago had seen this as well. His ship had already hit hyper-drive by the time the four tubes of light left the hull of the ship.

♊︎ ◆ ⚹ ● ⚹ ⚴ ♊︎

Chapter 29
Birth of a Legend

Saba paused at the top of the landing, wistfully taking a final look at the temple. "This will be the last time I ever come here," he whispered. The great story of his life was coming to an end.

Kippy stood waiting. "I don't ever want to play God again, even if it is just acting."

FLASH . . . BOOM!!!

Saba shuddered at the close proximity of the concussive wave. Pulling his head down, he hunched his shoulders as his hands reflexively covered his ears. He was temporarily blinded but felt more than saw as Kippy moved to a position to protect him.

"Easy big fella," said a familiar voice. "Look who I found."

It was a voice from heaven. Saba crossed himself in prayerful thanks as waves of relief washed the years off of him. Kippy leaped into his master's arms, almost knocking him and Kayla back into the tub.

"Hey boy," he said as Kippy unabashedly lapped at his face. "I'm glad to see you, too."

"Where were you guys?" asked the shaken Saba.

"Well, let's just say Lord Drago is gone and right now the Federation is watching our backs."

"And who is this beautiful young lady?" Saba asked, regaining his worldly composure.

"Kayla," she said, a slight flush on her cheeks.

Then another flash of light appeared and Oztin arrived.

"Hey guys," he said with a grin. "I've been doing all the hard work, where have you been?"

"So, you did it Oztin, you came through with flying colors. Well done, lad," Saba congratulated him. He noticed that he was wearing a bracelet, but it was on his other hand. It looked as if everything was going to turn out all right after all.

That should have about wrapped it all up. Let time sort itself out and let destiny's river resume its flow. But Saba's adventure was not quite over. Before he could catch his breath and savor the moment, the room filled with a phalanx of royal guards.

Purple clad, they followed Pharaoh with pride in their steps. Their benevolent leader had regained his authority.

$$e_T \mathrm{m} \cdot \blacklozenge \cdot \mathrm{K} \cdot \bullet \mathrm{K} \cdot \mathrm{m}$$

"Lord Sirius, I do not mean to interrupt," the monarch began. "Are these your friends?"

"Yes sir, they are," Kippy answered, relieved to see Pharaoh had recovered. "Let me introduce them to you. This is Richie, Saba, Kayla, and our very good friend Oztin."

Kippy watched the Pharaoh as he scrutinized Oztin. He could see it was making Oztin feel self-conscious.

"You are a friend of Lord Sirius?" he asked again, directing the question to Oztin.

"Yes?" Oztin said with a nod of hesitation.

"I should have known." Pharaoh's expression blossomed into a full grin. "No wonder we have had such good luck. Blessed are we with such an abundance of good fortune. You say you are Oztin, so you are, but you are also Bes, friend of all Egyptians."

"Who's Bes?"

"Bes is the Egyptian God of Luck, very ancient," Saba explained. "He is a favorite of all Egyptians. The God Bes is also a dwarf. I think that your diminutive stature has put you in some very good company."

The clarification seemed to make Oztin stand a little taller.

"He has brought good fortune to all of us," Saba answered for his tongue-tied friend.

"For a hero is not known by his stature, but by his deeds," Pharaoh proclaimed with affection. "In the eyes of our people, you will always stand tall, my friend."

"Man, I never knew there were dwarf heroes," Oztin said, beaming with pride.

"You will all join us tonight in celebration," proclaimed Pharaoh.

"I'm starved," Kippy said, his flapping tail confirming the decision made for them.

erℳ•◆•Ж•●Ж⤢ℳ

Kippy relished being the center of attention. Inside the great hall, he knew this would be a celebration to beat all celebrations. He studied his friends, who had been given personal attendants and dressed in Egypt's finest tunics.

Kayla was given four courtesans to help transform her from an American teen to an Egyptian princess. She was made up with kohl and minerals and her courtesans adorned her in an elegant hand-beaded tunic, draped with silk scarves. They placed handmade palm frond sandals on her feet and adorned her with gold cuffs and earrings.

The men were rubbed, scrubbed, washed, and dried. He noted that the boys felt a little self-conscious in the traditional tunic and mineral powder they were treated to, but Saba relished having the chance to live out his heritage.

As Lord Sirius, Kippy was given extra special attention by the personal retinue, all in preparation for an evening of celebration.

The gathered crowd bellowed in approval as he entered with his companions. Egyptian military trumpets blared, and a color guard stood at attention with dozens of colored banners angled out from their right side as they lined the processional walkway.

"Wow, look at this place," Kayla said, awestruck.

Kippy was pleased she had made the transition from a place where she had run out of hope, to now relishing the adoring accolades. It attested to how strong a girl she was.

To think, a month ago she didn't even know my master existed.

"Yeah, and smell all that delicious food," Kippy said.

"Everyone's got their priorities," Saba smiled with a twinkle in his eyes.

"Ole Pharaoh here knows how to throw a party," Kippy said to his companions. His nostrils were eager to find the plate of chops whose delicious aroma had his name on them.

Kippy led the procession into a grand dining room where streamers hung from beams polished to a high sheen. The room was cooler than he expected, he assumed it was the thick stone walls, and the floors were made up of mosaic inlays. But his attention soon focused on the tables, of which there were many.

Meats, bright trays of fruits, vegetables and steaming hot bread. There would be no shortage tonight. He did not know if they were as hungry as he was, but his taste buds began to salivate in gastronomical anticipation.

With the room filled with dignitaries, beautiful women, and their male escorts, whom Kippy assumed were the royalty of the Pharaoh's court, he relished that all of this pageantry was in honor of him and his friends.

"Marcal, Furan and Syed, I am so glad to see all of you. These are my friends, Kayla and Oztin," Kippy said, his tail wagging in greeting.

When Furan took Kayla's proffered hand and kissed it, Kippy suppressed a smile when she blushed.

They clean up pretty good.

Marcal and Syed shook hands with Oztin and Kayla, and they chatted until escorts led them to join Pharaoh's long table.

Kippy continued to be torn between the delicious smelling meats calling to him and the enjoyment of watching his friends and colleagues basking in the glow of respect. He eyed Saba and wondered if he should mention his little chat with Pharaoh. He knew Saba saw a noticeable difference in the man who was king.

"Oztin, come sit next to me," Saba said pulling the chair back for him.

Kippy took a seat on his other side, and then Richie and Kayla.

"Let's eat," Pharaoh said with a flourish and an army of waiters descended on the accumulated guests bearing silver trays of the finest foods Kippy had ever seen. He ate, looked up, and the servants were there ready with more.

There were speeches between the many courses and Kippy saw Richie just shake his head and laugh. "I don't know where you put it, buddy. Really, you are one of a kind," he said as he affectionately rubbed the tuft behind his ear. "But don't start farting," he mumbled under his breath.

"Man, I'm so full that if I take another bite, I could burst." This caused his friends to break into laughter.

When Pharaoh stood up, a hush descended upon the hall. Glasses were set on the table, napkins set aside, and everyone quieted down.

"If it were not for these heroes . . ." He paused, and then changed his thought. "Well, let us not think of that. As you know, we set out to build a temple to Sirius. But it seems that its intended purpose was not to honor our God as we believed, but instead, it was a cover for the perpetration of evil. Evil that was thwarted here today."

Kippy looked to his friends on either side of him as a great cheer rose and all eyes fell upon the strangers.

Pharaoh held up his hand for silence and continued. "When Lord Sirius appeared, before these awful impostors had fully taken over, I commissioned one of our greatest artists to create a centerpiece dedicated to his temple, and then I was locked away."

He paused and the hush in the room grew heavy. "But our artists never stopped working. Today I had a chance to spend a few hours with Sirius and we have decided that we will place this as a centerpiece atop the temple pedestal and then we will encase it in granite to last an eternity."

Kippy's attention was on one lonely piece of meat abandoned on his plate, and since everyone else's eyes were focused on Pharaoh in rapt attention, he took it.

"This temple will be refashioned for its original purpose, to honor the Great God Sirius. It will stand for an eternity to remind us all of the heroics of our good friends here. Ladies and gentlemen, I present this in honor of these fine friends and their service in saving our country."

Swallowing the choice morsel, Kippy watched as men drew back a rich silk curtain. Large, muscled servants entered carrying a giant statue of him riding high upon a board.

"Awesome," Kippy said in a not-so-humble voice. The artist had done a phenomenal job creating a three-dimensional illusion as if he were flying over them. The room around them was continuing its buzz of warmth, friendship, and merriment.

"So many things have been answered," Saba said. "But in the end, I have so many new questions. What is time? Is it like a river? Can we move back and forth? What about consequences?"

"Something is still bothering you, isn't it?" Oztin asked.

"Yes. There is something."

"What?"

"It's the battle back in the tunnels of El Cadiz. It just seemed, well, like it was too easy. I mean they didn't even put up much of a fight."

"Well I wasn't there, but from all I heard, no one could have survived. Do you think they did?"

"Yes, no, I don't know . . . just, well, in hindsight, it all seemed a little staged. As if they wanted us to think they had gone but hadn't. I guess I'm just paranoid. So what happens when we go back, I mean will we even remember all this?"

"Oh, yes," Oztin said. "And I believe there is more."

He paused, and Saba thought he saw the glint of mischief in the boy's eye.

"My father told me that once we entered the time portal that no matter what changes may result in the history of the world, our DNA is fused with the knowledge of what was and what might be. We will always know both realities.

"Things that have happened here—or could still happen here—will ripple across the eons. There are still some changes you can affect for the fortunes of those around you."

"Change the fortunes of others?" Saba asked quizzically. But he noted that all Oztin would give him was a smile and a wink, leaving him to ponder his comments while he circulated amongst the others. Saba was both relieved and bothered by Oztin's last statement. *What did he mean by changing fortunes? Why was he being so mysterious? Would his life continue as before?*

"My friends, it is time," Pharaoh announced. "Please, we have a grand chariot waiting out front, one more procession before the people. They want to see their heroes."

Saba let his young friends lead and he brought up the rear as the crowd erupted in applause and made their way to the front doors.

Once outside, Saba inhaled the night air. It transported him back to his days as a young boy, Miles's unofficial servant, he chuckled.

He recalled the day they entered the temple and the first time he saw the great statue of Kippy that now stood ensconced upon a gaily painted wagon. Two white stallions lifted their heads in majesty. He helped Kayla and Oztin, and once all five heroes had boarded, they made one final pass down the living streets of ancient Egypt.

The wagon started forward and they began the festive parade back to the temple. The procession led them through the city. The cool night air, awash in stars, held the scents of jasmine and frangipani. It appeared as if every citizen of the city had come out to say a final goodbye. A giant burden had been lifted.

"Look at all these people," Kayla said. "And look at Kippy," who stood waving.

"What a ham," Richie whispered to Saba.

Saba looked at the ancient people. They stood a hundred deep watching the canine God pass.

Saba enjoyed the rise, knowing this would be his last time ever in ancient Egypt, the country he was born in, the people he loved. When he finally reached the temple, he chorused his goodbyes along with his friends and with a final wave, followed them into the temple. Alone for the last time in the Great Hall of Sirius. It would be another five thousand years before he ever saw this place again. But the thing Oztin had told him, it was nagging and becoming an itch that had to be scratched.

What fortunes of others?

Saba wondered as he climbed the stairs for the last time. He stopped to take a final look at the place that had such an impact on his life. Sweeping his gaze across the expanse of ancient wonderment he sought to see his familiar symbols one more time. And then he saw it . . .

"Of course. Of course. Oh my God! Of course." He ran down the stairs on adrenaline of joy, like a code that once deciphered, unlocks a million mysteries, in his mind's eye he saw everything and wanted to whoop for joy. He had the energy of a kid again.

Wedged against the wall was the empty can of Fizz Cola. The one Kippy had knocked over. He picked it up and smiled.

"What was that all about?" Richie asked.

Saba was laughing so hard it was becoming contagious.

"Oh, just a happy ending," he said enigmatically. "I certainly don't want to be a litterbug."

He suggested they all climb into the tub together, one last time. In a flash, they were back at the cave. Saba climbed down the stairs and exited into the cool afternoon shadows as sunlight dappled though the pines at the outskirts of Santa Martina. He had brought his friends home safely. He felt like a proud parent.

"I want to thank you for taking me on this wonderful adventure and finally helping me to solve the biggest riddle of my life," Saba said giving the boy a warm hug. He then reached down to pet Kippy and followed with a shake of Oztin's hand along with a wink.

"Hello, Enoch," Kippy said. "You know they can't see you."

"I know," he said and reached into his pocket and pulled out two bracelets. He first slipped one on to Saba's hand, then the other on Kayla.

"Does that mean I'll being seeing more of you?" Richie asked with a smile of hope.

"Does a dog fart in the Pharaoh's palace?" Oztin asked which caused even Saba to laugh.

"Am I really invisible?" Kayla asked with a giggle.

"Yes, you are young lady. I hope you will keep our secret a secret though."

"Oh yes sir, I will."

Enoch then turned to Saba. "Can I give you a lift home?"

"Sure." He turned to his new friend and colleague. "Richie, call me in a few days, I'm sure you've got some explaining to do to your father. When you call me, I'll make sure Ms. Dangly will let you through."

Saba could feel the weight of the world being lifted from his shoulders. Watching the man from another world, he smiled as he gave Richie a warm pat on the back and had one last word for him before they left.

"Richie, this cave is special. I do not know who invented it nor do I know why it is here, but from what Oztin tells me, there was an old legend that said the chosen one will save the mother from dark forces. Well, it seems that legend has come true. I guess this is part of your destiny.

"I believe that no one else should ever know the secret of this place. Preserve it and protect it. I am sure there is a great and fascinating future about to unfold for all of you. Go in peace and may God always watch over you."

The great adventure was drawing to a close. They all said their final goodbyes and then just like that, the craft ascended and only three were left.

"I guess it's time to face the music," Richie said, and then added. "Somehow everything is going to work itself out."

Kayla took Richie by the hand and removed his bracelet as well as her own and squeezed his hand reassuringly.

Chapter 30
The End? Perhaps . . .

Saba watched his three exhausted friends exit the woods heading home. He followed Enoch into the space cruiser and sat next to Oztin.

"Well, Saba," Enoch began. "Oztin tells me you picked up the empty can of Fizz Cola. Good for you. You know we couldn't interfere, but now I guess if there is no can for Professor Miles to find, I guess there is no Miles Industries. Therefore, the cave is safe for the moment. Don't you agree?"

"For the moment," he agreed. "But there's more to it than that isn't there?" Saba asked. It was the twinkle in Enoch's eye that tipped his hand.

"You have a great responsibility ahead of you still," Enoch replied, avoiding Saba's direct question. "Richie and Kayla are just kids, wise but still very young. It would give me great comfort to know that you are keeping a secret eye out for their well-being."

"One of my few regrets in life is that I never had children of my own. And yet now, I feel as if they will be my adopted family. You need not worry about them," Saba promised.

"Good. Now there is something I promised to tell Oztin, I think you will find this of interest also. Why Earth is important to the grand scheme of things.

"You see, Earth is the center of God's creation. It is the alpha and the omega. Since before time, there has been a battle in the heavens between darkness and light. This battle is played out in each galaxy, each solar system, and each planet right down to the battle each of us struggle with against our own dark nature."

Saba leaned forward in attention.

"There is a prophesy that is widely known throughout the universe that darkness and light, what you would call good and evil, will collide in a final confrontation, and they have long suspected that this will happen here on your planet. Even in your own books of prophesy, I believe it is called The Revelation, it talks of a final conflict with the Dragon. This I think correctly translated would mean the Dragos."

Saba had once read the Book of Revelation, the last chapter of the Bible. He vowed to revisit it.

"And now that we know the Dragos are aware of this place, it is quite possible we may have entered the age when this prophecy may finally unfold. So you see, when I say keep a close eye on them, well . . . it's important for all of us."

Ꮛᛘ•◆•ᚻ•●ᚻᚷᛘ

"I'm not really sure how we are going to explain it," Richie said, as they arrived at the edge of the Radcliff's gravel driveway.

On their way back they had all agreed that Enoch was right, the fewer people who knew of this the better. Looking at his house, Richie was confused.

"Did someone paint this place?"

"And the yard, look, the broken fence I climb through has been fixed, and look at all the flowers."

"Geez, how long could we have been gone for?" Kayla asked.

One day? Two? Richie wondered.

Honk, honk-honk . . .

The blast of the car horn caused Richie to nearly jump out of his skin. They all stepped out of the way as a Range Rover edged past them into the driveway.

"Hey guys," Mr. Radcliff called, as he rolled down the window.

Where did he get that? Richie stared.

"Kayla! Your mom called, said it was alright for you to stay for dinner."

Richie looked at Kayla and his mouth hung open in surprise. "Did my dad just say that your mom is letting you stay for dinner?"

She just screwed up her mouth and shrugged her shoulders.

"Okay."

They entered the house, Richie holding the door for Kayla while Kippy followed, it was obvious his canine nose caught the unmistakable aroma of roasting turkey.

"Suddenly I'm hungry all over again." Richie rolled his eyes at Kayla who chuckled.

"Since when does my dad cook like this?" Richie said this casually, but with all the other strangeness about his home, he was a little trepidatious about what changes had taken place.

Did we alter history somehow?

"Is that you, my little star?" called a voice from the kitchen.

Richie's heart thudded and his breath stuck in his throat as he tried to suck in a gulp of air. His pulse quickened and he tried to say something but could not speak.

Is this some kind of a cruel joke? But there was that magical voice again.

"Dinner's almost ready. Bring Kayla and let's eat. I'm starving."

"Impossible," he mumbled. He rushed into the kitchen and saw his mother standing by the stove.

"Mom!" he cried out, tears streaming down his face. He wrapped his arms around her, willing this to be real. He began sobbing into her chest completely unaware of his two friends who stood dumbstruck at the kitchen's edge.

"You're alive, you're alive," he said over and over. "I wished and prayed so many times before. Mom, I love you!" he said, choking back his emotions.

"Of course I'm alive, honey. Did you think something happened to me?"

Richie released her and saw the look of worry on her face. He turned to see Kayla and Kippy basking in the glow of his happiness.

Richie recalled Saba's odd answer back at the temple.

'I'm making a happy ending.' And then he understood. Saba had retrieved the old soda can. *So, if there was no can for Miles to discover, it must mean there was no M.I., which means there was no mining truck there that day—which means Mom was not killed, which means Mom is really here.*

And that would explain the changes around the house. Changes for the better. Richie could see that Dad's life was back on track with the love of his life supporting him, and the weight of sorrow gone.

Was it gone? Or had it ever been there?

Richie did not know how to answer the questions that were popping into his head. History is a funny and wonderful thing, he realized, so grateful for all that had happened. *But what else may have been changed forever? What did his dad remember? What about the memories Mom will have for the years that have passed? How will I explain my amnesia?*

He realized that using the cave came with grave responsibility, but right now, he didn't care. He was just thankful for his family and his friends.

Richie pulled the dining table chair out for Kayla, joy surging through his veins. As they all sat down to eat, Richie asked if he could say Grace.

"Why son, I would love that," his mom said with a look of surprise on her face.

"Dear Father in Heaven, so much happens that only you can understand. I am so thankful for everything you do for us and for fulfilling our prayers. Bless this food and let us always cherish the time we have together. Amen."

"Amen," said his mom, smiling at her son.

As the happy family dug into their meal, Richie winked over to Kippy who was sitting patiently. He can't be hungry again, he chuckled.

Richie thought of all that had happened over the last few weeks. The world was wonderful. Mysterious, but wonderful. He looked across the table and smiled at Kayla and an odd thought floated up. The Egyptians had talked about the First Time. Who really did build the pyramids—Atlanteans?

Like a condensed movie reel, everything over the last few days played upon the screen of his mind's eye. As he feigned interest in the food before him, a nagging thought clawed deep within, and he knew it was important. It was a bad feeling and it needed to be understood. What is it? The world is now perfect. But it was an itch that demanded to be scratched.

Then with a shudder, an image formed inside his head. And with it came crystalline clarity. *Of course, it was all a great deception, they're still among us.*

He thought of all the cruelty in the world. The warlords and cruel dictators who had committed so many inhumane atrocities over the last five thousand years. But the thought was replaced by the joy of having his mother. He focused on what was right and good and found a warm fluttery feeling fill him with peace.

"So, what have you kids been up to today?" Richie's mom asked, pulling him back to the moment.

"What's with those crazy outfits? Was it Egyptian Day at school?"

Richie looked to Kayla and realized they were still dressed for the celebration. Even Kippy could not suppress a grin. Richie smiled as a thought came to him.

Can this cave take me into tomorrow and beyond?